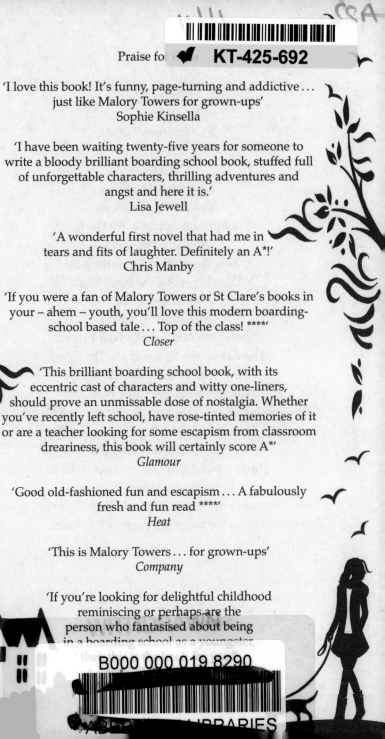

Praise fo KT-425-692

'I love this book! It's funny, page-turning and addictive...
just like Malory Towers for grown-ups'
Sophie Kinsella

'I have been waiting twenty-five years for someone to
write a bloody brilliant boarding school book, stuffed full
of unforgettable characters, thrilling adventures and
angst and here it is.'
Lisa Jewell

'A wonderful first novel that had me in
tears and fits of laughter. Definitely an A*!'
Chris Manby

'If you were a fan of Malory Towers or St Clare's books in
your – ahem – youth, you'll love this modern boarding-
school based tale... Top of the class! ****'
Closer

'This brilliant boarding school book, with its
eccentric cast of characters and witty one-liners,
should prove an unmissable dose of nostalgia. Whether
you've recently left school, have rose-tinted memories of it
or are a teacher looking for some escapism from classroom
dreariness, this book will certainly score A*'
Glamour

'Good old-fashioned fun and escapism... A fabulously
fresh and fun read ****'
Heat

'This is Malory Towers... for grown-ups'
Company

'If you're looking for delightful childhood
reminiscing or perhaps are the
person who fantasised about being
in a boarding school as a youngster

B000 000 019 8290

Also by Jenny Colgan

Jenny COLGAN

Rules

sphere

SPHERE

First published in Great Britain as a paperback original
in 2009 by Sphere
This reissue published by Sphere in 2016

13 5 7 9 10 8 6 4 2

Copyright © Jane Beaton, 2009

The moral right of the author has been asserted.

*All characters and events in this publication, other than those
clearly in the public domain, are fictitious and any resemblance
to real persons, living or dead, is purely coincidental.*

'Phenomenal Woman' copyright © 1978 by
Maya Angelou, from *And Still I Rise* by Maya Angelou.
Used by permission of Random House, Inc.
'The Night Mail' by W. H. Auden from *Collected Poems* by W. H. Auden
reproduced by permission of Faber and Faber Ltd.

All rights reserved.
No part of this publication may be reproduced, stored in a
retrieval system, or transmitted, in any form or by any means, without
the prior permission in writing of the publisher, nor be otherwise circulated
in any form of binding or cover other than that in which it is published
and without a similar condition including this condition being
imposed on the subsequent purchaser.

A CIP catalogue record for this book
is available from the British Library.

ISBN 978-0-7515-5328-4

Typeset in Palatino by M Rules
Printed and bound in Great Britain by
Clays Ltd, St Ives plc

Papers used by Sphere are from well-managed forests
and other responsible sources.

 MIX
Paper from
responsible sources
FSC
www.fsc.org FSC® C104740

Sphere
An imprint of
Little, Brown Book Group
Carmelite House
50 Victoria Embankment
London EC4Y 0DZ

An Hachette UK Company
www.hachette.co.uk

www.littlebrown.co.uk

For my father. A great teacher,
and an even better dad.

Acknowledgements

Thanks to the board; W. Hickham; every teacher (and pupil!) who took the time to write to me and tell me a little bit about their life; Ben Ward, for finding David's poem; and my beloved Beatons, large and small.

Characters

Staff

Headteacher: Dr Veronica Deveral
Administrator: Miss Evelyn Prenderghast
Deputy Headteacher: Miss June Starling
Head of Finance: Mr Archie Liston
Matron: Miss Doreen Redmond

Cook: Mrs Joan Rhys
Caretaker: Mr Harold Carruthers

Physics: Mr John Bart
Music: Mrs Theodora Offili
French: Mademoiselle Claire Crozier
English: Miss Margaret Adair
Maths: Miss Ella Beresford
PE: Miss Janie James
Drama: Miss Fleur Parsley
History: Miss Catherine Kellen
Geography: Miss Deirdre Gifford

Pupils

Middle School Year Two

Sylvie Brown
Imogen Fairlie
Simone Pribetich
Andrea McCann
Felicity Prosser
Zazie Saurisse
Alice Trebizon-Woods
Zelda Towrnell
Astrid Ulverton

A Word from Jenny

Hello, hello!

I know, a pre-introduction, that is WEIRD. Sorry. But I wanted to write a quick note to explain what this book is all about.

A few years ago, I wanted to read a boarding school book, having loved them when I was younger. But I couldn't find one for grown-ups. So I wrote a couple. We then decided, we being me and my publishers, to release them under a different name. I can't remember why now. It SEEMED like a good idea at the time.

Anyway, regardless, *Class* and *Rules* came out and they had lovely reviews. But as it turned out, absolutely nobody bought them at all, having never heard of Jane Beaton, which was perfectly understandable, but also made me very sad as I loved writing them and was very proud of them.

As the years have gone on though people keep finding their way to them, little-by-little, and finally last year somebody wrote the publishers a letter saying 'do please let me know what happened to Jane Beaton, as I kept checking the obituaries in case she died' at which point we thought, okay, ENOUGH IS ENOUGH. So we are now bringing them out again as Jenny Colgan novels this time, and hopefully I'll get to finish the series (there are going to be six of course), and hopefully everything will all work out nicely this time.

They are a couple of years old, but I haven't changed anything except one thing: when I wrote them originally I had in my mind for Simone, the scholarship girl, a pretty unusual surname I'd heard on a little-known lawyer back in a 90s trial and stored away.

For obvious reasons since then, we've decided to change the name 'Simone Kardashian' :). She will now be Simone Pribetich in honour of one of my dearest friends, Anouch, who is also Armenian.

Everything else – including 'Jane's' original introduction – which are of course, my feelings too – remains exactly the same, and I so hope you enjoy reading these books as much as I loved writing them. Do let me know, on @jennycolgan or track me down on Facebook, of course. As Jenny, probably, not Jane :).

With love,

Jenny xxx

Introduction

When I was growing up, attending my normal, extremely bog-standard Catholic school, I was obsessed with boarding school books. All of them. *Malory Towers, St Clare's, Frost in May, Jane Eyre, The Four Marys, What Katy Did at School*, the *Chalet School* books.

It's not difficult to understand why: the idea of a bunch of girls all having fun together, working, playing and staying up late for midnight feasts, as opposed to the tribal, aggressive atmosphere of my own school, exerted a powerful pull on a swottish, awkward child. None of these books, for example, had playground meetings that decided which girls were going to be 'in' or 'out' that week, cruel nicknames, long hours of Catholic instruction (OK, apart from Antonia White), or compulsory tiny mini-skirts for gym for the boys to line up and jeer at.

So I lost myself in pranks played on French mistresses; school plays (unheard of at my lackadaisical comp); lacrosse (whatever that was) and the absurd fantasy that you could speak English, French and German on alternate days. Incidentally, has there ever been a school on earth that makes you do that?

When the Harry Potter books came out, obviously its wizard lore and storytelling were a huge draw – but part of me still wondered how much of its success was down to the idealised boarding school life of Hogwarts, filled with delicious meals and having great fun with your wonderfully loyal friends, *sans* fear of parental intervention. The fact that boarding school applications rose sharply with each book published seemed to indicate that I might be right.

Of course in my adult life I've met plenty of people who did go to boarding school, every single one of whom has assured me it was absolutely nothing like the books at all – they know this because, oddly, my dormitory-bound friends seem to have read just as much boarding school fiction as the rest of us.

Perhaps it's the certainties of these schools – their rock-solid concepts of nobility, self-sacrifice, 'the good of the school' – as opposed to the reality of the lives of most adolescents and pre-adolescents: shifting sands of loyalties; siblings cramping your style; and the gradual, creeping realisation that your parents are just feeling their way and don't really have all the answers. Whereas boarding schools, of course, always have strict yet kindly pastoral figures – like Dumbledore, Miss Grayling, or Jo at the Chalet – who always know what to do and are liberal with their second chances. The repetitive rhythm of the terms provides solid ground, endlessly comforting to children in an ever-changing world.

As a voracious adult reader, I realised a couple of years ago that I still missed those books. The prose of Enid Blyton jars a little these days (and they do horribly gang up on and bully Gwendoline, for the sole sin of crying when her parents drop her off), although Curtis Sittenfeld's marvellous book *Prep* is a terrific contemporary account.

To Serve Them All My Days by R F Delderfield, though inevitably dated (which adds a wonderfully bittersweet twist to his stories, knowing how many of his boys were unwittingly bound for the battlefields of WW2), appeals to the adult reader, but as for my beloved girls' stories, there were none to be found.

So I decided to go about writing one myself. My previous book *Class* was the first in a projected series of six books about Downey House (of course! There must always be six. Well, unless you're at the Chalet school, in which case there can be about seventy-five). This one, *Rules*, is the second.

Although I'm writing this series for myself, when I've chatted about it I've been amazed by the amount of people (all right – women) who've said, 'I've been waiting for a book like this for such a long time.' I hope I don't disappoint them – and us, the secret legions of boarding school book fans.

Jane Beaton

Chapter One

Maggie was dancing on a table. This was distinctly out of character, but they *had* served her cocktails earlier, in a glass so large she was surprised it didn't have a fish in it.

Plus it was a beautifully soft, warm evening, and her fiancé Stan had insisted on watching the football on a large Sky Sports screen, annoyingly situated over her head in the Spanish bar, so there wasn't much else to do – and all the other girls were dancing on table tops.

I'm still young, Maggie had thought to herself, pushing her unruly dark hair out of her eyes. *I'm only twenty-six years old! I can still dance all night!*

And with the help of a friendly hen party from Stockport on the next table, she'd found herself up there, shrugging off any self-consciousness with the help of a large margarita and grooving away to Alphabeat.

'Hey, I can't see the game,' Stan complained.

'I don't care,' said Maggie, suddenly feeling rather freer, happy and determined to enjoy her holiday. She raised her arms above her head. This was definitely a good way to forget about school; to forget about David McDonald, the English teacher she'd developed a crush on last year – until

1

she'd found out he was engaged. To just feel like herself again, instead of a teacher.

'Isn't that Miss Adair?' said Hattie.

They'd been allowed down into the town for the evening from the discreet and beautifully appointed villa they'd been staying in high on the other side of the mountain. Her younger sister Fliss turned round from where she'd been eyeing up fake designer handbags, and glanced at the tacky-looking sports pub Hattie was pointing out. Inside was a group of drunk-looking women waving their hands in the air.

'No way!' exclaimed Fliss, heading towards the door for a closer look. 'I'm going in to check.'

'You're not allowed in any bars!' said Hattie. 'I promised Mum and Dad.'

'*I promised Mum and Dad,*' mimicked Fliss. 'I am fourteen, you know. That's pretty much the legal drinking age over here.'

'Well, whilst you're with me you'll obey family rules.'

Fliss stuck out her tongue and headed straight for the bar. 'You're not a prefect now.'

'No, but we're in a position of trust, and . . .'

Fliss stopped short in the doorway.

'Hello, senorita,' said the doorman. Fliss had grown two inches over the summer, although to her huge annoyance she was still barely filling an A cup.

Maggie and the girls from Stockport were shimmying up and down to the Pussycat Dolls when she saw Fliss. At first she thought it was a trick of the flashing lights. It couldn't be. After all, they'd come all this way to leave her work behind. So she could feel like a girl, not a teacher. So surely it couldn't be one of her—

'MISS ADAIR!' shrieked Fliss. 'Is that you, miss?'

Maggie stopped dancing.

'Felicity Prosser,' she said, feeling a resigned tone creep into her voice. She looked around, wondering what would be the most dignified way to get down from the table, under the circumstances.

Normally, Veronica Deveral found the Swiss Alps in summertime a cleansing balm for the soul. The clean, sharp air you could draw all the way down into your lungs; the sparkle of the grass and the glacier lakes; the cyclists and rosy-cheeked all-year skiiers heading for higher ground; the freshly washed sky. She always took the same *pension*, and liked to take several novels – she favoured the lengthy intrigues of Anthony Trollope, and was partial to a little Joanna for light relief – and luxuriate in the time to devour them, returning to Downey House rested, refreshed and ready for the new academic year.

This year, however, had been different. After her shock at meeting the son she gave up for adoption nearly forty years ago, Veronica had handled it badly and they had lost contact. And although there were budgets to be approved, a new intake to set up and staffing to be organised, she couldn't concentrate. All she seemed to do was worry about Daniel, and wonder what he was doing back in Cornwall.

She was staring out the window of her beautiful office, before term was due to start, when Dr Robert Fitzroy, head of Downey Boys over the hill, arrived for their annual chat. The two schools did many things together, and it was useful to have some knowledge of the forthcoming agenda.

'You seem a little distracted, Veronica,' Robert said, comfortably ensconced on the Chesterfield sofa, enjoying the fine view over the school grounds and to the cliffs and the sea beyond, today a perfect summer-holiday blue. They weren't really getting anywhere with debating the new computer lab.

Veronica sighed and briefly considered confiding in her opposite number. He was a kind man, if a little set in his ways. She dismissed this thought immediately. She had spent years building up this school, the last thing she needed was anyone thinking she was a weak woman, prone to tears and over-emotional sentimentality.

Robert droned on about new staff.

'Oh, and yes,' he said, 'we have a new History teacher at last. Good ones are so hard to find these days.'

Veronica was barely listening. She was watching the waves outside and wondering if Daniel had ever taken his children to the seaside for a holiday. So when Robert said his name it chimed with her thoughts, and at first she didn't at all understand what she'd just heard.

'Excuse me?'

'Daniel Stapleton. Our new History teacher.'

'Mom!'

Zelda was throwing ugly things in her bag. Ugly tops, ugly skirts, ugly hats. What the hell? School uniform was the stupidest idea in a country full of stupid ideas.

'Did you know I have to share, like, a bathroom? Did they tell you that?'

Zelda's mother shook her head. As if she didn't have enough to deal with, what with DuBose being so excited about the move and all. Why they all had to go and up sticks and live in England, where she'd heard it rained all the time and everyone lived in itty-bitty houses with bathrooms the size of cupboards . . . well, it didn't bear thinking about. She doubted it would be much like Texas.

4

'Don' worry, darlin,' DuBose had said, in that calm drawl of his. He might get a lot of respect as a major seconded to the British Army, but it didn't cut much ice with her, nuh-huh.

'An' we'll get Zelda out of that crowd she's been running with at high school. Turn her into quite the English lady.'

A boarding school education was free for the daughters of senior military staff on overseas postings, and Downey House, they'd been assured, was among the very best.

As Mary Jo looked at her daughter's perfect manicure – they'd been for a mommy/daughter pamper day – so strange against the stark white of her new uniform blouses, she wondered, yet again, how they would all fit in.

Simone glanced at Fliss's Facebook update – *Felicity is having a BLASTING time in Spain!* – and tried her best to be happy for her. The Pribetichs weren't having a holiday this year. It just wasn't practical. Which was fine by Simone, she hated struggling into her tankini and pulling a big sarong around herself, then sitting under an umbrella hiding in case anyone saw her. So, OK, Fliss might be having great fun without her, and Alice was posting about being utterly miserably bored learning to dive with her au pair in Hurghada, and she was jealous and she did miss them – but she was doing her best to be happy for them.

Thank goodness she'd been invited to Fliss's house for the end of the holidays, so they could all travel back together. Simone had tried not to let slip to her friends just how much she was looking forward to it – and even worse, to admit how much she was looking forward to going back to school.

It had been a long seven weeks, with not much to do but read and try to avoid Joel, her brother, who had spent the entire time indoors hunched over his games console.

She'd spent the summer dreaming of school and reading books whilst eating fish finger sandwiches. Her mother had tried her best to get her involved in some local social events, but it wasn't really her thing. She winced remembering an unbelievably awkward afternoon tea with Rudi, the ugly, gangly teenage son of one of her mother's best friends. His face was covered in spots and his hair was oily and lank. They were shuffled awkwardly together on to a sofa.

Simone's misery on realising that this was the kind of boy her mum thought she might like was compounded by the very obvious way Rudi looked her up and down and made it clear that he thought he was out of her league. She cringed again at the memory.

'You go to that posh school then,' he'd muttered, when pushed by his mum.

Simone had felt a blush spread over her face, and kept her eyes tightly fixed on her hands.

'Yeah.'

'Oh. Right.'

And that had been that. It was pretty obvious that Rudi, over-stretched as he was, would much rather be upstairs playing Grand Theft Auto with Joel.

Simone sighed. It would have been nice to go back to school with at least some adventures to tell Alice and Fliss. Still, maybe she could share theirs.

'Tell me about her thighs again,' said Alice, leaning lazily on shady manicured grass, watching tiny jewel-coloured lizards scrabble past and running up an enormous bill on the hotel phone.

'Jiggly,' said Fliss, under a cherry tree two thousand miles away in Surrey, tickling her dog Ranald on the tummy. 'Honestly, you could see right up her skirt and everything.'

'I never really think of teachers having legs,' mused Alice. 'I mean, I suppose they must and everything, but . . .'

'But what, you think they run along on wheels?' Fliss giggled.

'No, but . . . oh, it's so hot.'

'FLISS!' The voice came from inside.

'Oh God, is that the heffalump Hattie?' drawled Alice.

'I'm not going to answer,' said Fliss.

'FELICITY!' Hattie huffed into the orchard garden, her tread heavy on the paving stones. '*Felicity.*'

'I'm on the *phone*,' said Fliss crossly.

'Well, I have news.'

'Is she pregnant?' said wicked Alice.

'Ssh,' Fliss told her.

'Fine,' said Hattie, turning to go. 'So I guess you DON'T want to hear who's starting at Downey Boys this year?'

Fliss turned and looked at her.

'What are you talking about?'

'Just that I was down in the village . . . and was talking to Will's mum . . .'

And just like that, Alice was talking to an empty telephone.

'Come on.'

Stan was nuzzling her neck. 'Just one more cuddle.'

'I've got to pack!' Maggie was insisting. It wasn't too long before she had to go back and she wanted to be ready. Her clothes were strewn across the room, along with several books she'd wanted to collect to take back for her girls. Stan had a day off from his printing job.

Also, she felt nervous. Last year had been her probation year at the school. This year she'd be expected to perform.

'Cody and Dylan are quite something, aren't they?' asked Stan, moving away. Her two nephews had been playing with

7

them all day, and seemed to get more rambunctious every time.

'Quite brats, you mean,' said Maggie, who'd had to lift them bodily out of the biscuit tin at ten-minute intervals.

'Oh, they're just boys,' said Stan. 'That's what I used to be like. That's what ours'll be like.'

He tried to drag Maggie back on to the bed, but she resisted.

'Once you're Mrs Cameron, you're going to want little Codys and Dylans all over the place.'

'Yes, maybe,' said Maggie, extricating herself. 'But ours won't be allowed to do that to the neighbour's cat.'

Stan laughed. 'Boys will be boys.'

'I think that's why I only teach girls.'

Maggie softened. 'I do love Cody and Dylan, you know. I just worry – they're so crazy, and I know Anne is working all the time.' Anne, Maggie's older sister, ran a thriving hairdressing practice in Govan and was single-handedly raising her two sons. 'Sometimes I wonder what they're doing at that school.'

'Well, it was good enough for us,' said Stan.

Maggie gave herself up to his kiss, thinking about the rough Holy Cross where she and Stan had met, and where she'd later taught. It wasn't really a good school at all. Now, going back to Downey House for her second year there as an English teacher, she felt as nervous and excited as one of her girls when she thought of its four forbidding towers looming out of the hills over the sea. She fingered her new academic diary carefully.

'I suppose,' she said.

Fliss was nervous about having Alice to stay – she loved their large rambling house, but Alice was used to grand residences, and she hoped it would be smart enough for her. She needn't have worried. Alice's parents being in the diplomatic corps meant they moved every couple of months. Anywhere that had a lived-in feel, with a calendar on the kitchen wall and family pictures scattered on every surface, was heaven to Alice.

Simone, on the other hand, was far more intimidated. Felicity's house was HUGE! The garden alone was about the size of a park. There were loads and loads of rooms. In their terraced house in London there was a front room, a back kitchen and three tiny bedrooms. She and Joel had to share when there were visitors staying, which was all the time.

Fliss's mum and dad were delighted to meet her friends, if a little intrigued by the chubby girl who could barely utter a word at mealtimes. Fliss was embarrassed too. Why did Simone have to act so frumpily all the time? Why couldn't she show people how fun she could be? What, did she think Fliss's parents would look down on her? That was insulting!

The first night there all three had sat up gossiping late into the night. Mr and Mrs Prosser had finally let Fliss start drinking coffee, which to Simone, used from childhood to thick sweet grounds you could stand a spoon up in, was no big deal, but it made the girls feel grown up.

Biggest topic of the night was, of course, Will Hampton. Fliss had had a crush on him for a year, ever since he'd started playing in a local band. In fact last year she'd nearly managed to get herself thrown out of school for trying to see him. And now he was going to be at the boys' school just over the hill from Downey House! Fliss could hardly contain her excitement.

'Well, we'd better see this chap,' said Alice. 'See if he passes muster.'

'He still sings in the church choir,' said Fliss.

'Well, that will do,' said Alice.

It was some surprise to Felicity's parents when the girls announced on Saturday morning that they'd like to go to church on Sunday.

Mrs Prosser raised a heavily botoxed eyebrow.

'*Church?*' she said, in the same tone as she might have said '*The casino?*' Hattie was on the youth guidance committee for their local parish, but she'd had to drag Felicity there under the threat of dire torture since she was nine years old.

'Why on earth do you suddenly want to go to church?'

Felicity pouted. 'To give thanks and all that.'

'Yes, I'd like to go too, Mrs Prosser, if that's OK,' said Alice, with her usual adult assurance.

'And me,' squeaked Simone, promising Jesus in her heart that she didn't really mean it by going to a protestant church.

Hattie harrumphed loudly, but Felicity tried to ignore her. Undaunted, Hattie harrumphed again.

'Are you trying to say something, Harriet?' asked her mother, unable to keep the sharp edge out of her tongue. She loved her eldest daughter to distraction, but she could be terribly pi.

'I wonder,' said Harriet. 'I do WONDER if the male voice choir is singing harvest festival this Sunday.'

Fliss instantly coloured, and Alice spotted it.

'Are they?' she said. 'Actually, it was my idea to go. I do like to give thanks.'

Fliss's parents glanced at each other.

'We'll all go.'

In the event, not even Hattie's hateful sniggering could spoil Fliss's view, and she stood rapt in the third pew, watching Will's dark head as he bowed to his hymnal. His band had broken up over the summer, but he still loved to sing. *Notice me*, Fliss begged in her heart. What was wrong with her? Was she too short? Too fat? In fact, Fliss was blonde and pretty, with delicate features that could often be overlooked for the more striking dark looks of her friend Alice, but at fourteen she couldn't see beyond a touch of puppy fat and the occasional pimple. With all her heart she wished she was as confident as pert, cheeky Alice, with her dark shining hair and neat figure. Even Simone had big breasts. What did she have? Nothing! Oh, how she longed to look like a model.

Afterwards they filed out, Simone bobbing and crossing herself when she thought nobody was looking. Normally Fliss couldn't bear her mother hanging around to talk to the vicar and anyone else she came across, but today she lingered anxiously, wondering if she could find the courage to ask Will about his move.

Suddenly her heart stopped as she caught his floppy brown hair – and he was growing so fast, he must be nearly six foot already and he was barely sixteen – as he came out of the beautiful old church, so in demand for weddings from people who'd never even lived in the village.

As if in a dream, she watched as he slowly walked towards her. She bit her lip nervously. He couldn't be, could he? He couldn't be coming to talk to her? She felt like she was sinking underwater. Could she speak to him? Could she?

He stopped in front of her, and Fliss found she'd lost her breath.

'Uh . . . hi . . .' she stuttered. She felt like the whole congregation was watching them.

'Hi,' said Will. He had an easy, smiling manner about him, which made you feel like you were the only person he'd been waiting to speak to all day. Of course, he was like that with everyone.

'Have a good summer?'

'Uh yeah.'

Fliss's heart was pounding. Why couldn't she say anything interesting? Make a joke, say anything?

'Cool,' said Will. He looked around, to where Alice and Simone were trying to hover not-too-closely. Wow. Fliss's friend was really really hot.

'Hey, those your friends?'

Fliss couldn't do anything but nod dumbly. Will walked towards Alice.

'Hi,' he said, putting out his hand. 'I'm Will. Do you go to Downeys? You may need to fill me in on all its evil ways.'

Alice gave him a curt look, hiding her massive curiosity. She could certainly see what Fliss saw in him. Out of the corner of her eye she caught sight of her friend.

'Oh, I'm sure Fliss can help you out with all that,' she said.

Will nodded his head.

'I'm sure,' he said.

'Oh come *on*, Fliss.'

They were four hours into the drive, and Alice had yet to persuade her friend she hadn't been flirting with Will on purpose. Hattie was smugly sitting up the front, reading a book about lacrosse. Simone was in the middle – she'd volunteered – trying to stave off the tension. And Fliss was staring out of the window, thinking about Will and also the last thing her mother had said before she'd left that morning: 'Now, Felicity, you *will* be careful with all that stodge they serve at school, won't you?' She'd leant down out of earshot of everyone else. 'You don't want to end up like Hattie, do you?' 'What's that?' Hattie had said crossly, bounding down the stairs like an inelegant carthorse, her boater, schoolbag, hockey shoes and tennis raquet unraveling in her wake. 'Nothing, my gorgeous girls. Have a wonderful term!'

Maybe she would avoid the stodge, mused Felicity. Maybe that would help.

Alice sat back with a sigh, just as the sleek Audi crested the hill and, for the first time, the girls caught sight of the turreted, castle-like building that would be home for the next nine months.

'School! School!' shouted both Hattie and Simone. Simone's spirits lifted fully. Even Alice smiled. It did look like something out of a story book, the four towers of the main houses – Tudor, York, Wessex and their own, Plantagenet – nestled in the hills, with the cliffs behind, leading down to the still turquoise sea.

Chapter Two

'*Mon dieu,*' was the first thing Maggie heard as she stepped down from the railway carriage – this year, Stan had won the battle for the car.

Just ahead, her friend Mademoiselle Crozier, the impetuous French mistress, was wrestling with an elegant suitcase which had discharged its contents on to the platform.

'Claire!' she yelled excitedly, but didn't reach her before the guard and three passing men had all stopped to help. Maggie reflected that she could probably lose a leg under the train wheels before she could attract the attention of three passing men, but put the thought to the back of her mind.

'Hello,' she called. '*Bonjour!*'

'Maggie!' Claire ran up to her and gave her a big kiss. 'Eet eez *disaster*!'

Actually, her case was now being tidily zipped up by the hefty guard.

'Here you are, love,' he was saying. 'Can I help you down to your car now?'

The man was so overweight it didn't look like he'd make it much past the platform, but Claire just gave him her widest smile.

'Thank you zo much! That eez perfect, thank you!'

The man blushed to the roots of his moustache.

'How do you do that?' said Maggie, as they set off down the platform in search of a taxi.

'Do what?'

'Be so French.'

'I know,' said Claire seriously. 'Truly, I am from Liverpool. I did spend a long time working on ze accent.'

'POPS! No!'

'It's all I could get, Zelda. Calm down,' said Zelda's dad.

Zelda stared at the hummer in dismay.

'Dad, did you know those things are, like, totally destroying the earth?'

'No, hun, that's my nuclear bombs. Come on, get in.'

Zelda pouted and went back to applying lip gloss, then she heaved herself up into the giant armoured car.

'AND we have to stop for gas, like, every ten minutes.'

Zelda's mother glanced at her.

'Are you sure you should be wearing so much make up? There's none allowed during semesters.'

Zelda gave her mother a long look.

'Mom. This is the sixteenth school you've sent me to. I think I know what I need on the first day, OK? Dad's got his armour . . . I've got mine.'

Veronica could almost feel the approaching coaches and trains and cars, as she went through the school for the last time. Everything gleamed: the cleaning staff had done a fine job. The polished wooden desks reflected the soft September harvest light through the high, newly cleaned windows set into the strong stone walls of the four towers.

The refectory, with its long tables soon to be filled up with laughing girls and clattering noise, seemed oddly still. The only sound was the tap of her own heels in the long corridor outside, lined with pictures of headmistresses past, as she moved towards her own office. It was filled with her personal treasures – she had never wanted the headmistress's office to be just a place of fear or punishment, but neither did she want the girls thinking of her as a friend. She wanted to strike a balance between formality and balm. The girls should know the right thing must be done – but that second chances were always possible.

Her excellent and efficient proctor Miss Prenderghast stuck her head round the door, brandishing a large pile of post.

'Sorry to bother you already,' she said.

Veronica smiled and asked after Evelyn's new bassett hound.

'And don't forget,' said Miss Prenderghast eventually, 'the teachers' meet is at Downey Boys this year. Tomorrow night.'

Veronica winced. She was dreading this. An annual cocktail party to catch up with the teachers, plan the year ahead and make the aquaintance of any new members of staff at their counterpart school. Which, this year, would include . . .

'Yes yes,' she said, somewhat impatiently, fiddling with her plain gold necklace. Veronica, in general, was not a fiddler. 'What else?'

Miss Prenderghast felt awkward in light of Veronica's evidently unsettled mood.

'And there's the School Trade Fair in March, but that's a while off yet.'

Veronica put her hand over her eyes. 'Ah yes. The schools fair.'

This was a trade fair for public schools – essentially, a selling job. Veronica couldn't bear it. She would much rather

her school and its results spoke for themselves, and anyone who wished could come and have a look around the facilities. She disliked standing on a cheap stall trying to lure in people with money.

On the other hand, there was no doubt about it. Downey's emphasis on all-round education in its most traditional sense – the rounding of an individual – was showing in its results, against schools whose exam sausage-machines did nothing but cram information as tightly as possible into stressed, overburdened children with nothing on their minds except getting a sports car for five starred A-grade passes. It looked, in the rankings, like they were slipping.

Veronica despised this push for results as reflections on parents often too busy to broaden their children's horizons themselves. She felt it too often led to drop-outs and breakdowns at universities that encouraged self-directed learning, misery and bad behaviour in adolescents. However school tables were school tables, and she couldn't deny that they made a difference to what, in the end, however traditional, garlanded or revered, was still a business.

'Thank you, Evelyn,' she said. 'Another busy year.'

Miss Prenderghast smiled.

'We wouldn't have it any other way, Dr Deveral.'

The queue for taxis at the station was a mile long.

'Don't zey know we are teachers?' said Claire crossly, looking around for her friendly guard.

'I know, and I really want to check out the parents before they leave,' said Maggie worriedly. She wanted to meet the parents of the girls in her guidance class, now going into Middle School Two, just in case any issues she needed to be aware of had arisen over the long vac.

'*Brr*,' said Claire. 'I *never* want to see the parents. All they want to tell me is of their villa in the Dordogne and how their child ees French genius and can I spend all my time with thees French genius. An you know,' she added sagely, 'she is not genius.'

As she talked, a silver Audi drew up and honked loudly. Maggie raised her head warily – normally cars honking at her belonged to teenage boys, out too late from her old school in Glasgow. Instead, a nicely coiffed blonde head stuck out of the car window.

'Maggie? Is that you?'

It took Maggie a second to recognise her. When she did, her heart skipped a beat. It was Miranda.

Miranda had been David's fiancée, although to Maggie they'd never seemed very well suited – although she knew her own feelings for the English teacher might have coloured this view. They had broken up in the summertime. Maggie had wondered if it might have had something to do with her, but it couldn't have done, surely. She hoped Miranda didn't think so. She couldn't help remembering David's face, at the end of last year, when he'd asked her to go on holiday with him. She'd done the right thing staying with Stan, though, of course she had. She hoped Miranda was OK.

'Uh, hi there!' she said, leaning down to the window. 'How are you?'

'Fine, fine,' said Miranda.

Oh well, she couldn't suspect anything then.

'On your way to school?' asked Miranda. 'Want a lift?'

Maggie shrugged. It would be useful. 'Can you take my friend Claire, too?'

'Sure!'

Miranda signalled and pulled over, and the women put their suitcases into the immaculately tidy boot. Maggie sat in

18

front, still feeling nervous, even though technically she and David had never done anything wrong.

'Thanks for that, the queue is terrible.'

Miranda carefully pulled away. 'Yes, well, I'm going that way . . .'

She let her voice trail away as she looked out of the window. Maggie stole a glance at her. The antique ring on her fourth finger had gone.

They spoke in pleasantries until they had left the bustle of Truro behind and were heading out towards the country-side. Maggie, once again, after the tower blocks and heavy sandstone of Glasgow, appreciated its gentle beauty. Claire appeared to have gone to sleep.

'Maggie,' said Miranda finally, in a different tone.

Maggie felt her stomach lurch. Maybe Miranda *did* suspect something after all! Maggie told herself again she had nothing to feel guilty for, neither of them did . . . but as the nuns used to tell her at Holy Cross, there was sin in thought as well as deed.

'Uh, yes?'

'Have you . . . have you heard from David at all?' Miranda bit her lip. She looked pale; Maggie doubted she was used to asking for help.

Maggie shook her head. 'No, not at all. Didn't he go to Italy?'

'Yes, that's right, he said . . .'

Miranda signalled off on to the narrow country road and gave a half-hiccupy laugh.

'He is just so *damn* infuriating, you know?'

Maggie grimaced sympathetically.

'You know, he suggested maybe taking a break for a bit – we've been engaged for like a million years, we're obviously never going to bloody get round to it . . . And then, well, it just all came pouring out. I mean, it's OK for you, you guys are all teachers, so obviously it doesn't matter so much. But, you know, I'd just like a nice home, and someone with a bit of go-getting, you know? Some ideas and a bit of the get-ahead spirit. I mean, I work bloody hard, and I come home and there he is, nose buried in a book or messing about with that damn dog. I mean, is a bit of consideration too much to ask?' Her hands were gripping the steering wheel as her voice went higher.

'I don't *want* to work seventy hours a week when I have a baby, or live in some shitty rented flat all my life! I don't *want* to put everything I do to waste, just so he can get on with his precious boys! You can't believe the looks I get at the business group when I tell them he's a teacher. It's like that stupid old joke, you know? "Failed at everything? Try teaching."'

Miranda got a hold of herself and gave a short laugh. 'Sorry. I've just given you the same rant I gave him. And I know you're teachers too – sorry. I don't think you've failed at all, of course not.'

Maggie wasn't too sure about that.

But she could understand, a little, she supposed, Miranda's frustration. No doubt all her friends had blow-dried hair and nice manicures and husbands who worked in big cities for big pay cheques. She could see the attractions of an easy life. Though why it would make you throw over someone like David she could not comprehend.

'So . . . what's on your mind?' she asked tentatively.

'Well, he's annoying and distracted and always obsessing over something stupid and he never bloody stops talking. But . . . I don't know. I miss him. I'm not getting any younger. And the physical side is, well, it's kind of amazing. I just wish I knew what to do.'

Maggie very much did not want to hear about the physical side of things. Lifting her gaze, she felt her heart expand as, for the first time in two months, the four turrets of Downey House came into view. The car crunched expensive gravel under its smooth tyres.

'Oh, here you are,' said Miranda, looking up at the imposing building. She paused for a long time, then turned to Maggie.

'I'm not sure this is straight in my head.'

Maggie tried to look encouraging. 'Do you know what you want?'

'Don't be daft, I'm a woman in her thirties. Of course I don't.' Miranda attempted a watery smile, and Maggie felt her slightly forced friendliness melt into something more like empathy.

'I'm sorry,' she said, and meant it. She might think Miranda was crazy to pass up that man, but she knew what it was like to feel ambivalent about someone. She certainly did. And, odd though it may seem, perhaps she and Miranda could even be friends? After all, once upon a time they'd both liked the same man, so it wasn't as if they didn't have anything in common . . .

'Maybe I won't pop by the boys' school, after all,' said Miranda, placing her hands on the steering wheel. 'I obviously still have, uh, issues . . . Anyway.' She clasped her hands in her lap. 'I know you two are friends. When you see him, could you ask him to drop me a line? Please?'

'Of course,' said Maggie.

'And maybe we could go for a drink sometime? Girls' night out?'

Claire awoke with a start. 'Yes, please! So I do not keel myself!'

*

21

Zelda had a well-practised routine for starting new schools. First of all, find out if there were any more army brats just like her around. They normally understood each other. Failing that, hang back. Going in and trying to make friends was a sure-fire recipe for disaster, whereas if you were aloof and indifferent, they lapped it up. Not that it mattered, she'd be in Germany or Cyprus by next year, so, like, who gave a crap?

Now she threw herself on the spare bed in her assigned dorm, realising with some satisfaction that the other two girls were staring at her, wide-eyed. The dorm was two stories up – first years took the first floor – but otherwise conformed to a basic pattern: four beds, with their own side tables, and a corner sink.

Alice was still at her medical. Zelda patted her hair, which she'd back-sprayed until it was big – properly big. She didn't care if they were going to keep her in plaits for the rest of the year; today, she was having American hair.

'What kind of a shit hole is this anyway?'

The boyish blonde one spoke up immediately. 'I know. I protested about it last year. I nearly got kicked out actually.'

'Nearly, huh?'

'But I like it now . . . I mean, it's all right. It's a bit sucky.'

'So, what is it,' Zelda attempted a strangulated English accent, 'ginger beer and midnight feasts?'

'Are you American?' asked Simone eagerly. She'd never met an American before.

'Huh, well, guess my English accent isn't quite as good as I thought.'

Zelda threw her huge Louis Vuitton case on the bed. Fliss looked at it in horror; she thought it was vulgar. Simone thought it was amazing.

'It's not really midnight feasts, they're for kids,' said Fliss, trying to sound cool and unbothered though not particularly succeeding. Zelda was wearing a velvet miniskirt with long socks pulled up over her knees and a crisp white shirt with an Argyle-print, very tight tank top. Her bright yellow hair was backcombed over the crown of her head and she was wearing bright blue eyeshadow and a lot of pink lip gloss. She looked simultaneously a lot older and younger than her years, and very different from anyone the girls had ever met.

'Shame,' said Zelda. 'That's the only bit I was looking forward to.'

'My mum has sent me a big box,' chipped in Simone. Fliss wished she would get the puppy dog look out of her eyes. Come on, this girl wasn't *that* cool. 'We could have a midnight feast if you wanted.'

'Cool,' said Zelda. 'What else do people do for fun?' She took a long look out of the window and heaved a weary sigh. 'Push cows over?'

Maggie looked around her small suite of rooms, high in the west tower overlooking the sea, and gave a small sigh of contentment. It was odd, considering home was the ex-council house they'd bought in Pollock and made nice with a big telly and Ikea bits and bobs, despite far too many wires from Stan's Playstation, ideas for a surround-sound system which hadn't quite come off, and the trainers lining the hall. Here, the bare minimalism of the pale blue plaster walls, the small sofa with a delicate eau-de-nil print and the huge, gabled windows stretching out across the Irish sea felt calm and restful. And Claire, of course, was just through the other side of the study they shared. She unpacked carefully, not just tossing things around like she probably would at home, and remembered last year, when she had been so nervous.

This year was going to be different, she decided. She

wasn't going to feel out of her depth, or intimidated by the traditional surroundings of the boarding school. She was going to be calm, collected, never lose her rag—

There was a rap at the door.

'Miss Adair? Are you back? First assembly is just about to start, and I'd hate for one of my department to make a late showing.'

It was Miss Starling, Dr Deveral's second-in-command and Maggie's head of house, who always seemed to be telling Maggie off before she'd actually done anything.

'Yes, Miss Starling!' said Maggie, smoothing down her dark curls as best she could and heading for the door. Calm, elegant, inspirational . . .

Miss Starling was standing outside in the corridor, back straight as a poker, her fawn-tweed suit immaculate.

'Just got off the train, did you?' she asked Maggie. 'Shame you didn't have time to smarten up. Well, come on then, hurry up.'

'Yes, Miss Starling,' said Maggie, castigating herself as she usually did for speaking to her boss as if she were still a pupil. 'Uh, did you have a good summer?'

Miss Starling looked as if the question didn't make any sense.

'It was passable, I suppose. I've prepared a new review syllabus for your Middle School seconds I want you to take a look at.'

Maggie groaned inwardly. Miss Starling believed contemporary teaching to be namby-pamby in the extreme and believed that the girls should be spending their time memorising long screeds of Milton. Maggie didn't have anything against Milton per se, she just wanted to include and engage as many children as widely as possible; to build readers. And Milton wasn't always the way to do that.

'Yes, Miss Starling,' she found herself saying again, like a Victorian servant, as she trotted off at the deputy's fast pace down the corridor to the spiral stairs.

'She's going to be late!' Simone was fretting.

Fliss tutted. 'Matron will be checking her for tropical parasites again.'

Matron was stern and didn't suffer malingerers gladly, but to the truly sick she was a source of much balm.

Simone and Fliss – and Zelda, who had nothing better to do – were waiting for Alice, who was going to miss assembly if she didn't hop to it.

'She said she'd be here,' said Fliss, aware she was sounding childish. 'I wanted to show her my new Urban Outfitters dress.'

Zelda's ears pricked up. It looked like Alice was queen bee, which might be a bit more interesting than the fatso and the nervy blonde, who could be pretty if she wasn't dressed like a ten-year-old and tried a bit of make up on her pale, thin face.

'Where's she from?' enquired Zelda, world expert.

'Cairo at the mo,' said Fliss.

'Oh,' said Zelda. 'What's that like?'

Simone shrugged her shoulders. 'The country is, like, a total touchstone in bringing together East and West. It's geopolitically too imperative to be stable—'

'Hot,' said Fliss.

Simone swallowed hard. This may not be her old school, but still, her grip on popularity wasn't so strong she could go swotting it about all over the place.

When Simone, the lone scholarship girl from a poor background, had arrived the previous year, she'd hoped to find the pupils more sympathetic than at her old school, where she'd been relentlessly bullied for her studiousness and her weight. Instead, she'd found it just as cruel, with Alice, in particular, taunting her eating habits. Finally, falsely accused of stealing, she'd run away. Miss Adair and Mr McDonald – and his dog, Stephen Daedalus – had found her. Things had started to get a lot better after that and the girls were beginning to accept her, but she still felt insecure.

Just at that moment, a black-haired girl with dancing dark eyes and a mature air burst into the room.

'Bloody health certificate. I'm sure Matron wants to suck my blood.'

Fliss and Simone jumped up to go. Alice took a step back and regarded the newcomer coolly.

'Zelda Towrnell,' said Zelda, taking the initiative. Fliss watched the exchange nervously. Zelda, with her cool clothes and heavy make up, didn't look fourteen at all. Alice studied her, then appeared to make up her mind.

'Are you American? Whereabouts are you from?'

'Well, I was born in DC—'

'No way! My dad was posted there. I lived in Georgetown when I was seven.'

And they were off, chatting away nineteen to the dozen. Fliss turned away. Why did she have to be brought up in bloody boring Guildford, where everyone went to the same things and knew the same people and had visited Florida for Disneyland and that was it? She had thought they might be able to chat about her adoration of *High School Musical*, but that seemed silly and unsophisticated now Zelda and Alice were rabbiting away about bloody Jamba juice, whatever that was.

'We need to get to assembly,' she announced, suddenly conscious she was sounding like Hattie.

Alice and Zelda exchanged glances, and suddenly Fliss felt a cold hand clutch at her heart.

*

Veronica Deveral surveyed the large wood-panelled assembly hall, as four of her second years stumbled in late. She didn't mention it or pull them up. Miss Starling, recognising them as part of Maggie's guidance class, shot her a look. Maggie felt instantly cross with the girls – why did it always have to be her class showing her up?

Veronica simply paused in her short introductory welcome to new and returning students and waited till the girls had found seats at the back. Then, as if nothing had happened, she continued her talk, commending the young women in front of her to take part in the life of the school as fully as possible.

'I want you to work hard, play hard and think. Think about the kind of women you want to be, what you want to give to society and what you want to achieve in this life. We hope very much that Downey House can help you achieve it.'

She believed this, of course, wholeheartedly, but wondered too. With results becoming more and more important every year and grade inflation affecting A-levels, any school not churning out regular four A-starred medical students appeared to be slipping in standards. She took in the fresh faced, slightly anxious new girls, brown from holidays in Cornwall and Mustique, unusual-looking in the latest fashions they were allowed to wear on their first night. She wanted to take in these nervous girls and turn out poised young women, ready and prepared for everything the world could throw at them – not see them churned through some exam-passing machine and forced on to university courses and paths that wouldn't really suit them. Not everyone was a Simone Pribetich, she thought, her mind returning to the plump scholarship girl who'd topped the maths and science papers across the year before. The trick with Simone was to stop her working so hard and broaden her scope. But did league tables care about that?

Not a flicker of her concerns – or her trepidation at the teachers' cocktail party to follow – crossed her face, however, as she pleasantly exhorted the girls 'To try, to do. Winston Churchill once said, *I do like to learn, although I often do not like to be taught.* We understand that this can be true.' There was a scattering of laughter from the older girls. 'He also said, *Every day you may make progress. Every step may be fruitful. Yet there will stretch out before you an ever-lengthening, ever-ascending, ever-improving path. You know you will never get to the end of the journey. But this, so far from discouraging, only adds to the joy and glory of the climb.* And I hope you will also find this to be true of your time here.'

Maggie re-did her make up for the cocktail party. She had wanted to have a word with Fliss, Alice, Simone and the slightly alarming-looking new girl about their tardiness, but hadn't been able to find them after the assembly. Well, neither was it ideal to start term with a row, especially as she and Fliss had had their ups and downs the previous year, but they needed to know it had been noticed ... Especially, she grimaced to herself in the mirror, by Miss Starling.

And now, of course, she had to see David. She hadn't allowed her thoughts to wander on to him at all during the summer. In Scotland, and on holiday, that was easy. Their minor flirtation had seemed like a mere silly dream, an adolescent infatuation easily confused because of her new circumstances. Back with her parents, Stan and her sister, she could be much more grounded in real life. They were planning their wedding for next summer, at the Sacred Heart in Govan, with a reception in the church hall and a very loud ceilidh band and disco taking them through the night. They couldn't afford very much, but it was OK, they could bung a bit of money behind the bar, and her dad would probably want to do a few songs, and they could have a buffet rather than a sit-down, that would save them quite a bit. And Father McSorley had christened Stan and her; had made their first communions, taken their nervous first confessions; confirmed them (Stan's new name John, as plain as he could manage; Maggie's was Cecelia – she so hated the dullness of Margaret), looked disappointed when they stopped being regular attenders (and in Stan's case, an altar boy) in their late teens, but then found it hard to hide his delight when they'd returned and asked him to marry them. He would doubtless jolly up the wedding reception and probably want to share the karaoke wiith her dad. She smiled when she thought how different he was to the young Very Reverend Rackington, who took school services at Downey and always looked slightly terrified by the mass of young women giggling and passing notes throughout his tedious sermons.

But now, at the very least, she would have to pass on Miranda's message. Well, it would be fine. It wasn't like she was going to see him and turn to jelly, of course she wasn't.

There was a loud banging on the connecting door.

'We will be as late as your naughty little second years, *non*?' shouted Claire from her set of rooms.

Maggie heaved a sigh. Had *everyone* noticed it was her class that had been late?

'Come in!' shouted Maggie.

Claire found her still in front of the mirror. 'I do not want to go to this,' she sighed heavily. She had been embroiled in a secret affair with the Classics master, which had ended after he went back to his wife and left the school. Without even that excitement, Claire found being holed up in Cornwall very tedious indeed.

'Me neither,' said Maggie, with emphasis. Claire looked at her curiously, so Maggie finished up with, 'It's so dull, and Dr Fitzroy doesn't like me.'

The head of Downey Boys had seen Veronica's employment of a comprehensive teacher as a quaint experiment, like attempting to domesticate a monkey.

'He doesn't like women,' said Claire. 'Only the very strange work in schooling that is only for boys, yes?'

'Definitely,' said Maggie, as much to convince herself as anything. 'Definitely.'

Downey Boys, a smart fifteen-minute hike along the cliff path, was much older than the girls' school, dating back to the mid-eighteenth century. This, however, made it seem brighter and more contemporary than the forbidding, high-turreted Victorian gothic of Downey House. The sash windows were elegantly spaced, the rooms and dorms bright and sunny. The setting sun reflected off the clean glass in Dr Robert Fitzroy's large meeting room where teachers from both schools were mingling and discussing the plans for the year ahead. Handsome, gangling sixth-formers, smart in their navy blue uniforms or, for some of them, their Officer Training Corps garb, handed round drinks and canapés.

Veronica stood back on the threshold. Well, there was nothing else for it. She spied Daniel almost straight away, tall and good-natured looking, with a shock of strawberry-blond hair that was not unlike hers until she tamed it straight with some ferocity each morning. She took a deep breath, drew on her inner reserves of fortitude forged in a tough early life, and stepped forward to greet her estranged son.

'Mr Stapleton,' she said, without a hint of the torment raging beneath her neat cashmere twinset. 'How nice to see you again.'

Maggie caught her breath. David was standing next to the window, making Mrs Offili, head of music, and Janie James, the notoriously tough PE teacher, laugh raucously. The light reflected off his almost-black, unwieldy-looking hair, and caught his wide, slightly manic grin. He was as tall, skinny and angular as ever, with a light tan complementing his dark, quick eyes. Maggie probed her heart as one would a loose tooth. What did she feel? Did it hurt?

But she thought it might be just a general pleasure at seeing again someone she liked and respected. Yes, that was all it was. A friend. Definitely.

As she moved slowly into the room, she heard his voice cry, joyfully, 'Maggie!' Almost without thinking, she moved towards him, only to find her route blocked by Dr Fitzroy.

'It's Miss Adair, isn't it? Still with us?'

'Yes, sir,' murmured Maggie.

'Well, well. I thought you'd be pregnant and on the list for a council house by now . . . Oh come on, don't take me seriously, I'm only joking. Will you have a drink?'

He procured her a glass of white wine from a passing tray. 'So what were you thinking of teaching this year?'

Maggie glanced out of the corner of her eye. Sure enough, David was heading towards them. She felt her heart beat faster. In a friendly way.

'I thought First World War poets to my Middle School seconds.'

'Ah, capital idea. Though don't get too politically correct on us, will you?'

'I don't think there was much correct about the First World War,' said Maggie.

'Yes, well, perhaps. Don't forget Kipling, that's all I mean.' He took a deep oratorial breath. *'Have you heard news of my boy Jack?'*

'Not this tide,' joined in David softly, suddenly appearing at her side.

'Ah, hello, David! Yes, capital stuff.'

'Then hold your head up all the more, this tide and every tide . . . sounds like a Coldplay song now, of course,' added David.

'It sounds amazing,' said Maggie. 'I can't believe I've never heard it.'

Robert snorted.

'And don't start on my schooling again, please. Kipling is just unfashionable, that's all.'

'Political correctness gone mad,' sniffed Robert, but he cast her a smile as Maggie and David attempted an extremely clumsy social kiss and nearly clashed noses.

'Hello,' she said, suddenly shy. 'Did you have a good summer?'

'Magnificent,' he said, grinning. 'What about you?'

'Great,' she said firmly.

'Well, that's good.'

There was a pause as David rubbed the back of his neck, then headed for neutral ground.

'Are you going to teach the First World War poets?'

'What's wrong with that?'

'Nothing, I suppose. It makes my boys awfully drippy and they all get terrible crushes.'

'Oh yes. The Brooke effect.'

'They grow their hair floppy and walk about arm in arm.'

'Like public school boys.'

'Well, when you put it like that . . .'

'What are you teaching this year?'

'*The Beano*, I think. And *Loaded* magazine for Media Studies. Apparently we have to look to our grades now.'

'Now, McDonald, that's not what I meant at all and you know it,' said Robert sharply.

David rolled his eyes. 'Well, I wish they'd make up their minds. They can have grades or they can have an education and perhaps they can have both, but not always.'

Robert harrumphed and bore off to see his elegant head-teacher counterpart, who was looking a little distracted this evening.

'So,' said David, after a pause.

'Oh, I ran into Miranda,' Maggie said quickly – too quickly, she wondered? 'It was quite a coincidence. She gave me a lift from the station.'

'Coincidence, eh?' said David, giving her a look.

Maggie thought about it. It hadn't occurred to her that Miranda would look out for her on purpose.

'Oh,' she said. 'Well. Anyway.'

'How is she?'

Maggie looked frankly at him. 'Honestly? Between you and me?'

She thought about soft-soaping what Miranda had said, or subtly twisting it to make her seem unpleasant, but what was the point?

'She wants you back,' said Maggie. 'I think she wants you back really badly.'

David grimaced. It was obvious talking about his private life didn't come easily to him.

'She thinks she does. Then after a month she'll start talking about shoring up our equity options or something again and I won't understand it and she'll get jealous of Stephen

Daedalus and start hankering after the bright lights of Exeter and then it will all start over . . .'

Stephen Daedalus was David's loyal, beloved and somewhat boisterous mongrel.

He let his voice tail off, but his eyes were far away. Maggie sighed. He must still be thinking of her regardless.

'How did she look?'

'Gorgeous,' said Maggie, truthfully. Miranda was so tall and blonde and striking it would be ridiculous to imply anything else. 'She looked gorgeous. Sad, of course.'

'Well, of course,' said David, a shadow of his smile crossing his face.

'Are you going to give her a call?' asked Maggie bravely.

'How's Stan?' asked David, changing the subject. David and Stan had met the previous year and were like two alien species. Stan thought David was fey and peculiar. Maggie suspected that David never thought of Stan at all. She wasn't sure what was worse.

'Great! Great, he's great,' said Maggie. 'Celtic won the league, so . . .'

'That's good, is it?'

'Don't you follow the football?'

David looked embarrassed. 'I know, I know, it makes me less of a man.' He lowered his voice. 'I have a terrible affliction. I . . . don't like football.'

'Oh God,' said Maggie. 'How can you function?'

'With great difficulty,' said David. 'It's really awful, having to run your life when you're only interested in books, films, music, art, dogs, people and beer.'

'That does sound boring and empty.'

'It's very lonely, having to curl up in front of a fire on a wet Saturday afternoon with Stephen Daedalus and a book rather than hauling out with ten thousand other men to a muddy field in the rain to shout loud abuse at people wearing different colours from myself. I'm practically a girl.'

'Do you wear pink fluffy mules when you curl up on the sofa, eating chocolates out of a heart-shaped box?' teased Maggie.

'As long as it doesn't get in the way of my crochet,' he said seriously.

You see, just think of him as a girl, Maggie told herself firmly. A female friend. A friend.

'Hello, Daniel,' said Veronica gently.

Daniel steeled himself. He was nervous enough already about taking on his new job – it was quite a step up from his old role in Kent, and Downey Boys was a famous and established school. Originally a teacher, he had taken an inspector's position when the chance arose to visit Downey House, as he followed the trail of his birth mother. His evident qualities, however, hadn't gone unnoticed, and he'd been surprised and flattered when Dr Fitzroy had offered him a job – and even more surprised when he'd accepted.

He told himself that it had nothing to do with the fact that his birth mother was the headmistress of the girls' school across the way. His adoptive mother and his wife had both been very concerned, but knew better than to try and talk him out of something that loomed so large in his life.

'Hello,' he said. He held out his hand and she took it, gratefully.

'You look well,' she said. 'Did the children have a good summer?'

Daniel nodded. 'Relocating to Cornwall from the home counties . . . it's just been amazing. They're in heaven, they think they're on holiday every day.'

Veronica smiled at the thought. 'Living on the beach?'

'Living on the beach, playing in the sand ... I never thought I'd see Sam eat a prawn, but there you are. It's amazing.'

'I'm so glad,' said Veronica. 'I'm so glad you can be happy.'

She started again. 'I'm sorry about last year . . .'

Daniel's mouth twisted. 'So I suppose you haven't told anyone here yet?'

'I just wanted to wait for the right moment—'

'Which might never come.'

'I mean, it will be a shock—'

Robert came over and clapped Daniel on the back heartily. He wouldn't dare touch Veronica, of course.

'Dr Deveral, you know our new history teacher . . .'

'I do indeed,' said Veronica. 'You're extremely lucky.'

'I hope so. Got to pep up the old leagues.'

Veronica raised her eyebrows. 'Indeed.'

'Who ees zat?' Claire whispered to Maggie, staring in Daniel's direction. David had excused himself; Maggie wondered if it was to make a phone call.

Maggie craned her neck.

'He's one of the inspectors from last year, isn't he? I wonder what he's doing here. And anyway, he's wearing a big shiny gold wedding ring, so stay *well* away.'

'*Pff,*' said Claire. 'This is life, yes? It is nothing without a leetle risk.'

'Yes, a risk to you!' said Maggie firmly. 'Not to some nice guy with a nice wife who wouldn't have a hope if you sashayed over and Frenched him up with your raincoats and stuff.'

Claire frowned. 'Ah do not understand what you zay but I do not theenk it is very complimentary at me. But you, you are perfect, yes? In your life, always perfect.'

36

'*No*,' said Maggie. 'Was just trying to be helpful.'

Claire grimaced. '*D'accord*. Another glass of the pee of goat?'

'I think I'm going to head back,' said Maggie. David had gone to Stephen Daedalus, and she had said her polite Hellos to practically everyone else. 'I have a heavy class to prepare for tomorrow.'

Simone didn't know why she was nervous. She was clued up on the syllabus, she'd done really well last year, she was more than justifying her scholarship. Nonetheless at breakfast on the first morning, when Mrs Rhys provided the huge first-day spread that the girls often complained had to last them the entire year, she found herself mechanically slathering butter and jam thickly on white toast and cramming it into her mouth. Suddenly she caught sight of Zelda, who was picking listlessly at a fruit salad whilst boldly staring at her. Simone smiled, tentatively. She had started to come out of her shell a little, but still found it difficult to start conversations with strangers, especially tall, lanky glamorous strangers.

'What?' she said.

'Oh, nothing,' said Zelda.

'What?'

Zelda looked at Alice and Fliss.

'Well,' she said, 'it's just something we quite often do, like, in American schools? But I don't know if you'd like it here.'

The other girls' ears pricked up immediately.

Zelda genuinely didn't mean it to sound cruel. It just seemed obvious to her and she hated wasting time.

'What?' demanded Simone, getting irritated. She wasn't going to relinquish her hard-found acceptance to some mouthy American who looked like Miley Cyrus.

'A makeover,' announced Zelda, pushing back from her fruit salad.

The other girls gasped in admiration. It was one thing to talk about Simone behind her back, quite another to announce it in public.

Fliss was appalled. How dare this girl push in and decide she knew what was best for everyone? She hoped Alice was going to go for her with a really sharp put-down.

But to her amazement, Simone simply laid down her toast.

'OK,' she said nonchalantly.

Although Simone was trying to act as coolly as she could, inside her heart was beating incredibly fast. A makeover! How long had she dreamed of someone coming up to her and saying, 'You know, inside I bet you're really gorgeous. Let's bring out the real you.' She had a secret fantasy of one day meeting Gok Wan, and him buying her lots of lovely clothes and making her look great and feel fantastic about her body. This big-haired American wasn't quite as good, obviously, but she would have to do.

All the other girls were looking at her and smiling. Pretty, blonde Sylvie Brown was even clapping. They looked so happy and excited, and Simone enjoyed their reaction.

'You're really pretty,' continued Zelda. 'Bit of weight off, get the skin sorted out, a few new clothes . . .'

Simone didn't want to figure out how she could afford new clothes for now, she was too excited and flustered by suddenly being the centre of attention.

'Do you really think so?' All the girls said Of course, and made noises of agreement.

'Uh-oh,' said Alice in a low voice into Fliss's ear. 'We've created a monster.'

Fliss smiled, but she couldn't help feeling put out. Why

was Simone getting all the attention all of a sudden? She was used to her quiet, funny, mousy friend. She wasn't sure she wanted her turning glamorous. Alice was quite enough to cope with as it was. And as for Zelda . . . She had a sudden horrifying vision of the three of them all swanning around, dark hair swinging, wearing trendy clothes and leaving her out. She didn't like it, and slowly pushed her bowl of cereal away, the girl who couldn't even attract a boy from her home town.

Maggie tried to smile when she thought of herself this time last year, terrified of her first encounter with her class. Now she felt . . . Nope, she couldn't deny it. She was still nervous. She glanced at her notes. Just one new girl, that wasn't too bad. Miss Starling was taking the first years this year. She didn't envy them.

Smoothing down her new pale grey tea dress – heavily discounted in the Jesiré sale – she smiled brightly in the mirror. Rose-pink lipstick, a touch of blusher, a hint of her summer tan still there. Not bad. She thought briefly of Stan, who started work at the paper distribution plant at five o'clock in the morning and by the time he got home was often too knackered to notice what she looked like. Well, not to worry about him now. She headed towards her classroom.

Maggie was surprised to see the new girl loitering by the door, as the rest of the class took their seats inside. (She had said hello to Felicity and asked her if she'd had a good holiday. Felicity had tried not to smirk. It had been an uncomfortable moment for both of them.)

Normally new pupils tried to hide themselves inconspicuously amongst their new classmates. Maggie smiled in what she thought was a reassuring manner, remembering how scared she'd been the year before – and she'd been the teacher.

'Hello,' she said kindly. 'I'm Miss Adair, your form mistress and English teacher. Don't worry, I think you're going to like it here.'

Zelda had had the welcome speech about a million times before.

'Yeah yeah,' she said. 'Do you want me to introduce myself and say where I'm from and all that blah blah blah . . .'

Maggie glanced at the enrolment form.

'Well, Zelda, if you'd like to—'

'Yeah, whatever.'

Zelda squared up to the front of the class, and Maggie had no choice but to stand back and let her get on with it.

'Yeah, hi everyone,' drawled Zelda. 'My name is Zelda Derene Towrnell. I was born in Washington DC.'

She turned to Maggie. 'That's in America.'

'Yes, thank you, Zelda,' said Maggie tightly. She'd never been to America.

'And my dad's a major in the US marines. He's over here teaching your limey soldiers how to help kick butt in whatever place the United States of Ass-kicking gets stupidly involved in next.'

'Watch your mouth please, Zelda,' said Maggie, shocked. The girls were obviously enthralled by the tough-talking, undoubtedly glamorous stranger. They'd probably all have American accents in a week. 'We absolutely don't tolerate that kind of language here.'

'Yes, ma'am,' said Zelda, leisurely. 'Sorry. That was an outburst of independent thought. It won't happen again.'

Maggie gave Zelda her very sternest look, picked up a sheet and put a mark next to her name. The last thing she needed was a girl who probably wouldn't be staying at the school for very long and had no fear of consequences, encouraging the girls in impudent behaviour.

And another voice at the back of her mind said she did believe in free expression, didn't she? She did believe in encouraging the girls to speak their minds, engage in the wider world, however black and white their opinions might be. But there were opinions and there was rudeness, and this was definitely in the latter camp. On the other hand, it could be useful . . .

'Well, let's engage with what Zelda has said, shall we?' she added, indicating the girl to the empty seat next to Alice.

'This term we're going to look at the First World War poets, in conjunction with your History module. An entire generation of men suffered the whole breadth of horror and terror that life could throw at them – could throw at anyone. We can't know how many Beethovens and Einsteins, Picassos and Dickens were lost. But there were some who took that rage, that horror, and turned it into beauty, and its only possible redemption. We have it in their work. The men themselves, whether they lived or died, often could not be saved.'

Maggie noticed the mood of the class, previously perky and anticipatory with the smell of new schoolbooks and pencil sharpenings in the crisp air, had tuned in, become interested. Perhaps David was right, and they were all going to get caught up in the doomy romance of the whole terrible era. Well good, she thought. As long as they engaged.

'Are we allowed to conscientiously object?' drawled a voice. Zelda.

'And you, missy, can keep quiet in my classroom!' The second she'd said it, Maggie was furious with herself for losing her temper. Ten minutes into the start of term as well.

The rest of the class looked shocked and a little wary. Maggie took a deep breath and composed herself.

'Turn to page 356,' she said, brusquely. 'Simone, can you start?'

After a pause, there was a satisfactory rustling in the classroom.

'*What tolling bells,*' started Simone tentatively, '*for those who die as cattle?*'

Engaged.

'Not engaged?' Claire enquired crossly. 'Well, he asked you, so indeed you are engaged. And zat is zat.'

Claire, Maggie and Miranda were in a corner of the local village pub. Miranda had kept her word and rang them for a 'Girlie session', as she termed it. She was certainly very organised. There was only one pub, and teachers were discouraged from 'frittering' (Miss Starling's word) their evenings there. However sometimes needs must, and tonight was one of those evenings, so they sat choking over the unpleasant white wine.

'Yeah,' said Miranda, 'but he said I negated it when I took the ring off, threw it at him and told him it was a cheap piece of shit.'

'You did that?' said Maggie wonderingly.

'Well, I was under a lot of pressure at work at the time.'

'Men love passionate women,' said Claire, huffing into her glass. 'This wine is the piss of the dogs my uncle raised.'

'So what did he say?'

Maggie realised she had a slightly unhealthy interest, but couldn't help leaning forward anyway.

Miranda sighed. 'Well, he was holding his ground. But then I used my secret weapon.'

'*Non!*' said Claire. '*Formidable!*'

'What? What?'

'Men,' Claire went on with a knowing look, 'they cannot resist to see a pretty woman cry.'

'Really?' said Maggie.

'Well, it was just a *few* tears,' said Miranda.

'Did it work?'

Miranda shrugged. 'I think we're still on.'

'But do you still want him?'

By way of an answer, Miranda turned her gaze to a drunken old man sitting in the corner of the pub on his own. Nursing a whisky, his watery gaze was distant and vivid red veins mapped his face.

'It's not like my life is crawling with potentials,' she said, steeling herself and knocking back her glass. 'Anyway, what about you? You're engaged too, if I remember rightly? How are the wedding preparations going?'

Maggie smiled a little tightly. 'Oh, we're getting there. My nephews are very excited. They're going to be page boys and have Skean Dhus.'

'What is zis?' asked Claire.

'It's like a small sword you hide in your sock when you're wearing a kilt. I'm not sure letting my nephews anywhere with small swords is the wisest of plans.'

'Where is it going to be?'

'In a hotel near where we live that does a lot of weddings,' said Maggie, a tad defensively. She'd been to lots of parties and dances there growing up, it was within their budget and it seemed fitting.

She couldn't shake off, however, the idea that she should be more excited. She was, of course, but she felt a little as if she and Stan were married already, and this was just expensive fuss. Or that it wasn't, a very small voice inside her whispered, well, it wasn't her *dream* wedding. She realised thinking like that was stupid and spoiled. She made all right money, Stan got by. It would be completely and utterly stupid to spunk thousands of pounds they couldn't afford or get into debt just to hire a dumb castle or stately home, when all their friends and family would be delighted to be just where they were, all together.

'What about ze dress?'

'I think I need you to help me with that, Claire. Something French and chic. Otherwise I'll look like a big, white, upside-down mushroom.'

'You must get it made for you,' said Claire.

'When I get a jillion pound raise!'

'*Non*, it is a must. You must get it made for you. So it will fit like a glove.'

'Well, in that case I'd better postpone the wedding, give me enough time to slim down so they can get a measuring tape round me.'

'I think you have a gorgeous healthy figure,' said Miranda, politely avoiding gazing at the empty crisp packets by Maggie's glass. 'Don't change a thing.'

If you really thought that, you wouldn't be such a hungry-looking size eight, thought Maggie to herself, then felt mean, dissatisfied and not really a blushing bride.

Maggie rose early, feeling thirsty and worried about having drunk too much wine the night before. A walk, definitely, to clear the cobwebs.

It was fresh and very blowy, but the sun was strong for late September and she could feel her head clear as she hit the cliffs.

The warm tongue licking her hand didn't, as it might once have done, take her totally by surprise.

'Stephen Daedalus!' she cried in delight. The dog was overjoyed to see her again, and leapt up on her jeans.

'Now you *know* that is naughty,' she mock-scolded him, then gave in to the moment and rolled him around on the dewy ground, scratching between his ears in the way she knew he loved, which was how David found her five minutes later. Maggie scrambled up, pink-cheeked and out of breath.

'*Not* the most dignified of positions,' she smiled.

'Oh, I don't know,' said David, smiling back. 'You have a dandelion in your hair.'

'I missed him,' she said.

'He missed you.'

They fell into step, then both picked up a stick for the dog at the same time.

'Let's see whose he goes for,' said David. He hurled his far across the bracken. Maggie, who'd never been sporty, got hers about ten metres. Stephen Daedalus immediately aimed for that one.

'You are a VERY LAZY DOG,' said David, as Stephen charged back to Maggie's feet.

'You can't get over the fact that he likes me more than he likes you.'

'No he doesn't! He tolerates your weak throwing arm and inability to stop giving him treats.'

Maggie smiled. Then she told him about blowing up at the new girl.

'I can't just ignore it. They'll all start ... what's the American word?'

'Sassing you,' said David.

'Exactly.'

'The thing is, she really is quite cool.'

'Well, get her to express it then. Defuse her rebellious status. She won't be cool if the teacher thinks she's great. And get her to talk about her dad. Don't you think it would be good for your girls to hear about someone who really

45

puts their life on the line? Most of their fathers spend their lives jammed to their desks and those blueberry things.' He shivered.

'It doesn't sound like she'd have him come in.'

'That doesn't matter. Get her to share her experiences.'

'Like show and tell?'

'Yes! Exactly. Typical American – if you can't beat 'em, join 'em.'

'Maybe I will. I saw Miranda. She seems cheerful.'

David looked awkward. 'Yes, good. She's good, I think.'

'So it's all back on?'

'Uh ... well, we're thinking of having a trial period.' David pushed his long hands through his unruly black hair. 'Anyway. We'll see ...'

'Sure. Good,' said Maggie. 'I'm glad it's working out. Right. I'm off for breakfast.'

Stephen Daedalus pricked up his ears.

'That dog! You should teach him to say "sausages".'

David caressed his ears. 'Stephen Daedalus is far too intelligent and cultured to bother with sausages. *Foie gras*, maybe.'

'You think?'

'It's not his fault he's the best dog in the world.'

'It's not,' said Maggie, shaking her head as she went back through the wrought-iron gate at the bottom of the grounds. It was amazing, really, the affectionate way David talked about his dog, compared to how he spoke about his so-called fiancée.

Veronica was deep in thought. She had spent a sleepless night looking at her dilemma from every conceivable angle, trying to bring her usually logical problem-solving intelligence to bear on something which made her heartsick.

Perhaps . . . She couldn't simply announce to the world that she had a son, without facing so many intrusive questions, so many enquiring glances and curious eyes, so much gloating that the remote, untouchable headmistress had . . . Had given away her own child.

It could ruin her. Ruin the school. She looked around at her elegant office. She couldn't bear it. Everything she had strived for, longed for, wanted. All gone. Where would she go, unemployable at fifty? Nervously she fingered her rope of pearls.

But then again, she owed Daniel. She *owed* him. Her own flesh and blood. She had failed him once, she couldn't do it again. Oh dear. Why was life so difficult?

Miss Starling hardly waited past the knock to walk into Veronica's office, with the same, mildly offended gait she always displayed.

'June,' said Veronica.

'The treasure hunt,' said Miss Starling. 'I disapprove.'

Veronica felt much happier to be back on solid ground. There were a great many things of which June Starling disapproved, and being outside during lesson hours, fraternising with the boys' school and giving the impression of confusing learning with fun was quite high up there. Hence her usual assault on the annual second year's treasure hunt, held in early October when the foliage was at its loveliest.

'They never sleep, they get far too excited and I think it unwise to mix the schools, it makes the girls dreamy and unreliable.'

'They are teenage girls,' said Veronica. 'That could be expected in any case.'

The treasure hunt had been instituted a few years ago by Miss Gifford, the energetic and somewhat masculine young

Geography mistress. Essentially it was orienteering over the surrounding area, using fixed points, latitude, longitude and map-reading skills, and was usually highly successful in increasing pupils' understanding, apart from a small incident two years ago when one of the seniors had brought in a GPS and somewhat ruined it for everyone.

The boys' school and the girls worked together, making eight teams each, and it had become as fixed an event on the school calendar as the Christmas concert or the spring fete. Veronica knew that if June had her way she'd cancel both of those events, too, but she was also one of the best, most tireless and dedicated teachers the school had ever had. Veronica didn't like upsetting even someone so easily upset.

'We'll keep a close eye on them,' she said, in a mollifying tone. 'Miss Gifford says it's a really good way to jump-start their GSCE in Geography.'

'And misbehaviour,' said Miss Starling. 'It's a dangerous time.'

'I know,' said Veronica. 'Don't worry, there'll be plenty of supervision.'

It was after supper and the four girls were sitting in their dorm. Zelda was painting her toenails and Simone was watching with great interest.

Zelda was worried, though, although she wouldn't admit it. Normally her bolshy routine sufficiently impressed the other pupils and cowed the teachers so she wouldn't get too much hassle off anyone, but here it hadn't gone quite like that. The English teacher had been sharp – not that she cared, America hadn't even got into that dumb war till it was nearly all over – Miss Beresford the Maths teacher had stuck her at the back of the class on her own and ordered her to catch up, and Chemistry had left her competely bamboozled.

The international schools she had attended were mainly people passing through and having fun and learning a smattering of about six languages. The schools in the US were quite lenient. But here everyone looked really serious and bent their heads to their desks. Simone, Zelda's pet project, had answered almost every question in every lesson. It felt really strange that these girls, who felt so much younger than her in every way and whom she'd been ready to take pity on, were in fact streets ahead of her academically. She knew she wasn't stupid, she'd just never felt the need to work, and no one had ever seemed particularly bothered at home.

She covered up her surprise and nerves by reasserting how much cooler she was than the other girls. First, she'd sat Simone down in front of a special magnifying mirror she'd brought with her.

'Now look,' she said.

Alice and Fliss, fascinated, were hanging around in the background.

'Do I have to?' asked Simone, who was still marvelling that anyone would want to pay this much attention to her. 'Normally I don't.'

'You don't look in the mirror?'

'Well, I check I don't have anything in my teeth,' said Simone, feeling more uncomfortable now. She'd learned early on that the mirror was not her friend. Plus, one day she'd been trying to pose by sucking in her cheeks and Joel had come in and found her at it and laughed his head off, then impersonated her for weeks. Ever since then she'd scuttled past her reflection in shop windows. She found excuses not to be in photographs. It was such a reflex she didn't even consider it any more.

'Well, start,' said Zelda, who looked in the mirror a lot.

49

She forced Simone's face around.

'See? You have beautiful big dark eyes. But they have bags under them. You have to go to bed earlier and drink more water.'

'Can I go to bed now?' asked Simone nervously.

'But this is, like, for your own good,' said Zelda sincerely.

'You don't have to do it if you don't want to,' cut in Fliss, who was pretending to study at the desk by her bed but couldn't help glancing over.

'Sure you do,' said Zelda. 'It'll be cool.'

Simone glanced at Alice, who shrugged.

'You want to do it?' she said. 'It's totally up to you.'

'I do,' said Simone, a quiver in her voice.

'Cool,' said Zelda. 'Who's got tweezers? It's gonna be a *long* night.'

'Hey,' said Maggie on the phone. 'What are you up to?'

'Not having sex with my wife,' said Stan.

'Number one,' said Maggie, 'I'm not your wife yet. And two, isn't it half time? You're calling me at half time?' She heard the noise of the pub in the background. 'You totally don't miss me.'

'I do! Plus I need to ask you something. Oh yeah, some dry roasted peanuts, please. Three packs, aye.'

'Are you having dry roasted peanuts for supper?'

'*Supper?*' jeered Stan. 'What do you mean, *supper*? Do you mean tea, or do you mean something else altogether?'

Maggie rolled her eyes. OK, so she'd picked up some phrases from being down south. It was hardly a crime, was it?

'It doesn't matter what I mean. Three packets of dry roasted peanuts can't possibly be good for anyone.'

'Yes, miss,' said Stan, taking what sounded like a long

draw from his pint. 'I thought you werenae supposed to start nagging till after we got married.'

'What did you need to ask me?'

'Oh yeah. My ma wants to know what the colour theme for the wedding is. She wants to buy her outfit in the sales.'

'The what?'

'The colours, you know? What colour the bridesmaids will be wearing and what colour your flowers are and all that. I don't know, girl's stuff, isn't it.'

Maggie thought about it. She just hadn't considered it at all.

'Ehm,' she said, 'I don't know. Tell your mum to buy whatever she wants.'

'Well, she's not going to like that, is she? She just wants to know what will fit in.'

'But *I* don't know yet!'

'OK, fine, don't blow your top! I thought girls were meant to be all into this kind of bollocks anyway.'

'It's not bollocks, I just haven't had a chance to think about it, that's all. Just tell her to get something nice that covers her tattoos and we'll take it from there.'

There was silence on the end of the phone. She'd gone too far.

'Oh, Stan, I didn't mean it like that. Don't be daft.'

'Maybe you're too good for us now, down south, is that it?'

'No, of *course* not.'

'Maybe you're just too posh. Maybe you need a horse and carriage and all of that before you'll deign to walk down the aisle, is that it?'

'Of course it's not, Stan! Of course not!'

The background noise got louder and she could tell the match had kicked off again.

'So why haven't you shifted yourself? My mum is going to spend a lot of money and you can't even tell her what kind of dress she can have! And by the way, there's all sorts of letters and crap at the house from the venue about what kind of stuff we want and you didn't even take them with you.'

'I've been busy,' said Maggie weakly.

'Oh yeah, with your seven-week summer holiday,' said Stan. 'I'm getting back.'

'No, don't go . . . Let's sort this out.'

But it was too late. When she called his phone again it was switched off.

Chapter Three

The day of the October treasure hunt dawned mixed and muggy. The rain was holding off, just about, but there were ominous black clouds massing over the far cliffs. Miss Gifford was insistent that they went ahead, however. Second years were formed into dorm teams, headed by a senior pupil who was meant to be testing their leadership skills, told to put on waterproofs and wellingtons just in case and handed an Ordnance Survey map and their first clue per team. They had to find the grid reference point and work from there.

'Please not Hattie for team leader,' said Fliss through gritted teeth as she shrugged her way into her too-big waterproof. Simone squeezed into hers. She felt a little lightheaded; she'd only had fruit for breakfast, and hot water with lemon. She'd felt like an idiot filling her cup for the first time the previous week, but Zelda insisted this was what Scarlett Johansson had every day. Sure enough, within three days everyone was doing it.

The two schools met at the head of the cliffs. The boys were revved up and anxious for a challenge, almost straining at the leash. The girls glanced over at them and universally wished they weren't wearing the standard red cagoules. Fliss suddenly noticed Zelda was wearing hers knotted casually around her shoulders over a striped Breton top and wished immediately she'd done that too.

Shanthi, a gorgeous Indian girl from the fifth form, walked up to their group with a smile.

'Are you the Plantagenet seconds? All right, you lot, I've got you. I was hoping old Grassy Gifford wouldn't have changed the clues since we did it, but apparently she has, so I'm going to be no use to you whatsoever. And I'm not running either, it's bad for the skin. I'll be under that tree reading *Vogue*, and I don't want to hear from you lot unless you're actually bleeding from an open wound, OK?'

Slightly intimidated, the girls nodded.

'OK. Fine. Scram.'

'I won't be like that when I have to lead a group,' said Fliss. 'I'll be, like, really cool and stuff.'

'Yeah, I think you lost the coolness when you volunteered to lead the group,' said Alice, and Zelda sniggered. Fliss felt herself colour. It didn't get any better when she suddenly caught sight of Will Hampton standing on the other side of the hill, trying to contain a group of younger looking boys. Her heart leapt.

'Will's here!' she couldn't help squeaking to Alice, praying she wouldn't use the knowledge to tease.

Alice's eyebrows perked up. 'I can't believe you can make him out from this distance,' she said, but gave Fliss a reassuring smile. 'Shall we aim to beat them?'

Fliss smiled gratefully. 'Maybe just follow them.'

Simone glanced at the first envelope she'd been given by Shanthi. Just as she did so, Miss Gifford lined them up in a row. Will's team was some distance away behind them.

'All right, children. Line up. Now, try not to rely on your leader too much.'

'Shouldn't be a problem for us,' said Alice.

'Don't follow one another, the clues are all different.'

'This teacher is a complete obsessive,' David whispered to Maggie. They were hovering by the side with four other second-form teachers who'd been roped in to supervise.

'Well, maybe that's good for them,' said Maggie, looking doubtfully at the rainclouds. 'Teach them that if something is worth doing, it's worth doing . . . blah blah, you know.'

David smiled. 'And as long as something is worth supervising, it's worth supervising for five hours.'

'It takes *five hours*?'

Claire stomped towards them in a Burberry raincoat that, on her, was not in the least chavvy.

'Every year thees is the most boring theeng. I shall hide in ze woods and smoke ceegarettes.' She knelt down towards Stephen Daedalus. 'Dog. I do like you. OK, *d'accord*? But you must not jump on me. Zat would not be good for my jacket, dog, and therefore not good for you. Thank you, *merci*.'

Stephen Daedalus sniffed respectfully.

'*Bonjour, mademoiselle*,' said David. '*Allez-vous bien?*'

'*Oui, mais . . .*'

And they started to chat in French. Maggie tried to look interested and tapped her foot. Finally they stopped.

'Zees man is the only one between here and Boulogne who can speak at all,' said Claire to Maggie.

'Really?' said Maggie, hoping she didn't sound too jealous of their ability to casually slip in and out of another language.

'Yeah, she tells me all her deepest darkest secrets, don't you, Claire?' teased David, as Claire rolled her eyes at him and Maggie turned her attention back to the pupils.

The whistle blew and there was a great fumbling with envelopes.

'*For your first grid reference, multiply the number of chimneys on Downey House by the number of crenellations on the west tower,*' read Simone.

'I thought this was Geography, not Maths,' grumbled Alice.

'You know, in my old high school,' said Zelda, 'they'd, like, *totally* never make us do this. And we get to drive to school.'

'The drive from the dorms to the school isn't actually that bad,' said Alice, looking around for Fliss to try and make her laugh. But Fliss was staring, trying to make out a figure in a blue anorak who was disappearing with a group of laughing, haring boys, far away over the cliffs.

'It's a hundred and seventy-two,' said Simone. Then she turned round. 'Isn't *anyone* going to take part in this except for me?'

In fact by the time the girls had discovered the tiny red box, impossible to spot unless you knew its exact location, with its code inside hiding global positioning co-ordinates, they were quite excited. Occasionally they would hear the yelps of other teams galloping past them, including the Tudor girls, who had obviously got their sums wrong and were running back and forth asking if anyone had seen a box. The teachers followed behind them at a safe distance, refusing to answer clue questions (they knew better than to try and upset Miss Gifford's carefully constructed plans), but instead granting loo passes and diagnosing stinging nettle bites.

The clouds advanced relentlessly. Maggie glanced around suddenly and realised that it was dark; a huge black nimbo-stratus (as Miss Gifford had effortlessly identified, though sadly not forecasted) had appeared to crest the hill and now loomed towards them, ominous and heavy.

The girls were down in the small copse at the bottom of the hill that most of the pupils insisted on calling 'the forest'. The map references had led them directly into its heart, and they were on the look-out for something nailed to a tree. Zelda was jumping and nervous, and pointed out that in American forests there were bears, snakes, coyotes and prairie dogs.

'Is everything bigger there too?' said Alice. Fliss knew Alice winding her up was just her way of making friends, but Zelda didn't seem to mind in the slightest.

'Yeah,' she said complacently. 'It's just, like, you know . . . better?'

'What's that?' said Simone. They all stood still. It was very dark inside the forest now, the rainfall only drops away. Fliss, who'd seen *The Blair Witch Project* at a faintly scandalous Halloween party when she was twelve, went rigid.

'Ssh,' she hissed. Another twig cracked on the ground. The girls immediately panicked and started giggling and gathering close together.

'It's a witch,' said Fliss.

'Axe murderer,' said Simone.

'It's probably Mam'selle Crozier sneaking out for a fag,' said Alice with her usual perspicacity.

They huddled in horrified joy when the big fat raindrops first started down on them. Within seconds it was a downpour that bounced off their waterproofs but made a joke of their jeans and ran down the insides of their wellies.

'My *hair*!' shrieked Zelda, as the source of the foot-cracking revealed himself: Will, and a shivering group of boys behind him.

'Hey hey,' said Will, beaming at them. 'Are you the treasure?'

*

57

Maggie looked around. Apart from David and Stephen Daedalus, there were no other teachers to be seen. They must have taken heed of the rain coming in, but she and David had been talking about Matthew Arnold and she simply hadn't noticed where they were. In fact they were right by the cliff edge, a kilometre and a half away, at least, from either school. None of the pupils were in sight either.

'Oh God,' she started, as the rain began to pour. 'We're going to get absolutely drenched.'

'In the autumn, in England. It's outrageous.'

'Should we go and find the children?'

'I think children are mostly waterproof,' said David. 'And they've probably all dived for the trees and the school anyway.'

Certainly, there wasn't a soul to be seen on the crags. The rain intensified and soaked through Maggie's Primark coat.

'This isn't funny,' she said.

David glanced up at the drenching sky. 'We're not going to be able to stoic this out, are we?'

'I don't think so,' said Maggie, getting rain in her mouth as she opened it to speak.

'OK,' said David. 'Come on!' And he grabbed her hand. 'Follow me! Come on, Stephen Daedalus.'

He set off over the crags, and Maggie let herself go to run at full strength beside him. As she did so, trying to keep up with his long legs, she realised how long it had been since she had run – *really* run, not some half-hearted jogging at the gym or aimless strolling. Her legs and shoulders stretched as she flew through the raindrops and she found she was laughing as well as panting, sodden, but with an effortless, light feeling of freedom pounding through her veins.

'STOP!' hollered David, grabbing her back from the cliff edge. He glanced right and left. 'OK, it's here. Jump!'

And, without letting go of her hand, he threw himself over the edge.

Will advanced. Fliss felt her heart stick in her throat. Then he put on his big movie-star grin.

'Hey,' he said. 'We got lost. I think.'

'You got lost here?' said Alice, hollering above the noise of the rain on the leaves. 'It's about ten minutes from the school.'

'I'm new,' said Will. 'And from Guildford. This is like the rainforest to me.'

He looked around. 'Uh, anyone want to shelter?'

Fliss raised her hand before she realised she was alone.

Then she stuck it down again.

They – Will and his band of sniggering, slightly awkward-looking second-form boys – made a circle with their cagoules and let the girls shelter inside, even though Zelda was far too tall and popped out, getting soaked anyway.

'This is very chivalrous,' said Alice. Fliss was too over-whelmed to say anything at all. Here was Will, his chest exposed, sheltering her! She could feel a huge, nervous lump in her throat. All she wanted to do was . . . she couldn't even admit to herself what she would like to do. It made her feel hot and embarrassed and a little trembly. Nonetheless, she couldn't take her eyes off him.

'Naturally, ma'am,' said Will. 'We're from that posh school up the hill. Oh yeah, so are you.'

How could she do it? wondered Fliss as she heard Alice effortlessly chatting with Will about music, films, all sorts of things she knew about and could have offered an opinion on. Why didn't her friend get nervous like everyone else? It sounded like Alice and Will had known each other for years, when Fliss had been the one watching him for years from afar. She was talking to him like he was a completely normal person. And worse, he seemed to be enjoying it, laughing at Alice's wicked descriptions of the slightly toadish appearance of the Geography mistress.

One of the second-form boys let out a big sigh. Simone, who was standing next to him, glanced up. If she didn't know, she'd say he was much younger than his fifteen years. He was chubby, Asian, with a sweep of black hair plastered by the rain on to his head. He looked absolutely miserable.

'What's up with you, sucko?' said the boy beside him, who had pulled the hood of his cagoule so tightly around him that all that remained visible was a pair of sharp blue eyes. 'Too much of a gay baby for a bit of wet weather?'

If the boy was upset he didn't really let it show. 'Yes,' he said, 'I'm a gay baby. That's right, Stokes.' He turned away, as if he were imploring the sky.

'I just . . . I mean, why are we out in this? It's not like it takes more than ten minutes to figure out how longitude and latitude work. I mean, if you read Dava Sobel it's all in there anyway.'

'I *loved* that book,' said Simone instantaneously, without even remembering to be shy. Then she checked herself as the boy turned his dark eyes on her.

'Have you seen the Harrison c-clocks?' he said. He appeared to have a slight stutter. 'They're at—'

'The Greenwich observatory! I know, my dad took me last summer! They're amazing.'

'They are,' said the boy. 'Did you know Philip Pullman used H4 as the inspiration for his alethiometer?'

Simone didn't, and any discussion of one of her favourite writers meant that her normal self-consciousness was completely forgotten.

God, even *Simone* is talking to someone, thought Fliss, drenched, cold and miserable.

Well, this is cruel and unusual punishment, thought Zelda, as the rain trickled down the back of her neck.

'Where the hell?'

Maggie glanced around. She was on a concealed ridge, just under the crags. David had vanished.

'Where are you?'

'You ask a lot of questions,' came a voice from behind her. She turned quickly and, sure enough, just down the ridge a little was a dark cave.

'God,' she said. The rain was, if anything, getting stronger.

'Quick! In here!' came David's voice. 'Unless you're half fish.'

Maggie tentatively stepped inside the cave, giving her eyes time to adjust to the darkness. 'How did *this* get here?'

The tall dark shape of David was standing next to a white rock formation in the ceiling. 'There must have been waves up here once, millions of years ago. Amazing, isn't it?'

The cave went back about thirty feet, and smelled of the salt water so far below. Maggie glanced around and touched the slimy walls.

'Yes,' she said. 'I'm surprised half our sixth year doesn't come down here to drink beer.'

'It's almost impossible to find unless you know where it is,' said David. 'Stephen Daedalus came across it one day. Howled his head off. I thought I'd lost him.'

Maggie looked around. The rain cut off the entrance like a curtain. There was no noise from the outside world at all.

It came out of the blue. She had had no expectations that this would happen. But suddenly it seemed unthinkable that it would not.

'Maggie.' He said her name, but with a deep, questioning tone. Before he'd even finished she had turned towards him.

She had dreamed of this moment for such a long time. But she had never expected the passionate intensity with which he strode towards her, grasping the tops of her arms. His dark eyes burned into hers as he asked her a silent question and her body answered: yes.

His kiss was fierce, as if unleashing something pent up inside of him for a long time. Maggie felt light-headed, as if she was losing the ability to breathe, and she returned it with a fervour that took her by surprise; a passion so strong she found she wanted to be crushed, completely obliterated in him. She kissed him back with equal strength and they found themselves hard against the wall of the cave. Maggie felt as if a dam was breaking inside her and raised her arms, letting David pin them above her head. She could feel his long, hard body pressed against hers and all she could think was *more*. She was panting now as he continued to kiss her deeply and she found herself muttering words: 'Please,' she said. '*Please*.'

David pulled back. His eyes looked wild and his breathing was heavy. She noticed his hands were shaking.

'Oh, Maggie,' he said. 'Oh, Maggie.'

Maggie knew he was right to pull back, she was behaving wantonly, in the wrong place, at the wrong time . . . but the huge feeling of emptiness was nearly overwhelming.

'I know,' she said. 'But . . .'

He looked at her with such longing that it took her breath away.

'You're engaged,' he said shortly. 'We're at work. This is . . . this is *wrong*.'

The simplicity of what he said was so harsh. But so true.

As Maggie scrambled out of the cave, scarcely checking to make sure no pupils had seen her, her mind in turmoil, she could barely see straight.

She tugged down her ruffled clothing, tried to smooth back her hair, but nothing could quell the rapid beating of her heart or stop her head feeling like a washing machine. Partly she felt triumphant. That yes, he had wanted her. Did want her. Just as much as she wanted him. Her insides were gripped with satisfaction.

But the pain. Oh God. How could she be so stupid? The wedding was *booked*. She wasn't on the run from an unhappy relationship, or a cruel man. Stan was her own sweet boy. Not perfect, but nobody was. She wasn't one of her second-formers, with Chace Crawford posters on the wall. She knew what life was like: even if she was with David, she was sure he'd annoy her just as much as Stan sometimes did, have his own foibles and little ways. Everyone did. And a sure guarantee of unhappiness was to jump from man to man, chasing a dream that didn't exist until she was too old and bitter to attract anyone at all.

And it was wrong. It was plain wrong. She had promised herself – her body, her soul – to Stan. For ever. So far, for ever seemed to have lasted less than a year. What kind of person was she? She'd always seen herself as moral, someone who wanted to do the right thing. To be good. Yet here she was, throwing herself into doing the wrong thing, as recklessly as she knew how. If David hadn't stopped them, what would she have done? She shivered to think. Partly from shame; partly from a lust that was to give her many sleepless nights over the weeks to come.

The crazed rain had slowed to a trickle. Suddenly Maggie wasn't sure how long she'd been down there. She climbed ungracefully back to the clifftop.

Sylvie was running towards her, her beautiful hair plastered to her head.

'Miss Adair! All the clues got lost, miss! Or maybe we

couldn't find them. And Alice and Fliss are in the woods with a big bunch of boys!'

As ever, it took her pupils to shake her back to some kind of reality.

'Come on. Let's round everyone up, get them inside and warmed up.'

She looks like Diana, the huntress, thought David wistfully, as he saw her fleet of foot across the meadow grass, her long dark hair spreading out in the wind behind her, before he turned away and whistled for Stephen Daedalus. He hadn't planned anything in showing her the cave; nothing beyond the easy friendship appropriate under the circumstances. But the force of his feelings as she stood in front of him, pink-cheeked, her lips apart as she took in the cave . . .

'Come to me in my dreams, and then
By day I shall be well again.
For then the night will more than pay
The hopeless longing of the day.'

He threw a stick for Stephen Daedalus with far more force than he'd intended, until the dog looked at him warily.

From just over the ridge, Alice, who'd left the boys behind when she'd felt the atmosphere become slightly peculiar – and wanting to get out of the rain – watched them both emerge from the cliffs with some interest. Well, well, she thought. What on earth were those two doing down there? Goody two-shoes Miss Adair and that tasty teacher from the boys' school. That *was* useful to know.

Chapter Four

Maggie woke up with a horrible, hot stone in the bottom of her stomach. She had a foul taste in her mouth. At first she struggled to remember why. Then she sat bolt upright in horror. Oh God. Oh God. What had she *done*? She had ruined *everything*. Her life, everything. How could she have thrown it all away? All for one stupid kiss in a stupid sea-drenched cave. She had lost David's friendship, that was for sure. He was disgusted with her, and so he should be. And Stan . . . Stan. Her heart went out to him. How could she have done this to him? She wasn't fit for marriage. She wasn't fit for teaching: although she'd gone through it in a blur, she'd got a very sharp pulling up from Matron and Miss Starling when half her second-form Plantagenets ended up in the san, because instead of sheltering indoors from the rain storm they'd been cavorting about in the woods with a clutch of boys. She wasn't fit for anything or anyone.

Too upset even to cry, she moved slowly and painfully towards the window. After the grey storm clouds of yester-day it had dawned fresh and bright, the last fading greens of summer – autumn seemed to come late here – bathed in a soft morning light. Finally she choked out a sob. Just as she did so, her phone rang.

Stupidly, cretinously, she wondered for a split second if it might be David. Then she loathed herself all the more for even entertaining the thought. She picked the phone up tentatively, as if it were a poisonous snake.

'Hello?'

'Maggie.' It was Stan.

She closed her eyes. Could he see her guilt from Glasgow? She felt it was radiating off her in waves. Maybe . . . A horrifying thought struck her. Maybe he knew, somehow. Someone had seen them, or David had felt guilty and somehow got in contact, or—

'Maggie, I'm sorry.'

She thought she'd misheard. Shouldn't she be saying this?

'What do you mean?'

'About the other night. I'm sorry.'

Maggie struggled to remember. A row over his mother's outfit. God, it sounded so stupid and felt so long ago now. So innocent, when that was their only worry. She stifled a sob.

'Oh, Maggie, don't cry. OK. I really am sorry, I was just at the pub and, well, you know how it is.'

Now all Maggie wanted to do was bawl.

'I am too,' she stumbled over.

'You know, everyone says it's stressful putting a wedding together,' went on Stan. 'I just want you to enjoy it, OK?'

If anything could have been designed to make her feel worse, it was this.

'OK,' she said, feeling like a hideous fraud.

'When are you coming up?'

Maggie thought about it. It was half term next week – which Stan knew, of course – but she'd been planning on staying behind to catch up on work. Now, though, that seemed like the coward's way out.

'Actually, this weekend,' she said on impulse. 'Definitely.

If I catch the train Friday afternoon I'd be home by eight or so.'

'Do you mean it? That would be brilliant.'

Before the phone call, Maggie had been wondering whether she could, should, tell him. Suddenly she knew she couldn't. All she wanted to do was to be back, safe, in Scotland, where nobody thought she was sluttish, or careless, or borderline negligent. Just to be home.

'I'll check out timetables,' she said.

'Good,' said Stan, sounding extremely relieved. 'Yeah, that'll be great. We'll go to the pub, right? Just kick about, have a laugh. Not get anyone's knickers in a twist about the W word. Look, I won't even say it, OK?'

'Yeah,' said Maggie. 'We'll go to the pub.'

They hung up the phone. And then she really did cry.

'What on *earth* did you think you were doing?' Matron had asked the girls sternly, issuing them with rough clean towels and doling out large spoonfuls of medicine that tasted so unpleasant Fliss wondered if she actually boiled it up herself.

'When the weather comes on you, head for the nearest building. You' – she indicated Simone, who the previous year had got herself very lost on the moors – 'of all people should know that.'

'Sorry, Matron,' they had murmured. How could they say that the attractions of talking to a clutch of male pupils had far outweighed the possibilities of contracting bronchial pneumonia? Miss Gifford had put forward the idea of continuing the treasure hunt today, but had been shouted down by a team of teachers anxious to get their lesson plans back on track. So back to class it was for everyone, and it looked like Miss Starling might get her wish after all.

*

Maggie was desperately hoping her red eyes didn't show. She was also going to have to have a word with the girls who'd run into the woods yesterday, but would leave it for later.

'We're going to look at Rupert Brooke,' she announced to the girls as they looked up at her expectantly.

Fliss gazed at the picture inset in her book. He looked so dreamy and romantic. He looked a bit like Will, if she closed her eyes and squinted hard. She imagined herself in a long dress, something probably a bit like Keira Knightley would wear, waving off Will to war on a steam train. He would clutch her to him and say something like . . . she glanced at the book, '*Oh, never a doubt but, somewhere, I shall wake, And give what's left of love again.*' Then he would go far away to France and probably die, and it would be a terrible tragedy, but she would love him all her life long . . . She was adrift in a happy reverie when she heard her name called, and by the sounds of it, not for the first time.

'Felicity *Prosser*! Thank you for coming back to us.'

Miss Adair sounded exasperated. That rarely ended well.

'Yes, miss?'

'I need to see you after class – all of your team, in fact – so we can have a word about appropriate measures for rain shelter.'

The rest of the class giggled. Fliss didn't care.

'Is that, like, *against the rules*?' Zelda asked. 'Sahry, did I miss something? It's just, in America we don't, like, punish people without telling them what they can and can't do.'

Maggie raised her eyebrows at that.

'No, you're not being punished,' she said, suddenly feeling very tired. 'It's just some things are and aren't appropriate behaviour on field trips, and we should go over what those are.'

It wasn't even possible, she reflected, that any of her girls could have behaved worse than she had.

Simone grabbed two pears from the fruit bowl in the canteen.

'That's not your lunch,' said Fliss.

Simone raised her eyebrows. 'It is. Zelda says I need to eat something light every ninety minutes.'

Their lecture hadn't been too bad in the end. Miss Adair didn't even seem that bothered, she was miles away and just going through the motions of giving them a row. If it had been Miss Starling they'd have been in deep doodoo for months.

'Oh, *Zelda*,' said Fliss crossly. 'Everything *she* says is just *wunnerful*, isn't it?'

'What's that?' said Zelda, emerging from the lunch queue with two pears on her plate. That was the thing about Zelda, she never took offence.

'Nothing,' said Fliss. Alice was following up behind. She had three pears. Fliss looked down at her macaroni cheese.

'Come on, Simone,' she said, turning round. But Simone had gone.

'What's up with you?' said Alice, watching Fliss push her macaroni around with her fork.

'Nothing,' said Fliss. 'It's just, I was kind of looking forward to coming back here this year. But now I'm back and it just seems a bit rubbish.'

Alice raised her eyebrows. 'It's school,' she said. 'This is what it's meant to be like. That's why they call it, you know, "school" and not, "having a really good time".'

'Yeah, I've sure known worse,' commented Zelda, taking

69

a bite of her pear. 'Well maybe not, like, *much* worse. When do they switch the heating on in this place?'

'November,' said Fliss. 'Dr Deveral says it's bad for our skin.'

'Jeez. I take back that statement. This is, like, the worst place ever.'

Alice looked smug.

'What?' said Fliss. 'What are you looking smug about?'

'Oh, I don't know,' said Alice. 'It's not like I have any secret gossip that could cause a HUGE scandal.'

Both the girls turned round straightaway.

'What is it?'

'I can't tell,' said Alice, delighting in her power. 'No way.'

'Please let it be about Hattie,' said Fliss.

'I can't possibly say,' said Alice. 'But life at school might be about to get a *lot* more interesting.'

'Tell us! Tell us!'

But Alice just looked smug and refused to say a word.

She couldn't help it. She had to know. Carefully, Simone retraced her steps to the little copse where they'd found the second red box, just before the skies opened. It was still there! Carefully she keyed in the three-digit code she'd derived from subtracting the ages of the two schools. The box popped open. Inside was a small piece of rolled-up paper.

'Take the number of letters in the capital of Iran, multiply by the height in metres of Everest (to the nearest 10,000) and subtract from $\overline{L}$ to get the first line of the grid reference . . .'

At one stage it looked like it might rain again, but in the end it didn't and Simone, with one eye on her watch, doggedly marched through the clues in her lunch hour. By ten to two she was homing in, she was sure of it, with the grid reference definitely sending her towards the lighthouse, at the far end of the cliffs. Short on time she ran there, remembering Zelda's imprecations to incorporate exercise into her daily life. Puffing slightly, she ran up towards the steps and looked around, wondering what to do. Presumably these days all lighthouses were computerised, so there wouldn't be anybody—

Just as she was thinking this, the door at the bottom of the lighthouse opened and a bearded man stepped out. He shielded his eyes.

'Are you from the school? I thought we were going to see you chaps yesterday.'

Simone couldn't quite get her breath back, but tried to explain.

'We were . . . the weather . . .'

The man looked confused.

'You let a bit of weather scare you off? I don't know what schools are coming to. Is it just you?'

Simone nodded. Suddenly, however, she heard someone panting behind her. She turned round. Making hard work of getting up the hill towards the outpost was the chubby boy from yesterday. When he saw that it was her, she saw his face drop with disappointment. Not for the first time, she thought ruefully. She did seem to have that effect on boys.

'Why are you here?' he said accusingly, as soon as he could. 'The treasure hunt was called off.'

Simone shrugged. 'I wanted to see where it went. Why are you here?'

The boy shrugged back. 'How can you have got here so fast? It's impossible. Did your teacher help you out with the clues?'

Simone was stung. 'You think it's impossible that a girl might beat you to the clues?'

71

'I would say it's unlikely,' said the boy.

The lighthouse keeper sighed. 'Uhm, could you two have this conversation another time? I have a Panamax coming up from Finisterre, and I'd like to keep an eye on it.'

Simone and the strange boy immediately lapsed into silence when the adult started talking.

'All right,' he said. 'I have this box here for the team winners, which I suppose must be you two.'

'We're not really on the same team,' said the boy.

'Well, the girl was here first then.'

'It's all right,' said Simone. 'I'm sure we can share it.'

The lighthouse keeper brought out a box and bade them farewell. Although it was well past lunch hour now and they were some distance from school, Simone didn't give in to her customary panic, but instead sat down on the damp grass to open the box. The boy stood hovering around her, giving off irritated vibes.

'What's your name anyway?' she asked.

The boy shrugged. 'Ash.'

He was so rude!

'I'm Simone.'

'Fine. Are you going to open the box?'

Simone did. Inside was a beautiful gold-coloured sextant with *Dorm winner, 2009 Geography Hunt* inscribed on it.

'It's beautiful!' she said, genuinely taken aback.

Ash gave it a look. 'How are we going to share that then?'

'I don't know,' said Simone. She glanced at her watch. 'I have to get back. It's Geography now, weirdly enough.'

Ash was still looking at the sextant. Simone was exasperated.

'Look, do you want it? Do you want me to tell everyone you got here first and you won the treasure hunt?'

For a second Simone thought that was exactly what he

wanted her to tell everyone. But he looked at it for a long time, sighed, then said, 'No. You won it. You take it.'

'Thank you,' Simone said. Then, 'I'm sorry we couldn't share it. Want to borrow it sometime?'

'No, thank you,' he said. 'But I do have the new Garth Nix book.'

Simone's eyes lit up. 'Can I borrow that?'

'If you like,' said Ash. 'See you around.'

And he started off back towards his own school, his face flushed and his hair damp with the exertion. What an odd chap, thought Simone, holding her prize close to her chest.

'Simone Pribetich, is that you?'

Miss Gifford couldn't believe Simone would be late of her own accord, she could hardly say boo to a goose. 'I'm going to have to tell Miss Adair about this.'

'Sorry, miss,' said Simone. What had seemed to her a great adventure last night when she thought of it suddenly seemed terrifying – she was going to get reported! After sheltering with the boys too! Simone never got into trouble, and now she was frantically worried. Would it affect her scholarship? Would she get sent down, or worse? Her hands started to shake.

'Were you off school property in school hours? Are you aware this is not allowed for Year Two pupils?'

Simone could feel a lump start in her throat.

'Um, yes, Miss Gifford.'

The rest of the class – which included the Tudor girls, as this was a mixed session – watched in delighted horror. Simone never ever got into trouble. What on earth could she have been doing? Simone felt her heart quicken. Could she ever manage to speak up for herself? Stand up and talk? She imagined Alice in this situation, or Zelda. They'd just say what was on their minds and be done with it, they wouldn't stand here like big scarlet puddings, struck dumb just because a teacher asked them a perfectly reasonable question.

'Um,' she said again. Then she brought out of her rucksack the golden-coloured sextant. Miss Gifford gasped aloud.

'Where did you get that?'

Simone brought out the pieces of paper. 'I went out at lunchtime to follow the clues ... I wanted to finish the hunt ...'

Miss Gifford took them off her. 'And you did this all by yourself?'

Simone looked modest. 'Well, I'm really sorry, it made me late ...'

Miss Gifford didn't know what to do. On the one hand, lateness and heading off school property was completely unacceptable. On the other, her heart burst with pride that a pupil was so keen to finish her Geography treasure hunt that they would actually break school rules to do it.

She tried to keep her voice neutral, however.

'Very well,' she said. 'I'll have to inform your class mistress. And I would like you to take a detention. But we'll say no more about it, at least you were in the services of Geography.'

Simone stood, unsure of what to do.

'You may sit.'

'But ... what about the sextant?'

Miss Gifford eyed it up. 'Well, I suppose it belongs to the Plantagenet dorms now.'

A great cheer went up from half the class, whilst the Tudor girls looked sulky and muttered things about cheating and not giving everyone a fair chance. Simone's face was still red, but now for a different reason.

'All right everyone, settle down,' said Miss Gifford. 'Back to erosion, please.'

'Well done,' said Alice as Simone sat down. 'Your first detention!'

Simone grimaced. She'd never had a detention in her life before, and had absolutely no desire to start. It would go on her record and everything. Her chest tightened. It wouldn't stop her from going to university, would it? Or get her scholarship into trouble? She'd hardly even worried about the discipline side of things, so sure was she that she'd never do anything to get herself into hot water. And now, here she was, being late for class and roaming out of bounds. Meekly she bent her head to her work, her mind a whirl of confusion.

Miss Starling could hardly control her glee in being proved right, as she led the detention class. Along with a couple of known troublemakers from York House there was Astrid Ulverton, one of the most talented musicians in the school, who was there for forgetting to finish her History prep for three days in a row. Her protestations that she was deep into a new Carl Nielsen concerto had cut no ice with Miss Kellen, the sombre History teacher whose low, slow voice, full of import, was known to have a deadly effect on her students on sunny days just after a heavy lunch.

But Simone Pribetich was definitely the prize.

'Out of school grounds?' she'd said. 'Surely after last year you'd have learned your lesson?' It didn't get much worse than getting told off by Miss Starling. Still, thought Simone, to comfort herself, at least she would have to skip dinner. That would fit in with Zelda's regime.

*

Maggie sleepwalked through the rest of the week leading up to half term. As the girls sighed over Erich Maria Remarque and Siegfried Sassoon, Maggie arranged for a Wednesday evening double showing of *Regeneration* and *Gallipoli* in the film lounge, which sent all four houses into mass hysterics and earned her a stern ticking-off from June Starling about age-appropriate media. All of it just washed over her. She was counting down the hours until Friday, when she could fly home. Would she crumble at the sight of Stan? Would he see it written all over her face? Adulteress? Would he even believe it? He'd shown little but contempt for the gangling, weirdy intellectual ponce from across the crags.

Of course she definitely didn't want David to phone. Definitely not. Which was just as well, because of course he hadn't.

She'd gone through a thousand times in her head what she might say, but every time she looked for a way of explaining it that didn't make her look too bad or reprehensible, she had to see it again for what it was: her cheating on Stan. Throwing herself at a man she fancied. With whom she had a professional relationship. Ten months before her wedding day. Every time she thought of it, she wanted to cry again.

Nope, not an email, not a text message – not, she suspected, that David knew how to text message. He wasn't a text message kind of person. More of a handwritten letter type of person. She hadn't had any of those either, apart from a badly scrawled card from her nephew Dylan, imploring her to COM HOM SOON!!!

'What ees wrong with you?' Claire asked her on Thursday. 'Are you coming out tomorrow night? Miranda and I thought we go into Truro and see if anyone anywhere has heard of what a cocktail might be.'

Maggie tried to smile, but even though the girls were becoming good friends, the idea of seeing Miranda suddenly filled her with dread and self-loathing.

'No, I can't,' she said, grateful to be getting out of it. 'I'm going to Scotland.'

'Ah, a deerty weekend with Stan, *non*? Super!'

'Something like that,' said Maggie.

'You mees him so much . . . ah have noticed you have seem a leetle down, a leetle sad since you come back here.' She looked around. 'I'm not surprised. It like prison.'

'If you hate it so much, Claire, you don't really have to work here,' Maggie surprised herself by saying. 'Go teach French to businessmen in London or something, you'd have scads more fun.'

'What, and leave these girls to your English ways! *Non, non, non*, I could not abandon them.'

Maggie knew Claire was only half joking.

'And, I am a very good teacher.'

That was certainly true. Mam'selle Crozier was feared for her impetuous rages and imaginative scoldings, but admired as glamorous and as having the ability to drag some kind of accent out of the dullest-spoken of girls.

Her words sobered Maggie up a little. If Claire of all people could understand why she was in teaching, and what for, surely Maggie should be able to focus more on what was truly important: her pupils. Mooning around after someone she couldn't have was ridiculous, as was letting impressionable teenage girls cry themselves sick over Mel Gibson in a World War One uniform. She was going to have to focus. Pull herself together. Stay in the real world.

'Thanks, Claire,' said Maggie.

'What for? I do not buy you a cocktail, *non*.'

'No, but you're a tonic,' said Maggie.

'*Bof*, your Breetish humour. Eet is not funny you know. *Monty Python* ees not funny, Ricky Gervais he is not funny, Peter Kay ees not funny.'

'No, he's not funny,' admitted Maggie, 'but—'

'I shall never understand. Never!' said Claire, and she stomped off, rifling in her Hermès bag for her Gitanes.

Chapter Five

Come Friday, half the school disappeared with glee. Many of the girls, however, stayed at Downey House over the half term: those with parents abroad, or who couldn't take time off. Simone was staying, although her parents had insisted on driving down one day to see her. She was planning on writing the best Geography paper Miss Gifford had ever seen. Alice was staying too, and was planning on lying in bed as late in the mornings as was humanly possible.

Maggie's good intentions to devote herself steadfastly to teaching lasted about as far as Bristol. She had set out to get organised and plan for the spring term but, gazing out on the dirty, cold November day, with evening already closing in fast and the train packed and noisy, instead of reading D.H. Lawrence she found herself turning to an old favourite: W.H. Auden.

'This is the Night Mail crossing the border,
Bringing the cheque and the postal order,
Letters for the rich, letters for the poor,
The shop at the corner and the girl next door.
Pulling up Beattock, a steady climb:
The gradient's against her, but she's on time.'

As always, she found the rhythm of the piece comforting and relaxing. Trying not to knock over the three cans of lager the man in the next seat had lined up on his table, or get too distracted by the incredibly noisy hissing and thumping of the man in front's headphones, she let her eyes close briefly.

'Past cotton-grass and moorland boulder
Shovelling white steam over her shoulder,
Snorting noisily as she passes
Silent miles of wind-bent grasses.'

Before she knew it, Maggie was asleep.

David screwed up his face. He couldn't believe he was doing this, but he was no good on the phone and email was such a horrible method of communication. But he should do the right thing, nip it in the bud properly. It was the gentlemanly way to behave after their . . . slip up; not just running away or fumbling apologies. David prided himself on trying to do the right thing, but this had left him totally flustered, in a way he could never remember feeling before. This would have to be face to face. Just to sort things out, get everything straight in his head. It was only fair.

He suppressed the thought that really it was because he was desperate to see Maggie again. That wasn't the case. He was just doing the right thing, he told himself sternly, as he strode across the hills. God it was a bleak night. He knew she often went to the pub with Claire on a Friday night, so he'd check in there first.

The little village was quiet out of season, whilst it bustled all through the summer with people exploring the beautiful northern coves, yellow beaches and big waves famed in the region. With the night drawn in – Stephen Daedalus was staying very close to his master – the Smugglers' Hole looked cosy and inviting, its old-fashioned lanterns casting a warm pool of light across the little cobbled street, and convivial chatter spilling from inside. David brushed the rain from his mackintosh, braced himself and pushed open the door.

Maggie woke with a start to find the train pulling into Central Station. She hadn't realised just how tired she was, but a week full of sleepless nights and a full teaching schedule had left her drained. There weren't even that many people left in the carriage, just a lingering smell of ketchup and crisps and wet wool and old magazines. She blinked and stretched, taking a long drink of water and marvelling at how dark it was outside.

She felt a hand of fear grip her. She must remember: she did *not* kiss anyone. She was *not* unfaithful. Nothing happened. Nothing worth talking about. It was a moment of madness and she didn't need to poison Stan's mind by telling him about it. He had that slip up himself last year, she reminded herself. Once, after they'd had a fight, she hadn't been able to get hold of him all night and he'd told her later he'd had to fend off a girl. He'd said it hadn't gone anywhere. She thought it had. People do slip up occasionally. But if they truly love each other, it doesn't matter.

She lifted her bag down from the overhead compartment, feeling stiff and a bit spacey. The familiar rough Glaswegian tones welcomed her to Central Station and reminded her to collect all her bags and belongings. She picked up her *Norton Anthology of Poetry* and pen, reflecting sadly on how little work she'd actually managed to complete and, bracing herself, pressed the button to open the door.

*

'Hey,' said Stan. There was no running into one another's arms, of course. They had been together far too long to be doing that. It was for new lovers, thought Maggie. She shouldn't be sad or cross about it. It just showed how secure and comfortable they were, that was all. They didn't have to make public displays.

'How's it going?' he asked, after a clumsy kiss. The air of their last few conversations – stilted, at cross-purposes – still hung in the air.

'Fine,' said Maggie, wondering if he could read the guilt seared all over her face. She pressed it into his coat. 'Fine. Bit tired. Slept most of the way.'

'It'll be all of those nine to four days,' said Stan. Maggie waited for him to pick up her bag, but he didn't.

'Want to go and get a pint then?'

'I'm really hungry,' said Maggie.

'Well, they'll probably have a pie. Or we could get some chips on the way.'

'Let's do that,' agreed Maggie, incredibly relieved that he hadn't seemed to notice any difference in her. But did that mean she was always evasive and a bit grumpy? 'Yup. Great.'

'Are you sure? Was I supposed to have booked us like a posh dinner or that?' Stan looked a little sheepish.

'Why?' she said. 'Do you think I've picked up all these poncey southern ways?'

'Well you have, love,' he said. 'It's just a fact, isn't it?' He looked at her as she hauled her own bag towards the car park.

'I haven't changed,' insisted Maggie.

Stan looked at her, a little sadly. 'You can't even hear it, can you? You even sound different.'

'Well, sometimes I have to speak more slowly so the girls can understand me.'

'Throw the r away,' said Stan, with a touch of bitterness in his voice.

'No,' said Maggie. 'It's stupid, really, Stan. You can't just hate the English all the time. They don't hate you.'

'No, they just think they're better than me.'

Maggie stretched in the car. 'Stan. Can we not . . . I mean, I've come all this way and . . . could we not—'

'Of course,' said Stan. 'Sorry. Come here, darling.'

And as his lips touched hers she briefly, instinctively, drew back before she remembered where she belonged.

David could see Claire tucked into the corner of the snug talking to someone. OK. She was here then. His heart pounding, he approached to ask them what they wanted to drink.

'Hello, David!' said Miranda, holding up an enormous glass of wine next to a nearly empty bottle. 'Why haven't you been returning my calls then?'

David flinched. Why was she calling him? Had Maggie told her? He hadn't realised they were such great friends now. Claire's face was giving nothing away.

Miranda paused for a second, then smiled. 'Are you getting the drinks in or what?'

She couldn't know. She couldn't. David felt a huge wave of relief. Guilt, and relief.

'Of course,' he said. 'White wine?'

Miranda nodded immediately, even though her glass of wine was only half empty. Claire shook her head.

'No more for me, thank you. It is strange, but I have never taken to thees British idea you have of being very sick in doorways.'

'Suit yourself,' said Miranda, as David headed for the bar. When he returned with a fresh bottle and two glasses, she patted the seat next to her. 'Come on, sweetie. Tell us what boring poetry you've been terrorising the fourth-form with today.'

'Where's the other member of your coven?' said David, faux jokily.

'Maggie has gone to Scotland,' said Claire.

Of course. That hadn't occurred to David; that she would just go. To be with her future husband.

Miranda, swigging quickly from her glass, saw an opportunity.

'Yes, she's gone up to do wedding stuff, I think. Wedding, wedding wedding, it's all she's ever on about! I think the name for it is, what, Bridezilla?'

Claire looked a trifle confused, but Miranda was undeterred. If she wanted to get David back, she reckoned this was her best shot – show him that she wasn't like other women.

'I was never like that, was I?' She put her hand over his.

He registered its familiar softness, the beautifully tended nails.

'I do think it's a shame when women are happy to trade their independence for a man,' said Miranda.

David raised his eyebrows. 'I always thought women were meant to be allowed to do whatever they damn pleased.'

'Oh well, of course they are,' said Miranda, filling his glass. 'It's just, you know, a bit sad to get so excited about an outmoded institution. What's he like anyway? Maggie hasn't said much about him.'

'I thought you said she was talking about him non-stop?'

'Uh, yeah, about the wedding . . . The groom could be Ken Barbie for all she mentioned him!' laughed Miranda.

'He ees nice,' said Claire, loyally. 'He has red hair and loves football.'

'Scottish, then,' said Miranda.

'He is nice,' said David, drinking faster than he normally would, angry with himself. He might as well admit it. It was a stupid, dangerous game he'd got involved in, and he'd lost. Served him right.

'"Nice" is always what people say when they mean, "has no distinguishing characteristics whatsoever",' grumbled Miranda. 'At best it means hopelessly average; and at worst it means you hate him and want him killed.'

'It means personable and well-mannered,' said David. 'Which at the moment is more than can be said for you.'

Miranda tossed her long golden hair towards him and gave him a teasing smile.

'Oh, come on,' she said. 'I'm just being honest. You love it really, don't you?'

'I must go,' said Claire.

'Oh, no, Claire, we haven't finished the wine,' complained Miranda.

'Ah theenk you two should stay and feenish it.'

Miranda rolled her eyes as the French mistress stood up and left. 'Subtle, isn't she?'

'Is that better or worse than nice?' said David.

Miranda eyed him thoughtfully. 'You look tired. Have you been missing your Miranda?'

David looked at her pretty face, her enthusiastic smile. He thought of their shared history.

'*Do you remember an inn, Miranda?*' he said.

'Stop! I may be pissed, but I am absolutely not pissed enough for your endless bloody stupid poetry. Just answer the question.'

'OK. Fine. Sure.'

In fact, they ended up having a good night in the pub. Well, Stan did. Of course all his mates were there and pleased to see Maggie, and she did her best to get on with their girl-friends, some of whom seemed alarmingly young. They all worked around Glasgow, and talked about the cool bars they'd been to and the bands they'd seen. It made Maggie feel like a country bumpkin suddenly; she couldn't even remember the last time she'd seen a movie. Most of her evenings were spent quietly with Claire in their joint study, reading and listening to music, or curled up in her sitting room – Claire couldn't bear British telly, so she did that alone. With her long walks along the headland and quiet weekends it could feel like a lonely existence, but it didn't, of course. The presence of three hundred girls easily put a stop to that.

But listening to these girls with their sunbed tans, poker-straight hair and pale pink lipstick talk about the new collections at Cruise or the latest underground nightclub made her feel as if she were getting old before her time. She didn't have much to add that wouldn't make her sound stuck up and pretentious, and nobody seemed terribly inter-ested in asking her about school – and why should they? They weren't long out of school themselves. Probably hated all teachers. They probably thought she was the squarest person there. Maggie sighed and felt sorry for herself and decided she needed to drink some more. And change out of this ridiculous skirt, she was the only person there not in jeans.

'Come on then, mopey. It's a big day!'

Anne had taken a Saturday off from the salon to help Maggie look at wedding dresses, so she wasn't about to let a bit of mumping spoil her day. Maggie had wanted a lie-in – she'd drunk too much last night, they'd moved on to some lurid turquoise shot glass thing and it had made her feel absolutely dreadful. But she'd finally had fun though; ended up trading jeans with Jimmy Mac's girlfriend, what was she called again? Anyway, it had been highly funny, someone had got stuck in a toilet and they'd all burst out at the same time, hysterical. Stan had been delighted with her, kept snogging her behind the snooker table like they were teenagers again, and she hadn't minded a bit – in fact, was delighted to be snogging her fiancé in public, showing everyone how much in love they were, even though they were old fuddie duddies getting married and she was a teacher.

They'd gone back and had drunken fumbly sex just in time before they passed out. Now Maggie was reaping the consequences of having severely cut down on her alcohol intake whilst at work. Her tolerance was minimal, her hangover severe.

'This house smells like a brewery,' said Anne, who, despite the ongoing chaos of Cody and Dylan, managed to keep her little council flat neat as a pin. Whilst Stan had clearly made a cursory attempt at cleaning up, Maggie could see that this meant simply pushing everything under the bed and spraying air freshener about. Given that his mum was back to doing his washing, this wasn't very impressive.

'I know,' said Maggie. 'Well, we were celebrating, of course.'

'Yes, it looks great fun,' said Anne sceptically. 'Come on, get dressed. I don't want to think what Stan thinks passes for coffee in here, let's go out.'

'He's still sleeping anyway,' said Maggie. 'Best not disturb him.'

There was a grunt and a farting noise from the bedroom.

'Ah, married life,' said Anne. 'Bring your make-up bag.'

'Why?'

'Because if you try on wedding dresses looking like that you'll get so depressed you'll probably want to call the whole thing off.'

Maggie groaned.

'Don't cry,' Anne was saying. 'You look beautiful.'

'Many girls cry when they come here,' said the very well-spoken and turned-out lady who ran the wedding dress shop. Or boutique, as she insisted on calling it.

'Yes, but from happiness,' said Anne, in a warning tone.

'I look like two melons in a hammock,' wailed Maggie from behind the curtain.

Anne stalked in. 'You do not.'

Maggie snivelled in response.

'Strapless is very in this year,' said the assistant.

Maggie came out and the assistant made her stand on a chair.

'There. It's beautiful. You look beautiful,' she said robotically.

Maggie took a deep breath and stared at herself in the carefully lit mirrors. The dress was strapless, covered in pink roses on the bodice, and became a large, white skirt with more roses following down the train. It had looked rather romantic on the hanger. Now . . . how could she possibly say "This is hideous"?'

'I don't think strapless is the way to go for me,' she said. Although she wasn't fat, she could see little dimples of flesh bunch over the corseted top of the dress. This was a dress for the bird-boned.

'I don't want to spent the whole day holding out my arms so I don't look like I have bingo wings.'

'Strapless is very popular,' said the lady again. Maggie ignored her.

'Plus, everyone wears them. Then you get the photos back and all the head shots make the bride look totally naked.'

'Well, that's true,' agreed Anne.

'And that's . . . it's just an awful lot of my back on display, don't you think? It's like about a square metre of . . . *skin.*' Maggie peered dubiously behind herself.

'We have lots of others you can try on,' said the woman, looking like Maggie had personally insulted her.

'OK. Do you have something with, uh, sleeves?'

The woman looked momentarily non-plussed. 'Perhaps in our plus-sized section.'

'Oh, let's not start with that, shall we?'

They collapsed at a table in Princes Square, the posh shopping centre. Neither of them spoke for a moment or two, until Anne ordered two large glasses of white wine. When they arrived, she leant forwards.

'OK. What's up?'

Maggie shrugged. 'Nothing.' She took a deep gulp of her wine. Hair of the dog, that might do it.

'We're going shopping for your *wedding dress*. Your *wedding dress*, Maggie. But you look like I'm dragging you to the vets to get neutered.'

'What?'

'Oh, I had to do it to the cat . . . she looked just like you do now.'

Maggie stuck out her bottom lip. 'I'm just tired, that's all.'

'That's not all,' said Anne. 'Don't play the numpty noo with me.'

Maggie took a deep breath. She was tempted to come clean, it would be such a relief to confess everything, get it off her chest, try and make sense of her feelings.

Then she remembered Anne's heartbreak when she found

out her boyfriend, Dylan and Cody's dad, was cheating on her with that slut who worked down the karaoke bar. Her devastation and misery that someone could do that to her. She thought of the endless battles over money; about Cody and Dylan growing up without a father. She thought also about how much Stan was part of the family – he was still going to her mum and dad's for Sunday lunch, he was practically more of a part of the family than she was.

And it was only a kiss, she told herself stubbornly. Just a stupid little kiss like anyone might do in a drunken piece of nonsense. Of course, she hadn't been drunk. But still, the same thing applied.

'Oh, I don't know,' she said finally. 'I'm just feeling a bit stressed with school and everything. The wedding is like the last thing on my mind.'

'I thought you'd be thrilled,' said Anne. 'Everyone else is. Do you not think it's fancy enough for you?'

'That's bullshit,' said Maggie crossly. This was the second time she'd been accused of becoming a snob about it. 'I don't want to hear it.'

'OK,' said Anne. She glanced at the menu. 'I'm going to have the carbonara.'

Maggie sighed. 'I suppose I'll be on the green salads till the wedding.'

'Well, that is a joyful way to think about it.'

'Hmm,' said Maggie.

'Anyway,' said Anne. 'There's something I want to talk to you about. *Real* problems.'

Maggie raised her eyebrows. 'Oh yes, sorry for bothering you with my being exhausted.'

'Well, if that's all it is you shouldn't have done WKD shots till four in the morning, should you?'

'No,' conceded Maggie. 'What is it?'

'It's the school. It's really gone downhill lately. A kid brought a knife into Dylan's class, Maggie.'

Maggie managed not to ask whether or not it had been Dylan. She loved her nephews, but they could be hard work.

'The whole area ... The teachers can't cope, Maggie, they're just getting completely overrun.'

'That's awful, Anne. Can't you take them out and send them somewhere else?'

'The other schools are just the same. And I'm hardly going to send them private, am I? I'm hardly like the mums from your school. Am I?'

Maggie didn't know how to respond to that.

'No,' she said.

'Anyway, you know I've heard they're looking out for new teachers?'

'I'm not a primary school teacher, though, Anne.'

'No, they're looking for a teacher to handle the senior school, too. Look, I cut it out for you.'

Maggie took the ad Anne proffered.

SCHOOL LIAISON OFFICER
*Teacher with administrative experience required to liaise
between Holy Cross secondary school and the feeder schools
of the district in order to facilitate better links between
intake expectations and ongoing achievements ...*

'I mean, do you think that's something that could help?'

Through the horrible management-speak, Maggie figured it out. It meant the school was looking for someone to go around collecting the new little shits and trying to stop them being such little shits. It was a completely thankless job that they were looking for some underpaid skivvy to do, and she couldn't think of anything worse.

Anne looked at her hopefully. 'I just thought, someone like you, keeping an eye on the primary schools, sorting them out. I mean, it would be great for the boys – for everyone, really – and you'll be looking for a job up here anyway, and I just thought this would be perfect.'

Maggie didn't know what to say. She would have to come home one day, that much was clear. She didn't think she was going to get Stan down to England without actually knocking him unconscious, and who'd ever heard of two married people living in different countries? That was completely impossible. She'd need to start looking for something at some point.

'Mm,' she said. 'Well, I'm kind of committed to this school year . . .'

'I know it doesn't work like that,' said Anne impatiently. 'Dylan's had three teachers already this year.'

Maggie winced. That really was bad. She hated to think of the boys falling behind.

'OK, well, give it to me and let me think about it, all right?' She finished off the rest of her wine. 'I'll see what . . .'

She let her voice trail off, unable to commit too much.

'Great!' said Anne. 'I'll tell Mum, she'll be so delighted.'

'Don't!' said Maggie. 'Even if I do apply, it's not certain I'll get it.'

Anne pshawed. 'Yeah, like there are a million applicants for these jobs. Dylan was on supply teachers for two months.'

Maggie knew this was true, but didn't want to think about it. There was no doubt that if she applied for the job, she'd probably get it. The interviewers would be very impressed by her time at Downey House, and it would work well with her background . . . And it was, potentially, an interesting job. One where she could make a difference to the hordes of scared, young first years who arrived at big school each year terrified and panicky, who then took refuge in gangs or misbehaviour to bolster up their self-worth. If she could tackle that before they even started . . . well, wouldn't that be worthwhile? Isn't this what she'd always told herself she'd do? So why did she feel so dismayed at the thought? Just how selfish was she?

David leant over the bed to pick up his watch. There, stretched out, her blonde hair fanning the pillow, was Miranda. Even in sleep she looked glamorous, untouchable. He sighed. Was he making a big mistake? Was she? Was this what they wanted?

Miranda stirred and her eyelids fluttered. 'Mm, good morning, handsome,' she murmured. 'You really are getting disgustingly skinny.'

'I've always been like this,' said David, slightly peeved.

'Exactly. You look like a teenager, but you're a grown man. It's not right.'

David rolled his eyes. 'So you want me to do what, exactly? Eat doughnuts for breakfast?'

'Ooh, breakfast,' said Miranda. 'I'm starved. Did you offer? Can I have a latte and could you chop me up some melon? *Please?*'

'I can't work your coffee machine, remember? You told me it was a wilful refusal to engage with the modern world.'

'Oh, I didn't mean it like that!' said Miranda. 'Just bring the pressure gauge up to . . . Oh, never mind, I'll make the coffee.'

'I'll chop the melon,' said David, obediently, following her into her hi-tech and barely used kitchen.

Chapter Six

Post-half term, everyone's attentions turned to the Christmas festivities, much to Simone's horror.

'I'm really very very hungry.' Simone was lying on her bed, groaning instead of doing her prep.

'Yes, you've mentioned that about five times,' said Alice. 'Go eat a big pie or something, nobody's forcing you.'

'No!' said Zelda. 'Stand up!'

Simone reluctantly did so. Fliss pretended to be ignoring everyone and working on her French homework.

Zelda pushed Simone in front of the large and unflattering mirror fixed above the sink in the corner of their dorm.

'Look!' said Zelda. Simone had instinctively cast her eyes downwards. Apart from checking she didn't have anything caught in her teeth, she normally avoided mirrors like the plague. Or rather, if she knew herself to be all alone (which at school was incredibly rare), she would ignore her body and try out her face from different angles, trying to find one where you couldn't see the double chin.

'Look at yourself! Jeez!' said Zelda in quite a scary tone of voice. Simone took a deep breath and stared herself straight in the eye.

'See?' said Zelda. 'You're looking better already. Look, all those spots on your chin are nearly gone.'

It was all Simone could do not to stick her hand up over her chin. Those spots were the bane of her life. However much she scrubbed at them, ignored them, squeezed them or covered them in stuff Fliss lent her, they never went away. They were like a small forest, there to stay.

But now, after a few weeks of eating less – a lot less – and doing as much exercise as she could fit in, they seemed to have . . . Had they . . . they had gone!

Simone gasped. And could it be? It could. Instead of having to contort her face into the normal position where she looked her best, she could see, definitely see, that her double chin had reduced; had almost disappeared. Her cheeks, too, had slimmed down.

Alice came over and stood behind her. 'You really have changed, chipmunk.'

Zelda grabbed Simone's trousers by the hips. 'Look at these! They're far too big for you. Look! Hip bones! You have hip bones!'

'And the dance is coming,' teased Alice.

The Christmas dance was the big social event of the year for the Middle School: a mixer with Downey Boys, with both traditional country dancing and a disco. First-formers were banned, and the Upper School had its own affair with, it was rumoured, *wine*. The girls had talked of little else since half term – who would wear what, who would ask who to dance. The entire year was in a fever of hormonal excitement and the formal dancing lessons were about to start. As PE teacher Janie James wryly observed, it was the only time in the year that sport captured everyone's attention.

Combined with the end of term and Christmas on the way, a vein of excitement ran through the Middle School seconds, and everyone, even Simone, was getting caught up in it.

Fliss had watched the preparations in dismay. Everyone else seemed so sure they were going to have a wonderful time. But she really, really needed to stand out. What could she do?

Simone grabbed the trousers back from Zelda. 'Don't be silly,' she said. But she was growing pink with pride.

'Anyone going to supper?' said Fliss.

'Not me!' said Simone.

'Me neither,' said Fliss. But she left the room anyway.

'What's got into her?' said Zelda, looking at Fliss's departing back.

Alice shrugged. 'Teenage hormones?'

Simone looked after her, torn. Part of her wanted to keep looking at herself in the mirror – maybe even try on some new clothes – and part of her wanted to run after her friend.

'I'm going to see her,' she said.

Alice raised her eyes and got up heavily. 'Well, if it is suppertime.'

'Fruit only!' ordered Zelda. 'No bread.'

Alice rolled her eyes. 'Hey, American,' she said, 'pipe down, OK?'

'I still think we should do our *High School Musical* workout,' said Zelda, unabashed.

'We've got formal dance tomorrow, don't you think that's enough?'

'I *hate* formal dance,' said Simone with feeling. 'We should be doing hockey.'

Alice looked at the rain lashing the windows. 'Inside is *definitely* better,' she said.

'Yeah, but it's just, like, a dance, isn't it?' said Zelda. 'Throwing shapes and shit?'

'Throwing shapes and shit,' mused Alice. 'Uh, not exactly. Does nobody read the syllabus?'

Simone didn't mention that Alice had two elder sisters at the school and a bit of a heads-up on the rest of them when it came to some of Downey House's more arcane rituals.

'So what is it?' said Zelda. 'Some Jane Austen shit?'

'A bit further north,' said Alice, as they left for the dorm.

Zelda tutted. 'Like I know about the geography of this place. Is this country even big enough to *have* geography?'

Miss Gifford happened to be walking ahead of them into the refectory and shot Zelda a very stern look, which Zelda completely missed. Simone instantly went pink, she still couldn't bear to be reminded of her detention.

Fliss was sitting alone at the corner of their usual table, pretending to be engrossed in a magazine and picking listlessly at a tangerine.

'Has she fallen out with us?' said Simone, wonderingly. She hoped it wasn't something she had done. Fliss had been in a mood with her for ages, she couldn't even cheer her up by doing impressions of Miss Adair being cross and Scottish, like she usually did. She didn't realise that Fliss was still jealous of Alice for getting Will's attention; and was now jealous of the attention even she, Simone, was getting for losing weight. Simone was so used to thinking of Fliss as glamorous, popular and blessed, it never even occurred to her that Fliss could feel that way.

Alice snorted. 'What have we done?'

Fliss felt herself colour under the scrutiny of the other girls. She knew they were talking about her. What could she say? What could she do? It sounded so awful; she couldn't shout at Simone and tell her to stop losing weight and getting pretty, it was hard enough that everyone else in the dorm was already prettier and more attractive, which was why Will liked Alice more than her. And they all seemed to find it so easy not to eat, but she found it really difficult. Well. She'd show them. She could eat less and exercise more than any of them. Surely if she was the slimmest and prettiest, Will would notice her after all, especially at the dance?

'What's up with you?' asked Alice. Fliss felt even more annoyed. Why was Alice always so bloody confident all the time? Nothing ever bothered her.

'Nothing,' she shrugged. 'You know. We're *slaves* to our hormones.'

Alice raised her eyebrows. 'Just in a shitty mood?'

Fliss didn't add, 'No thanks to you.' She just sat there, toying with her food.

'You know it's formal dancing tomorrow?' said Simone.

'What?' said Fliss.

'Preparing us for the Christmas ball.'

'You are joking?'

'Dunno,' said Simone. 'Alice knows all about it.'

'It's just stupid poncing about for the boys, isn't it?' said Alice loftily. 'So they can put formal dancing down on our forms like good little ladies.'

'I'm going to refuse to do it,' said Zelda. 'And if they make me, I'm going to sue them.'

But Fliss wasn't listening. Suddenly, her bad mood forgotten, she drifted into a reverie . . . Of herself, slim and perfect in a white dress, with a blue sash to match her eyes, spinning gracefully round the dance floor as Will nudged his friends and asked who she was again, he'd hardly noticed her before, but now he could see her in an entirely different light.

'What kind of dancing?' she asked.

Alice rolled her eyes. 'Just like on *Strictly Come Dancing*,' she said. 'You get the costumes and everything.'

'Really?' said Simone. She adored *Strictly Come Dancing*.

She wondered if she'd be thin enough by Christmas to get into something sparkly, with sequins.

'No,' said Fliss. 'Alice is just winding you up.'

'And big feathers in your hair,' Alice went on. 'And a celebrity to dance with.'

'I wish it *was* like *Strictly Come Dancing*,' mused Simone. 'That would be great.'

It was, of course, nothing like *Strictly Come Dancing*. Janey James, the strict but generally fair sports mistress, lined them all up along the walls of the large gymnasium. It was clear she felt this was a total waste of sports time and really thought they should all be outside doing cross-country running.

Simone was particularly nervous. She remembered her first ever school disco. Not quite yet known for her swottiness, she was still fairly optimistic about secondary school. She wasn't the only heavy girl there, and there were lots of nice-looking boys, and she was doing well at Maths; people even spoke to her occasionally in class. Maybe big school wasn't going to be quite as awful as she'd been dreading after all. And her mother, of course, was keen for her to go to the dance; had even made her a special dress for the occasion. Simone remembered every stitch of it. It was red velvet with a white collar, material pulled far too tightly across her emergent bosoms. But it had a swirly skirt that moved when she did, and the colour suited her dark hair and skin. Her mother lent her a slick of lip gloss, and her father dropped her off at the unusually lit-up school with a kiss, telling her she looked beautiful.

That feeling had lasted for precisely five minutes. As she walked into the rec hall, which was covered in flashing disco lights and banners and playing Girls Aloud at high volume, she realised, to her horror, that not a single other girl there was wearing a dress. They were wearing super-tight jeans with little tops, or tracksuit trousers with lots of gold accessories, or miniskirts that slit right up to their bums, with G-strings hanging out over their backs. But not one was wearing a childish, homemade dress. Or anything like it. Everyone looked so *different* out of school uniform . . . Well, she'd had no idea, really. Everyone was looking at her. She could tell. Estelle Grant, the meanest girl in the school, walked slowly up to her. The year group watched to see what Estelle would do. Simone felt her heart pound painfully in her chest.

Estelle stood in front of her in her Kappa top, black string-vest and black miniskirt. She looked like one of the Pussycat Dolls. She certainly did not look like a schoolgirl.

'Nice threads,' she said to Simone. 'What are they, Prada?'

The trio of girls who followed Estelle around regularly all threw back their heads and howled with laughter. Simone tried to walk past her to see her friend Lydia, who was sitting by herself at the edge of the dance floor wearing the white blouse and black skirt she normally wore to waitress in her family restaurant. At least she faded into the background. But Estelle was blocking her way.

'Did nobody tell you you're allowed to wear your *own* clothes?' she said again. 'Not, like, something you stole off a doll?'

Out of the corner of her eye Simone could see Mr Graves, the Biology teacher, approaching the situation rapidly. Simone knew, of course, that letting a teacher deal with the situation would only make matters worse in the long term. She should really say something clever and witty back to Estelle, or even better, just whack her one. That would stop it. But the pounding of her heart and the lump in her throat made any kind of retaliation impossible. All she could do was stand there, feeling her face flush hotter and hotter.

'Everything all right here, girls?' said Mr Graves.

'Oh, yes, sir,' said Estelle. 'I was just telling Simone how nice she looks.'

'She looks less of a dangerous liability than you, that's for sure,' said Mr Graves. Estelle scowled and mouthed 'Paedo' out of his eyeline.

'Is that right, Simone?'

Simone could do nothing but nod. She and Lydia had spent the entire night sitting against the wall drinking fanta, as everyone else danced and laughed and had a fantastic time. Only once, when The Killers came on, their absolute favourite song ever ever ever, did they get up and move, unsteadily and clumsily, from foot to foot with each other in the darkest corner of the dance floor.

'How was it?' her father had asked anxiously. Simone would never know, but he'd kept his car parked outside the entire evening. Just in case.

Simone shrugged. 'It was OK.'

It broke her father's heart to see her unhappy. He loved her so much. What could he do?

'Want to go and get cheeseburgers and milkshakes at McDonalds, huh?'

Simone had looked up at him, sniffing a bit. 'Yes please, Daddy.' And he took her hand in his and gave it a big squeeze.

This is going to be different, Simone was thinking to herself. I am different now. It is different. It's like Zelda said, I am a positive person. I make my own destiny.

'Pribetich! Over there!' came Janie's penetrating voice. Simone glanced up. She was being herded to one side of the room with Zelda, big lanky Astrid Ulverton, poor Bessie from Tudor House, whose parents were always taking her out in the middle of term to send her to fat camp . . . Simone's heart sank. She didn't even have to hear JJ say it.

'All right. This wall here. You're going to be the boys.'

'And hop and back and swap your partners to the left, and one two three, and *one* . . .'

This was hard work. Especially when you were going to have to remember it all again in reverse, thought Simone dolefully. They were changing partners every turn and she had to remember to step twice up in the circle otherwise she held everyone else up. She was so intent on counting out her steps that she didn't notice Fliss taking her hands.

'Isn't this great?' said Fliss dreamily. She followed the steps perfectly, twirling daintily and spinning away. Simone watched her in awe.

'You're a really good dancer,' she said.

'I'm going to have to be,' said Fliss.

As dance class progressed, though, they did improve – particularly Felicity Prosser, Janie James noticed, who was obviously practising in her own time, though she was looking a little thin and drawn. She'd mention it to her form teacher, Maggie.

Really it was amazing that the girls memorised any of the steps at all. All their time seemed to be taken up with chattering about which boys would be there: Gabriel Marsh, the tall captain of the cricket team with the curly hair who looked like something out of *Hollyoaks*? Mohammed, the liquid-eyed minor prince from the Middle East? Will Hampton, who'd had his own band? And how much make up *could* they wear, please, miss?

*

'I just surely wouldn't want to see my girl going to a school that's biased and against my true ethics, that's all.'

Once upon a time, Maggie remembered, when she'd been teaching at Holy Cross, she'd given Fallon McBride a suspension. Her mother, a terrifying woman with huge tattoos all over the tops of her breasts, had marched up to the school, Fallon in tow, and threatened to give Maggie a 'doing' if she didn't scrap it. 'Ah cannae have her roon the hoose, she does mah head in' had been the reason.

Maggie had rather hoped to avoid this kind of confrontation at Downey House, so had been surprised when she'd answered her office extension to hear a molasses-slow southern voice, of a type she'd usually only heard in films, introduce himself as 'DuBose Towrnell, Zelda's pa', then proceed to ask why she'd been teaching such peacenik garbage in class.

Maggie had been too surprised that anything she'd been teaching Zelda had been making the faintest impression – as well as enjoying the sound of his voice – that she didn't know what to say.

'So you gotta see both sides, yeah? I just don't like all this propaganda.'

At first Maggie had been shocked. Then, on balance, she'd reflected on two things: first, even though she couldn't be further apart in her beliefs from an American soldier on the subject of war, perhaps it was right that the girls knew there were two sides to every story; second, and more importantly, perhaps this might be the thing to stop Zelda handing in the bare minimum of work and spending most of her days in class surreptitiously experimenting with lip gloss. Her excitement at this caused her to overlook the note from Janie James about checking Felicity Prosser; Felicity had always held a sullen air in her class and she hadn't noticed any change in that.

'All right, everyone,' she announced brightly. 'Today we're going to look at the war poets from another angle – from those who believed in and supported the war. Thanks to Zelda's father, by the way, who suggested it.'

Zelda dropped her head to her hands and let out a huge groan. 'Aw, *man*! I *told* him not to say anything!'

'Now, Zelda, I'm sure he was just trying to get involved.'

'Yeah, poke his nose in where it's not wanted – typical bloody US soldier.'

Some of the class nodded approvingly. Maggie sighed.

'Zelda! No more cheek, please! Turn to page ninety-five, you'll see it starts, *There's a breathless hush in the close tonight, Ten to make and the match to win . . .*'

Zelda let out a huge sigh. Maggie looked up.

'One more word out of you and you'll not be going to the Christmas dance.'

At this the whole class let out a groan of dismay. Maggie bit her lip. All she wanted to do was be a good teacher. Why did she keep ending up as the bad guy?

Simone had her hand up.

'Yes, Simone?'

'Uhm, sorry, but isn't this the poem about how only the upper classes know how to behave themselves in war by killing everyone?'

And I've even betrayed my own principles, thought Maggie, reading on: *'Play up! play up! and play the game . . .'*

Veronica hadn't even known why she'd taken the dune path down towards the beach. It had been such a sharp Sunday morning but the sun was in the sky, and after another one of the reverend's particularly tiresome sermons, she'd felt the need to get away from everything for a bit; from the school, the other teachers, the day to day niggles of roll calls and applications.

She scrambled slightly down the slope, feeling a small pain in her ankle, but recovered quickly enough.

The winter beach was deserted in both directions. Even in summertime it was too out of the way and windswept to garner much in the way of tourists. The waves crashed grey and ominously on the shore, cold and relentless. Veronica pulled her scarf tighter around herself. The colour of the sea suited her mood.

As she walked along the shingle, keeping a brisk pace against the chill wind, gulls overhead calling shrilly, she realised that in fact she wasn't quite alone; there was a group of figures rushing around about a hundred metres away. They were too small to be school children, and as she grew closer she realised they were toddlers, bundled up in warm jackets and hats till they looked like fat penguins, wobbling up and down with buckets and spades. Veronica smiled to see them. Then, drawing closer, she froze. The children were with Daniel, and a woman with long blonde hair blowing in the breeze who could only be his wife.

They hadn't seen her, or hadn't realised it was her yet. There was still time to turn back. The little family – two boys and a girl, she knew – looked perfect, playing beautifully in the surf, a lovely little family unit . . . She felt her heart wrench. She knew families weren't perfect, she saw the results of that in some of the girls who passed through her doors every year. She knew marriage was difficult, had proven too hard for the majority of her own friends. That raising children meant sacrifice, and that her own life had been built on hard work and making the best of the difficult hand she had been dealt. It didn't stop, though, an almost primal yearning; a desire, a want in the very pit of her stomach. It was all she could do not to shout out loud. It was so unlike her, and she was frozen to the spot.

At that instant Daniel lifted his head from where he'd been attempting to unravel a kite for his eldest boy, and caught sight of her. She immediately clasped her hand to her mouth and backed away, as she saw his face squint in the weak sunlight. He'd recognised her.

Veronica felt like a stalker. Imagine if he thought she'd followed them here to stare at his children, or worse. She continued to back away, but he shook his head. Then he beckoned his wife over and spoke in her ear. His wife checked the children then looked at her husband. Daniel then beckoned Veronica.

Despite the cold, Veronica suddenly felt the heat in her face. What was he going to say? Was he going to order her to stay away from his family? He couldn't, could he? They'd decided to move to Cornwall, after all – that wasn't her fault, was it? Was it?

Slowly, tentatively, she moved towards the group. Daniel moved in her direction. She clasped her coat more tightly around herself.

Finally they were standing face to face. The woman with Daniel was quite exceptionally pretty, with a kind, open face and glorious streaming blonde hair, which the children appeared to have inherited.

'Susie,' said Daniel, gently, turning to his wife. 'Uhm, this is Veronica. My, uh, my birth mother.'

Susie smiled a warm, nervous smile and held out her hand. 'I've heard a lot about you,' she said.

Veronica's heart leapt. Had he spoken about her? Well, that was silly, of course he had. But of course Susie would already have a mother-in-law, and—

'Who's this, Mummy?' A small, freckle-faced boy of about five, with his mother's beautiful hair and his father's shrewd green eyes, raced up, followed by the other two.

Veronica knelt down in the sand. 'Hello,' she said. Frosty as she may appear to adults sometimes, she knew how to talk to children. 'My name is Veronica. I'm a friend of your daddy. What's your name?'

'Rufus,' said the boy. 'I like submarines.'

'Ooh, me too,' said Veronica. 'You know, I've been on one.'

The boy's eyes widened. 'Really?'

'Really,' she said. 'Maybe one day I'll tell you all about it.'

Daniel smiled at her as she got back up. 'He's obsessed.'

Veronica glanced out to sea. She thought she knew a bit about the reasons for that.

'I know it's a freezing day,' said Susie, 'but I just had to get them out of the house! You know what they're like when they're cooped up.'

Veronica smiled like she did know.

'They're lovely children,' she said. Their little girl – their baby – was sitting by the water's edge trying to eat sand. 'Is she all right to be eating so much sand?'

Susie smiled. 'Oh, they've all done it. Didn't kill the other two. I just pretend they're getting lots of roughage.'

Veronica felt her heart tug. She liked this woman. She liked this family. And she was so inextricably connected, but . . . She glanced out to sea. There was one thing she could do. That she owed Daniel.

'Would you like to come to tea one day soon?' she said. 'So we could talk?'

Daniel looked taken aback. He immediately glanced at his wife.

'Um . . .' said Susie.

'I'm sorry,' Veronica cut in at once. 'I didn't mean to spring that on you.'

'No, it's not that,' said Susie. Daniel seemed struck dumb.

107

'Well,' Veronica started to retreat, 'of course, you know where to find me.'

'We do,' said Susie, taking her husband's hand.

'Anyway, I must go,' said Veronica quickly. 'Goodbye, Rufus!'

Rufus turned from where he was struggling with the kite and gave her a cheery wave. 'I want you to take me on a submarine!'

'Rufus!' said his mum. 'Sorry.'

'Take me on a submarine PLEASE,' came the voice.

'My door is always open,' said Veronica, smiling sadly as she turned back to pick her way against the wind along the beach.

And then, three days later, he had rang. Just like that. Yes, he would like to come for tea. Yes, Tuesday at four would work well.

They were stilted on the telephone, but Veronica still felt a profound joy, mixed with extreme nervousness. She had the fire laid in the grate, and extra scones sent up from the ref. The winter chill had really set in now December was here, and the girls no longer walked the perimeter of the four towers to get to class, as they did in sunnier weather, but raced through the unheated corridors, cheeks pink. It cut down on a lot of tardiness, not heating the corridors. Veronica had thought Miss Starling was being a little cruel suggesting it, but it had turned out to work rather well.

Her office today, though, was warm and cosy, its well-chosen furniture and treasured works of art adding to the room a sense of calm. She looked around, trying to see it through his eyes. She didn't want to make it seem . . . well, too comfortable, almost. As if her life had been good without him.

*

It had not been an easy decision for Daniel to make. He had lain awake, talking to Susie, who longed to help him do the right thing but wasn't entirely sure what that was. In the end, it had come down to one thing: I have to know, Daniel had said. I don't know why, but I have to know all I can. She's my mother.

Susie, close to his adoptive mother, counselled caution. 'You just don't know her,' she'd insisted. 'And everything you have to do with her makes you unhappy. Plus, I don't like this whole thing about keeping you a secret. If it were me I'd want to shout it to the world. And I don't like the idea of you making Ida unhappy.'

'I know,' Daniel had said. 'I know all that, I do. But there's so much about myself I have to learn. And . . .' He'd been surprised to hear himself defending her. 'She's a good woman. She is. She's a legendary headteacher, all her pupils adore her.'

Susie had sniffed a bit at this.

'I mean, she does have her reasons for the secrecy thing.'

'Yes. Bad ones.'

Daniel was silent. Susie leant over in the bed and kissed him.

'Sweetheart. Do whatever you must, OK? But stop worrying about it so much.'

'You know, I think she'd love to meet the children properly.'

'One step at a time, OK?'

The night before their meeting Susie had drifted off peacefully enough. But he had tossed and turned the hours away, endlessly playing out scenarios in his head. The worst, of course, being some nightmare about his real father – rape, or incest, or any one of a million horrible things. He couldn't think like that. He couldn't.

As he entered, Veronica could see straight away how nervous he was; it was mirrored in her own compulsive re-ordering of her desk, lining up the teacups when Evelyn brought them in. She wanted to put him at his ease but didn't have the faintest idea how to go about it.

'Hello, Daniel,' she said. 'Please, sit down. I lit the fire . . .'

'Yes, it's getting perishingly cold . . . feels like it might snow.' He attempted a weak smile. 'Didn't get this in Guildford.'

Veronica smiled nervously back at him. 'So I imagine. Tea?'

Daniel concurred and Veronica poured. Daniel felt the softness of the armchair and the peace and calm of Veronica's room begin to work its magic. It was hard to believe there were three hundred unruly girls somewhere in the building; they could be miles away. And it was hard to believe that he was about to hear things that might upset him – or worse, fail to answer his questions at all.

Veronica put down the milk jug decisively.

'Now, Daniel, I hope you won't mind if I tell you this all at once. Perhaps you could save any questions until I've finished.'

She lowered her head. 'I hope you understand . . . I haven't discussed this with anyone for nearly forty years. It's not very easy for me to think about.'

Daniel nodded to indicate that he did understand. Inside his heart was beating wildly.

'Once upon a time . . .' began Veronica. She smiled. 'I realise that is a silly way to begin. Still, all stories start somewhere. Once upon a time, there was a reasonably daft, certainly under-educated girl who lived in Sheffield. Her

110

name was Vera. She lived with her father, a steelworker, her mother and her three brothers in a terrace in Darnall.

'If I were describing her as one of my girls, I would say she was a dreamer. A bright girl, not really encouraged in her school work – her father didn't believe in education for girls – but a big reader. She liked Jane Austen, Tess, *Wuthering Heights* and all sorts of silly romance stories, and she truly believed that in love one had a great passion for which one would sacrifice just about anything.'

Veronica's voice sounded far away. Daniel heard a northern timbre creep into it.

'One day, Vera's father left his lunch behind, and her mother sent her down to the docks with it, skipping like Little Red Riding Hood. I think that perhaps Vera's mother had forgotten that she was no longer the sweet little girl whom the other workers would pet and give lollipops to. Instead she was growing too quickly into a body she didn't understand, full of curious passions and unexplained yearnings.

'After she'd found her father, she wandered slowly home between the cranes and delivery trucks on the dockside.'

She paused.

'And then, out jumped the wolf . . . or rather, a man, Bert Cromer. An acquaintance of her father whom she'd noticed before, at church with his own family or staggering out of the pub on week nights. He had dirty, sharp teeth and a sniggering way of looking at her that was uncomfortable and unpleasant.

'"Well, well, Miss Vera," he said, stepping out in between two large canisters, in a secluded part of the shipyard. "What have we here?"

'"I'm taking ma da his lunch," Vera said, looking for an easy exit. She couldn't see one.

'"Are you indeed?" said the man. "So you just happened to be down here, on your own, flouncing about dockside? There's a name for ladies who do that. Do you know what it is?" He moved closer to her. She could smell him; he smelled of stale beer and bad breath.

'"Do you, little Vera? Is that what you're going to do for a living now? They won't like that down the chapel. Always got your nose in a book, I've seen yer. That won't do yer much good, will it? But maybe it's taught you a few things."

'And he reached out and put a hand on Vera's dress. She jumped back, but couldn't see anywhere else to go. He was blocking the route ahead, and behind were only the empty crates, carrying Sheffield steel and Sheffield cutlery all round the world.

'Vera let out a little sound.

'"New to this, are you? Well, we might make it easy on yer." He was completely facing her now, pushing her backwards to one of the crates.

'"Let me go!" said Vera as strongly as she could manage, suddenly terrified. "Get off me." Her voice sounded pitifully weak and girlish.

'"Walking down the docks, in clear daylight. Brazen as brass," said Bert Cromer.'

Daniel swallowed. He could see the tension in Veronica's face and shoulders, could see her reliving the event as if it were yesterday. He wanted to cry, put his arm on her, apologise for the horrible horrible event, for his foul father. He felt, obscurely, that somehow it was his fault; it worried him to imagine what he himself was capable of, what darkness he might have inherited.

'I said no,' Veronica went on. 'Quite clearly. I said no.'

There was a long pause as they both gazed out on to the

112

frost-spattered lawn outside Veronica's window, into the darkening sky and the shadowy outlines of the headland.

'Then he was there,' said Veronica simply. 'Right there. I don't even know how he got there, or how he heard us. He must have been working nearby, the ship was nearby.'

'Who?' Daniel hadn't meant to interrupt, but he couldn't help himself. It didn't seem to matter though, Veronica hadn't even noticed. Her eyes had taken on a dreamy expression.

'I didn't even know what he said. It was just a kind of gut-teral, angry stream of sounds. But you could tell what he meant all right. And then he hit Bert on the head for good measure. Then he pulled out a spanner and offered to hit him some more with that, if that's what he wanted.'

She smiled to herself.

'He was very poetic of gesture. Bert was a coward really. All bullies are, of course. As soon as Piotr hit him, he scarpered off like a skelped rabbit. And he stayed well away from me after that.'

She paused, and sipped her tea, tidily.

'It took me about two seconds to fall in love. Piotr Petrovich Ivanov. You had to use his full name, and that was it. I used to think there were so many people in Russia, you needed to use all the names to differentiate. But it's just their patrimony. That doesn't matter, of course. I loved it anyway. I used to roll it round my mouth at night. *Piotr Petrovich Ivanov*. It was so beautiful, so exotic.

'He wasn't even meant to be off his boat. They weren't allowed in those days, do you remember? In case he got infected with evil Capitalist ideas. He'd come off for a look around, because he never let anything like that get in his way. He was puffing on one of the stinking black Russian cigarettes he smoked – they were absolutely filthy things. I adored the smell, I must have reeked of them. I can't believe my parents wouldn't have noticed that before.'

As if coming back to herself, Veronica sat a little straighter in her chair.

'He spoke no English, barely a word. A little more by the time he left, three weeks later. Not much. *Cee-ga-rette*. *Ve-ron-eeka* – that's what he called me, not Vera. Like a nickname. *Ya tebya ljublju*.

'I adored him. He was strong and brave and good and handsome and I loved everything about him.'

'What happened?' asked Daniel, fascinated.

Veronica looked at the high-cheekboned face, the pale eyes with the dark hair.

'You are so like him to look at. In terms of what you're like . . . well, I suppose I never truly got to know either of you.'

She looked down.

'Of course in those days there wasn't any internet, or mobile phones, or even a reliable mail service to Russia. It was a closed continent, unimaginably vast and mysterious. And I am sure, you know, he had a wife and a family and so on back there. He was a man, I was a girl. In a funny way, too, at that age, I almost . . . there was a part of me that knew. That knew it would be a tragic love affair. I was so full of silly stories and great passions . . . I did not expect, though . . . well, you.'

She smiled apologetically.

'I wrote and I wrote to the address he gave me. Nothing, of course. Was it a false address? Did I write it out wrongly? Did the state intercept his letters? A wife? I have so many questions too, Daniel. And I cried a thousand tears. Oh yes. Well, he never . . . he never came back for me. And then I started to show of course, in the way of it, and that bastard Bert spread it around that I was the shipyard slut . . . I thought my father was going to smack that baby out of me. So my mother sent me away. The gossip, the fuss ... you wouldn't think it was the seventies. But it was.

'If I had been brave ... If I had been brave, like Piotr Petrovich Ivanov was brave, then I wouldn't have given you up. Not for a second. And if things had been different ... I do believe love does not always need language or culture. We could have perhaps ... well, I will never know, of course. I think as far as the Communist tragedy goes, we were very much amongst the better off.'

Veronica looked to be straightening herself up.

'And after everything I decided that, after all, books were safer; studying life was better than living it. So here we are.'

She said 'So here we are' in the most matter-of-fact way she could muster.

Neither Daniel nor anyone else looking at her would have guessed for a second that, in her mind, she was sitting on the front of a bicycle Piotr Petrovich Ivanov purloined one night, riding round the shipyard at midnight after she'd crept out of the house, both of them screaming with laughter and frozen joy as the black water of the port lapped at the dock's edge.

'So I'm half Russian?' said Daniel, wonderingly.

'You are Daniil Petrovich Ivanov,' said Veronica. 'That is what I wanted to call you. Of course they wouldn't hear of it. Russians are godless, the nuns said. So I called you after the man who slew Goliath, who plucked the thorn from the lion's paw. My own name I changed as soon as I was allowed. I hated Vera anyway. I may have lost him, but I get some comfort from that. In my head, you know, I spell it with a k, and always will.'

Daniel stared into the fire.

'More tea?' said Veronica.

Chapter Seven

'Boys and girls together. I'm telling you, it's a disaster. Always.'

'Yes, Miss Starling.'

Maggie felt mutinously sure that she was the only teacher still new enough to the school to have Miss Starling give her a long lecture on why she didn't believe in the mixed school dance. Especially since she'd done nothing since half term except put her head down and work really really hard. She'd agreed, in the end, to buy the dress she'd tried on. It was in her price range, and when you came down to it, wedding dresses were all the same, weren't they? They'd also put the deposit on the venue. There was either whisky or vodka for everyone on arrival, red or white with dinner and champagne for the toasts. When they got closer to the time they could decide if they wanted chicken or salmon. So, it was all practically organised and everyone could stop bugging her about it. She bit her tongue at that. They weren't bugging her, of course. They loved her. They were excited. So should she be.

And she was doing well, she knew she was. Her second-year group seemed to be doing all right – Simone Pribetich for one was looking much better. She'd lost a lot of podginess and Maggie was really proud of her. She liked to see

116

teenage girls, normally so unaware of their own beauty, look good and make the best of themselves. They should know how beautiful they were – Maggie envied them their long smooth limbs and shiny hair. Felicity Prosser was looking pinched and sullen; Maggie would have to have a word. She sighed. If only she didn't find that little madam quite so difficult, she'd pay her more attention.

Her other classes were doing well, though, and Maggie had even conquered, over long nights of painstaking figuring out, her own distaste for the lyric poets. She had her priorities straight: work, family, a wedding. It was all good. Did she truly envy the tearful hysterics of second formers, wild with excitement of whether a boy would ask her to dance? Well perhaps, if she were honest, hearing their excited chatter, just a little. But everyone had to grow up sometime.

So even the idea of tonight – the school dance – seemed unusual: she had given up going out almost altogether. She didn't want to join in Claire and Miranda's cosy girls' nights. Miranda was obviously very happy at being back with David and she didn't want to rain on that parade, or even risk having a couple of glasses too many and saying the wrong thing at the wrong time. She'd enjoyed her nights alone up in the tower room, a glass of wine and a book of poetry, curled up in front of the fire. Sometimes she worried she might turn into Miss Starling. But not often.

'It always leads to *derring do*,' Miss Starling was continuing. Maggie thought that perhaps she haunted the corridor outside her rooms, waiting for her to emerge so she could continue one of her harangues.

'Derring do?' enquired Maggie. That sounded rather a grand name for what was likely to be a little vomiting in the bushes and some snogging that would be picked over and probably regretted the following day. Maggie smiled briefly as she imagined Miss Starling at one of Holy Cross's Christmas parties, which were famous for their debauchery. The teachers usually behaved just as badly as the pupils, too. They normally had to get professional cleaners in afterwards.

'*Mis-be-haviour,*' said Miss Starling, as usual overemphasising the wrong syllables.

'Ah,' said Maggie. 'Well, you look very nice.'

As usual, Miss Starling was wearing a synthetic blouse with a brooch and a knee-length skirt of no distinguishing characteristics whatsoever. She had a slender figure, but Maggie couldn't imagine she had ever been pretty – had her mouth always been so pursed? Her nose always so thin and pinched-looking?

Maggie was wearing her red dress again. It was the only nice thing she had really, or at least that was suitable for a school dance rather than a holiday in Spain. It set off her dark hair nicely, and after adding some cherry lipstick she was rather pleased with the result. It had made her briefly remember the last time she'd worn it and David had looked at her with those melting brown eyes, and they'd been caught alone under the mistletoe and she'd come so close to . . . She shut her thoughts closed with a snap. That was all in the past now.

'Shall we go down together?' She smiled sweetly at Miss Starling and led her off towards the spiral staircase, just before Claire, running late as usual, came careening out of her room, draped in an exquisitely printed dress and cursing like a navvy as to the whereabouts of her shoes.

The atmosphere in the girls' dorms was absolutely fierce. Boy-starved since the ill-fated Geography field trip, the levels of primping, expectation and nerves were approaching fever pitch, regardless of how many salutary, ardour-dampening chats they'd had from Miss Starling in the preceding weeks.

Skirmishes were breaking out over mirror space: 'One between four. This country is barbaric,' Zelda pointed out, as well as reminding everyone that in America the dorm would be the size of one girl's normal en-suite bathroom. Everyone, as usual, ignored her grumbling comparisons.

Fliss was in a dreamworld of her own. For the last few weeks she'd danced every spare second she could find, practising the steps. Some of the girls did extra dance classes on Saturdays, but up until now Fliss had never been that interested. Now she badgered little Sylvie Brown to show her *ronde de jambes* and arabesques until her muscles ached and Sylvie begged for mercy. She'd scheduled these practise sessions for mealtimes too, so she would have a legitimate reason for skipping supper. Matron, who kept a weather eye on these kinds of things, was about to have a word with Maggie about it. It wasn't right. Fliss's pale face looked more drawn than ever, her blue eyes huge and vulnerable-looking in the peaky face. Her hip bones had started to stick out.

Alice had noticed, but considered it none of her business. Naturally slim, she looked upon any kind of controlled eating as a form of attention-seeking. Fond of her friend, she didn't want to give Fliss that indulgence. Plus, Fliss seemed to be actively avoiding her. Alice couldn't believe it was because she'd talked for five minutes to that Will guy, she'd hardly given him a second glance. It couldn't be. It would blow over.

Simone, on the other hand, was giving Fliss all the reinforcement she didn't need and shouldn't have.

'Ohmygod you're so thin!' she said every day. 'You look like a model or something.'

Alice wanted to say she didn't look like a model, she looked like a warning poster for drugs, but bit her tongue. She sensed that on one level Fliss wanted nothing more than a big argument with her and she didn't want to start it.

Fliss gazed at herself in the mirror. Her blue party dress was falling off her. It was ridiculously big. Fliss hugged herself with delight. Also, it was freezing in here. Why couldn't they heat the place properly? The amount of money her parents paid, it was an absolute disgrace. Up until now she'd been hiding under big jumpers, but tonight her gorgeous new figure could be revealed. She hadn't eaten anything at all today except for an apple at lunchtime, and she'd drank a lot of water. And danced, of course. She was going to take this place by storm, she knew it. She pulled an emerald scarf of Zelda's tightly round her waist. She looked tiny, there was no doubt about it. It would all be worthwhile. And Will would see her . . . But at first, of course, she would ignore him, accept the invitations of other boys who were bound to come her way. She felt a momentary flutter of anxiety about this – the other boys would ask her, wouldn't they? – but dismissed it. She'd be with Alice, who knew half the boys anyway because they were friends of her sister, and Zelda, who'd have so much make up on the boys would ask her out almost by accident. Of course they'd notice her too.

Then, perhaps a few dances in when she was being as thin and graceful as Keira Knightley, Will would not be able to take it any longer and he would make his way across the dance floor – maybe he would separate her from dancing with another boy, that would be good – and ask her to dance and she would look up at him like this – she practised in the mirror – and—

'Jeez, what are you *doing* in there?' screamed Zelda at the

120

top of her voice. 'Not all of us have naturally straight hair, you know! We need a little more time!'

'Coming!' shouted Fliss. She felt a little light-headed for a second, and leant her forehead against the cool of the mirrored glass. Cool, that's all she needed to be. Cool, calm and collected, and she would be fine.

Simone looked at the stiff brown velvet and sighed.

'You are lucky, you know, angel,' her mother had said. 'How many other girls' mothers love them so much they make their own clothes?'

'But can't I at least choose the pattern?'

'I know what suits my beautiful girl best.'

That was entirely debatable, Simone thought, but, as usual, she'd acquiesced for a quiet life.

Still, at least the dress didn't pull around her chest any more. In fact, it was noticeably looser on her. She felt pleased.

Zelda stopped in front of her.

'Simone,' she said, shaking her head. 'Simone Simone Simone.'

'My mum made it,' Simone muttered.

'Why wouldn't you let us take you shopping?'

Simone flushed. How could she say that she didn't have any money for shopping? It didn't compute to Zelda, she thought shopping was just something one did, like reading a book, or breathing, and she couldn't bear the thought of accepting their charity, however kindly meant.

'Is that really all you have?'

Simone shrugged. 'I could go in my pyjamas if you like.'

'This is *not* a time for jokes!' Zelda frowned and went over to her own cupboard (or closet as she called it), filled with beautiful clothes perfectly put away.

'Let me see, let me see.'

Simone didn't want to be a part of this. Zelda may be tall, but she was slender too. Nothing she owned had the faintest chance of getting over Simone's chest, even now she had lost some weight.

'You're no sylph yet, Sims, but I bet we can find something. And you have to let me make you up, you have eyelashes like a cow.'

'Uh, thanks. I suppose.'

'Yeah!' Zelda was firing everyone up. 'We're good to go! Everyone is HOT! SOOO HOT! Yeah! Give us a twirl!'

Simone stifled a giggle. But she couldn't help feeling excited. In the back of her closet, Zelda had found a long draping black dress. It was meant to be baggy, but on Simone looked clinging and curvaceous rather than stretched. Simone never wore black – someone had told her once it was the colour fat people wore, so she'd always avoided it – but it went well with her dark wild curls, finally set free from the frizzy braids she normally wore, and smoothed down with about a pint of Zelda's relaxing serum. Her dark eyes had been made even larger and darker with three coats of mascara, and a cherry red stain on her lips and cheeks had given her a dramatic gypsy look.

'You could get served in a bar,' said Alice, semi-admiringly.

As a final dramatic touch, Zelda took a red scarf and loosely knotted it round her hips.

'Do you think?' said Simone doubtfully.

'All she needs is the rose in her mouth,' said Alice.

Simone sighed. 'Well, it doesn't matter to me anyway. If I'm not allowed to wear my glasses it's not like I can see anything anyway.'

'Hush, you doubters,' said Zelda. 'I am Queen of the Makeovers, and I say, HOT!'

Fliss hadn't really been able to listen to anything, she felt a little spacy and light-headed with excitement. She was sitting on the bed, her right foot twitching.

'Can't we just go?' she burst in. 'What if everyone's already there and they start the dancing without us?'

'No,' said Zelda carefuly. 'We have to make an entrance.'

'Well, no one is going to miss you,' said Alice. Zelda had conformed to the dance guidelines: her dress was below the knee and had straps. However it somewhat contravened the spirit, given that it had a huge split up one leg, was silver, and the straps were made of Swarovski crystals that glittered and reflected the light.

'Do you think the teachers will mind you wearing a dress that costs more than their entire salary?' asked Alice mischievously, glancing at Fliss. But Fliss was still sitting on the bed, twitching and staring into space. Alice fervently hoped that tonight she would pull a boy, learn how to snog and get over this ridiculous phase, it was pulling them all down. She herself looked elegant and appropriate in a pink silk fifties-style dress with a tight belt pulling in her tiny waist.

'Ya think?' answered Zelda, frowning. She always took everything literally. 'I mean, you know, they're always welcome to borrow it.'

Alice laughed. That was Zelda all over – not the sharpest tool in the box, but endlessly generous.

'I think it would suit Miss Gifford,' said Simone. Post-detention, Miss Gifford was the only mistress Simone felt allowed to slag off, so she did so on occasion, feeling terribly daring.

'No, old JJ,' said Alice. 'It'd be good to see her muscles poking through.'

The girls laughed.

'You could put it on Dr Deveral,' reflected Zelda. 'She'd probably make it look sorta classy.'

'Well, that's more than you're doing,' said Alice.

'Come on!!! Let's GOOO!' said Fliss, anxious beyond endurance.

Once again, Harold Carruthers, the caretaker, and his team had done the school proud. The refectory, normally a clashing maelstrom of chatter and banging cutlery, with steam rising from large catering vats, had been completely transformed.

Now the wooden walls were hung with heavy Christmas wreaths, thick with red holly berries. Candles had been posted in the high windows to add flickering shadows to the room. All the tables and long benches had been cleared away and the canteen area itself closed off. Refreshments – orange or apple juice, hot sausage rolls, jacket potatoes, stuffing sandwiches and horseradish crisps all followed by slices of the school's special Christmas cake (that Joan Rhys still sent to old girls around the world every year, it provided a flourishing business on the side) – would be set up on a long buffet table at the back at nine p.m.

The band were a local folk group who could play music in a variety of styles, and there was also a mobile disco to be set up later after the formal section had been completed. There were two hundred and fifty pupils there in total, stiff, nervous and anxious in new shirts and dresses, desperately trying to give off an air of worldly sophistication that, however privileged their upbringings, they couldn't pull off quite yet.

Maggie felt her heart soften as she looked at them all. In the classroom they could be bumptious, aggravating, clownish, but here they were just extremely young women- and men-to-be, filled with the worries and anxieties of every person that age who ever lived. Am I normal? Am I all right? Will they accept me? Will anyone ask me to dance? It seemed like yesterday that she'd been in exactly the same position. When Stan, of course, had asked her to dance.

Having managed to lose Miss Starling, who was demanding to see the DJ's 'song list', as she called it, to make sure he didn't play anything too risqué or suggestive, she and Claire took up an unobtrusive corner overlooking the dance floor. They weren't there to supervise, not really, just to generally fend off any unnecessary behaviour with a light touch.

Slowly, tentatively, the room began to fill up – nobody wanted to be first to arrive. But as all the boys had arrived together in a clump, speed-marched from over the hill (there would be a coach arriving to take them all back at 10.30 p.m. precisely), girls were emerging from everywhere to get a good look at the talent.

Sylvie Brown was wearing a light-green prom dress that made her pale eyes look enormous. Her blonde hair cascaded like a cloud down her back. Maggie and Claire saw the stir she made amongst the boys and smiled at each other. There was nothing quite like a petite blonde. Andrea McCann, the second year's star hockey player, slouched in in a plain black dress, looking like she'd much rather be out in a muddy field, even in the dark, than tarting herself up for some dance. Zazie Saurisse was far too glamorous and chic for the event and looked as if she'd scare the boys rigid.

Some girls walked in confidently, a little older and already aware of their ability to turn heads, to be liked and admired in male company. Long, clean hair swinging, smooth limbs in pretty prom dresses, Maggie would have felt churlish to deny them their confident smiles, the flashes of white teeth, even if she couldn't avoid feeling just a little jealous. Then there were others, not quite so confident, looking around nervously to see what the other girls were wearing, who the boys were looking at.

The boys, in dinner jackets or lounge suits, did look rather dashing, Maggie had to admit. Not like the spotty little scamps with the shaven heads, tracksuits and nascent pot bellies she remembered from her old school. They looked like young Hugh Grants in the making: callow, clean, polite, but unmemorable somehow, although Maggie had no doubt that wasn't how they appeared to the girls. To them, they would be great heroes of teenage romance, carrying expectations they couldn't possibly hope to fulfil.

She caught sight of David, chivvying the boys along. Well, of course. That was hardly unexpected. She ducked her eyes before he could see her. He was wearing the same dated velvet jacket he'd worn last year. It suited him. She would keep out of his way, that was all.

'Shall we spike the punch?' she asked Claire.

Claire nodded vigorously. 'Normally I dislike the English tendency of endless drinking,' she said. 'But tonight, to get through thees, I may have to make exception. Or let them all get pregnant. I have not yet decided.'

Maggie's response, however, was knocked out of her as she registered the little group entering through the refectory's double doors.

Linking arms, the four of them entered the ref. Maggie was not the only one to notice and react accordingly. Most of the girls in their year leapt forward, startled.

'*Mon dieu,*' said Claire. '*Regarde le papillon.* Simone is your leetle butterfly.'

Indeed she was. Maggie almost couldn't believe that the nervous, near-silent scholarship girl was this curvy, smiling, vibrant-looking beauty. It was a different girl altogether. Incredible.

That hadn't been what had made Maggie gasp, though. It was her own idiocy. How could she have been so caught up in her own obsessions, her own problems, as to ignore what was happening in *her* guidance class, right in front of her very eyes. The very thing she absolutely knew to watch for in teenage girls going on right under her nose, when these young women were meant to be in her pastoral care.

'Oh my God,' she said. 'Look at Felicity Prosser.'

Claire was shaking her head. Fliss's bony shoulders protruded from a dress that could hardly keep itself up. There was almost no difference between the front and back of her. Her eyes looked wide and spacy.

'Dear me,' said Claire. 'Dear me.'

Maggie wanted to rush up to her with a blanket, haul her upstairs, put her to bed and forcefeed her toasted cheese sandwiches till she could stand up again. Her ankles didn't look able to support her body.

Maggie could hear murmurs around the hall. Her Plantagenet girls were certainly being noticed. Zelda looked ridiculous, of course – her hair was about a metre in the air and she looked like a forty-year-old cocktail waitress in Vegas; Alice looked perfect as ever, and Simone looked like someone had just handed her a big pile of gold bananas. But Fliss . . . what was the matter with her? After last year's travails she'd been getting better marks, doing well. She had friends, didn't she? What on earth was going on?

Maggie realised she was making excuses for herself. She should have noticed. She should have seen it.

'Maybe I'll go up and have a word,' she said.

'Not now,' counselled Claire. 'This is her big evening. Don't embarrass her.'

'But everyone's going to be talking about her, whispering . . . it's not right.'

'So you're going to bundle her off to bed, yes? In front of everyone? *Non*, Maggie, thees is not right. Eef there is a problem here, thees will not solve it.'

Maggie reluctantly realised Claire was right.

'I can't . . . I just can't believe I didn't notice.'

Claire patted her kindly on the arm. '*Bof*, all these young girls, they are exactly the same, *non*? One moment they are up and the next they are down and unless we put them on the scales every week of course it is hard. I did not notice either.'

But it wasn't Claire's job to notice, thought Maggie. It was hers.

'You cannot think of it tonight,' said Claire. 'And look at your beautiful Simone.'

Simone couldn't believe it. As soon as she'd entered the room she could feel everyone's eyes on her. At first she thought they were going to point and laugh, that they were staring at her because she looked so terrible and ridiculous and she was going to be the laughing stock of the school.

But then Astrid Ulverton – who would never make a cruel joke, there wasn't a mean streak in her body – came dashing up to her with Sylvie.

'Simone, is that really you? You look incredible!' gasped Sylvie.

Astrid nodded. 'You do. You look really pretty.'

And that was like the cue for all the girls from her class – and some from the other houses, too – to come over and make admiring and somewhat envious remarks. Simone blushed pink and couldn't hide her pleasure. If those girls from St Cats could see her now!

Fliss stared in amazement. When all eyes had swivelled towards her as she entered the ref, head held high, she'd felt pleased, as if it was her due. She'd worked hard, starving herself for this. But now the girls were coming over to congratulate Simone, and their glances slid off her and they looked away, uncomfortable. One or two of them whispered to one another.

Jealous, thought Fliss furiously. They were all just jealous, that was it. They were all sucking up to Simone because she was still comfortably fatter than any of them, so they were just patronising the fat girl, that was it. But they couldn't talk to her, because they knew she was thinner and better than any of them. She felt her fingers tighten.

She didn't feel any better when Hattie, surrounded by her annoyingly twittish bright and breezy hockey chums, bounced over. Fliss had been avoiding her for weeks. Hattie stopped in front of her. For once she wasn't wearing the smug, supercilious look she usually put on around her little sister. She looked actually, genuinely, shocked.

'Felicity! What . . . what the hell is the matter with you?'

'Hell' was very strong swearing for Hattie. In truth, though her sister annoyed her with her attention-seeking ways and pretty, delicate demeanour (Hattie had always been the 'clodhopper' in the family. Her father thought this was funny, contrasting her with the paler, altogether less ruddy-looking Felicity. Hattie hated it. Why couldn't she have been dainty too?), she was genuinely shocked by how skinny her little sister had got. She looked like she was suffering from a disease. She couldn't deny it. She looked anorexic.

Felicity stuck out her chin. 'Nothing. Did you get that dress in the DFS sale?'

Now it was Hattie's turn to flush. Her mother had bought

the dress, a supposedly sophisticated black number, in the January sales. Now she was far too big for it and could feel her shoulders bursting out of the fabric. Why couldn't she stop growing? She felt twice the weight of all the boys there and was sure that Fliss was going to get asked to dance before she was.

'We're not talking about me, we're talking about you. Why have you lost so much weight?'

Fliss shrugged. 'I haven't, not really. Haven't really noticed.'

Hattie bit her lip. 'You look like something from the Irish famine.'

'You don't,' shot back Fliss.

Alice could sense a nasty situation developing. 'Hi, Hattie,' she said, desperately. 'You look nice.'

Hattie glanced at Fliss's smart-mouthed friend. She usually had a hidden agenda. 'Hmm,' she said.

'Where's the juice table? I'm parched.'

'Forget that, where's the MEN table? I'm parched!' said Zelda, blissfully oblivious to the atmosphere. She linked arms with Simone and Fliss and the party moved on.

The band were fantastic. After playing a medley of popular hits to get everyone into the room and relaxing a bit, Dr Deveral stepped up in front of them. Maggie was dying to shout 'Give us a song!' but of course wouldn't dare on pain of death. Nonetheless, there was always something forbidding about her boss that brought out the naughty schoolgirl in her.

Veronica was wearing a beautiful deep-green velvet dress that made her look elegant and somehow timeless. Against the old wooden panelling of the refectory walls, with their heavy boughs of holly and mistletoe, she herself seemed part of the school, something fundamentally rooted there.

As she turned to face the hall – there was no need for a microphone – an instant hush descended.

'Welcome, everyone!' she said. 'Our Downey girls, of course, all of whom are looking very beautiful tonight.'

There was some clapping at this.

'And our brother school, Downey Boys. You are our very welcome guests here.'

This was said lightly, but no one was left in any doubt that they would be expected to behave as very good guests indeed.

'Christmas is a time to celebrate, to bring light out of the dark, as many of us believe the Christ Child led the world out of the dark. It is a time to wassail our neighbours, to laugh and make merry, and throw the cares of the year behind us.'

Veronica glanced briefly to where Daniel was standing with his group of charges. He let a small smile cross his face.

'So please, make merry and have fun. Because, for some of you, next year brings exams . . .'

Veronica smiled as the hall groaned, but then the band struck up the first dance, a Gay Gordons.

Almost instantly, as if repelled by magnetic forces, the boys and girls who had been milling in the middle retreated to opposite sides of the room, the walls lined with chairs.

The agony in the boys' eyes was clear to see. Not much making merry here, Maggie reflected. For all their bourgeois self-confidence, scratch the surface and they were just little boys after all.

Dr Fitzroy, resplendent in a pair of most peculiar tartan trews, soon dispelled the awkward atmosphere. He strode up the boys' line, loudly and furiously imprecating. 'Come on, men! Are you men or mice? You don't want to confirm what they say about boys' schools, now, do you? Come on!

Look at those beautiful women over there, knockouts every single one of them. Get yourselves a partner immediately, or I'm taking you all home and putting you on all-night detention.'

Maggie smiled and watched as he made a courtly bow towards Dr Deveral, who acquiesced and lent him her arm. They led off on to the floor, as, tentatively, some of the older boys moved across to chat and tease the older girls they already knew.

Famke Medizian, a pretty but unthreatening fourth-form girl on the debating team – and thus well-known to the boys – was the first to be picked, by a tall boy with a protuding Adam's Apple. She took his arm immediately, which was the cue for the floodgates to open.

Simone was content to bask in the compliments of the other girls. She had no expectations of being noticed by the boys too, and sat down quite happily. Fliss, on the other hand, was hyperactive, nervously glancing up and down the line of boys. Will was at the end and didn't seem to have seen any of them.

'Oh, for goodness' sake, Humph,' grumbled Alice, as she was swept away by one of her older sister's admirers. 'If you stand on my feet you will BLOODY regret it.'

Humph blushed companiably. He had accepted it as his lot in life to always be unsuccessfully in love with at least one Trebizon-Woods sister.

'You wanna get into this?' came an American voice next – it was Forest, a tall black boy whose father was also stationed at the base. He and Zelda had spent some weekends together looking for proper milkshakes and complaining about breakfast cereal. The girls thought he was handsome, but Zelda was helping him as he prepared to come out to his parents.

132

'You are the only person who is going to be worse at this that me,' said Zelda happily. 'And I know the man part, so you can be the girl. Perfect.'

'Shit, girlfriend, I can *move*, you know? Just not to this shiz.'

'Shiz?' said Zelda. 'Forest, you're getting more American on purpose.'

'Well, I am sorry, ma'am,' said Forest with a courtly bow.

That left Simone and Fliss. Fatty and Thinny, thought Fliss bitterly. Simone didn't even care, she was just so pleased to be at a dance without people teasing her. Well, it was early, and Will hadn't even seen her yet, so . . .

The floor was now a thicket of dancers, bouncing, spinning to the sound of the violins and accordions. It looked like fun. Fliss told herself again it didn't matter. This wasn't even her best dance anyway. When Hattie came round in the circle, led by a spotty Chemistry specialist she knew from the lab, Fliss looked away from her like she didn't care.

Simone knew how important this dance was to Fliss, even if she didn't know exactly why. She desperately searched for the right words to say.

'You look lovely,' she said awkwardly. 'The boys probably can't see you, you're looking so slim.'

Fliss didn't even answer. She felt her face flush and the horrible word 'wallflower' bubbled up inside her, as the dancing segued into an eightsome reel and the dancers changed partners or kept to the floor. Nobody was approaching them. She glanced nervously at the other girls sitting around the side of the room. All of them looked the same, pitifully embarrassed and upset.

There was Hilary O'Fielding from Wessex House, whose acne hadn't responded well to the sunbed treatment at all, which meant she now looked spotty *and* bright red; Phyllis

133

Mason, whose strong, newly found religious beliefs this term prevented her from dancing (Fliss wasn't sure why she was attending), and a large clump of boys hovering round the punch and refusing to dance. They were guffawing loudly about something. Fliss envied them.

A short boy who looked too young to be there started sidling up to them. Fliss glanced at him without much interest. He looked like a midget who'd snuck in from Year One. She didn't want to dance with him, she was about four inches taller than him. She'd be a laughing stock. She decided to turn him down gracefully but quite clearly, so that everyone else could see that she had been asked, she was just being picky.

The boy sidled up uneasily, looking as if he were trying to creep up without being noticed. He had the most peculiar side-slipping gait. Fliss didn't recognise him. One of the weirdos from Downey Boys, she supposed. Just her luck.

'I hate this,' said the boy.

Fliss wasn't expecting that. She glanced up, brow furrowed. But the boy wasn't talking to her at all.

'Why did you come then?' said Simone reasonably.

Ash pouted. 'For the good of the school,' he said crossly. 'And to stop them calling me Pussyballs for about five minutes. And Cassiopeia is coming into our orbit tonight,' he went on. 'That's a constellation.'

'I *know* what it is,' said Simone.

'I'd rather be with my telescope.'

'Well, just sneak off then.'

'You don't look like you're having fun either.'

'Well, that's where you're wrong,' said Simone. 'So there.' Ash was so annoying.

'You look different,' he said after a while.

Fliss let out a huge groan of boredom.

'Your tuxedo is too big for you,' commented Simone.

'I know,' said Ash. 'I don't care. It's stupid.'

But he made no move to go. Instead he sat up by Simone. Even though it was only the boys' school weirdo, Simone still felt herself flush. A boy! Sitting beside her!

'I feel like Holden Caulfield,' said Ash. Simone looked at him. Someone further to what her imagination (rather sexily) conjured Holden Caulfield to be, she couldn't imagine.

'They're all phoneys,' she said helpfully.

'Yes!' said Ash, in genuine surprise. 'That's it! That's exactly how I feel!'

'And now,' announced the bandleader, 'it's time for the ladies' choice.'

Fliss felt her back straighten. Ladies' choice? She hadn't known there was going to be a ladies' choice. Instantly all the girls were back on this side of the room, giggling and fluttering like excited birds. Zelda moved over to where Fliss was.

'Come *ahn*, Fliss!' she hollered. 'Are you going to have some fun at this thing or what?'

Alice glanced around the room. Suddenly, she stopped. It was as if she'd never seen him before. She even blinked. But there he was. Fliss's crush. Will Hampton.

He was in front of the punch bowl, telling a joke to some friends. And she couldn't tell if it was in the cheeky crease of his grin around his eyes; the upward pitch of his eyebrows that meant, even when he wasn't, that he always seemed on the point of laughter; his sparkling blue eyes; or the way his beautifully cut dinner jacket fit snugly across his broadening shoulders. He threw back his head to laugh, the flashing lights off the mirrorball catching his finely cut profile, and in that instant Alice saw everything Fliss could see, wanted everything Fliss wanted – and more.

Fliss's hands were twisting uncomfortably in the lap of her dress, the knuckles white. It was now or ... Could she? Dare she? She thought of the prospect of his hands in hers, his shoulders next to hers ... Already girls were sprinting cheekily across the dance floor and grabbing their prizes as the boys learned to accept their place in the pecking order of life. Sylvie Brown had cheekily asked Mr McDonald, the cute English teacher. Right. It was now or never. Trembling with nerves, feeling hot and cold, she set off in Will's direction.

Will had been part of the boys' group laughing by the orange juice. He wasn't really bothered with the formal dancing, he just wanted to watch the girls and then see if anything good would happen at the disco later. Suddenly, on instinct, he turned his head and his breath caught. Alice. That friend of the Prossers, that was her name. He'd thought she looked hot before, but nothing had prepared him for tonight. Her flushed cheeks as she caught him looking, her long, shining hair cascading over her shoulders, the suggestion of the curve of her waist under the pale pink silk. Dumbstruck, they gazed at one another.

Suddenly, he noticed someone standing in front of him.

'Uh, Will?' said the voice. He glanced down, blinking. Was that really Hattie's little sister? She looked absolutely terrible, like she'd been ill or something. All scrawny and twitchy, she looked about ten years old.

'Hey,' he said, trying to glance over her shoulder to see if Alice had moved. Would she come over? She had to, surely.

'Uh, do you want . . .'

Will remembered it was ladies' choice. The force of his feelings struggled with his innate good manners, and the manners prevailed.

'To dance?' he said. 'Sure.'

And once this was over, he'd find her.

Alice was shocked by how much she minded when she saw Fliss had got there first. A huge brawny chap who looked like an all-England rugby player caught her eye and grinned hopefully at her. She let him take her arm without thinking. Only one name filled her head. *Will*.

'Would you like to, mm, maybe, mmm, dance?' stuttered Simone. She was surprised at herself. Normally she would-n't have dreamt of saying anything like that. It must be the dress. She couldn't believe she'd even opened her mouth.

'NO!' said Ash.

The dance was Strip the Willow, which involved one couple forming an arch for the others to dance through. It reminded Fliss of a wedding. Every time they had to hold hands to dance through the arch, Fliss looked up at Will hopefully. He didn't return her gaze – in fact he seemed very distracted. Fliss decided to concentrate on showing him how daintily and prettily she could twirl and skip. She wanted to enjoy the music, the candles twinkling, the rustle of skirts, scent of perfume and clashing of polished shoes on the ancient wooden floor. Here she was finally, lighter than air, hand in hand with the boy of her dreams. She *would* be happy. She would. Alice twirled in front of her with some tall rugby boy, and Fliss gave her a little wave, to show her that it had all worked out, she was with the boy of her dreams, her love.

Alice ignored this, however, and as soon as the dance was over made her way to where they both stood. Will bright-ened immediately as she approached.

'Hey, it's the Dashing White Sergeant next,' he said, with an enthusiasm that would have surprised his dance teacher. 'Shall we?' And he offered an arm to Alice, and one to Fliss.

The Dashing White Sergeant was a complicated dance, involving two groups of three – two boys and a girl and two girls and a boy – forming a circle, then breaking into lines. The boy or girl in the middle of the three then had to dance with each of his or her partners before the line went on around the room to form another circle. It was fast, tricky, fun and romantic. Fliss would have preferred to have been the one girl between two boys, but didn't want to complain – it was Will asking her for a second dance!

'MAGGIE!'

Miranda's educated tones rang out across the noisy room. Dragging David in her wake she crossed the width of the dance floor. She was wearing a slightly unlikely tartan dress with a huge bow on the shoulder.

'Where on *earth* have you been?' Miranda kissed her forcefully on both cheeks. 'I know you've got the wedding of the century to arrange, but it is just *no fun* drinking wine and complaining about men without you.'

Maggie instantly felt a little ashamed. Miranda just wanted to be friends, and she had indeed been avoiding her. But she couldn't sit and listen to her crowing over how David had come crawling back to her, full of apologies for breaking it off, determined to make a go of it . . . From the way Miranda had talked about it, he had turned into a cross between George Clooney and Santa Claus to win her affections, even though she still mocked his efforts. Well, they were a couple. David had probably always loved her. It was right they were back together. She still found it painful though.

'Hello,' she said. 'You look good. Hello, David.' Maggie didn't meet his eye.

'Come dance with us,' said Miranda. 'It's that mad one where they need threes.'

'Oh, I'm not sure I really know how to—'

'Come on! It's a bloody jocks' dance! You've got to, I'm completely hopeless. Come on, otherwise those bloody cow-eyed teenagers will start pestering David again and I'll be forced to cop off with one of those hot sixth-formers.'

There was no getting away from Miranda's emphatic charm. Smiling apologetically at David, who had gone slightly pink around the ears, Maggie stepped with them on to the dance floor.

'And . . . eight to the left and eight to the right and form a circle . . . Now your partner on the right, now the left, swing round, swing round, swing round, swing round . . .'

The caller talked them through the steps as Maggie stood nervously in their circle. Opposite them Claire was looking queenly in between Dr Fitzroy and the young History teacher.

'Why are we doing thees when we could be sitting down talking Philosophy and eating a good deener?' enquired Claire loudly.

'*Pour encourager les autres!*' boomed Dr Fitzroy, as the music started up and David took Maggie's hand.

Maggie felt it there: strong, with long graceful fingers, warm and dry. Apart from the day he'd grabbed her in the rain, it was the first time he had ever taken her hand, but somehow it didn't seem that way. It felt like it had always belonged there. He didn't squeeze it, although she had thought that he might.

It was very loud. Although it was some time since Maggie

had been to a ceilidh, she'd certainly attended plenty in her time and the rhythm of the music pounded hard through her DNA as they started to circle.

Miranda had not being lying about being bad at dancing. She had absolutely no idea what she was doing. As David stepped to the side and then tried to spin her round, she careered wildly into Dr Fitzroy and let out a loud, snorting laugh.

Then it was Maggie and David's turn to face one another. She was still unable to meet his eye. In fact, it turned out, she didn't have to. Somehow their arms linked instinctively, their feet moving in perfect harmony. As he spun her round, the red dress streaming behind her, she felt as if she were floating, or spinning on ice. She landed right in the heart of the beat, her arm outstretched, his hand automatically where it needed to be to take hers, to carry on the dance.

Fliss danced her *pas de bas* as neatly as she could. But, she began to notice with a growing sense of dread, it didn't matter. Whichever way she twirled, however daintily she proffered her arm for the spin, Will's eyes were always elsewhere, flickering, following Alice's dark hair bouncing and shining in the light of a hundred candles. When Will had to spin her, he did so politely (in fact, though she didn't know it, he was terrified of breaking her). When it came Alice's turn, he whizzed her round as fast as he could, even picking her up by the waist and pushing her around, both of them laughing and teasing one another. When they had to put up their arms to move around the room, he pretended to tickle her armpits. He playfully bumped hips with her on their way round. There was no doubt, truly, who he was dancing with. As the music seemed to grow louder and faster, as the whole room became a mass of swirling colours and whirling bodies, Fliss felt a black gloom fill her up like oil, piling up and choking her till she could barely move.

The music seemed to be even louder and faster now. Miranda had dropped any pretence of trying to keep up and was now swearing manfully and throwing herself around on purpose. Maggie and David, on the other hand, couldn't put a foot wrong. Everywhere she turned, there he was; they did not need a count, or a beat, but each found the other wherever in the dance they needed to be. Maggie felt she had entered an altered state where time had turned liquid, where they were swimming through the dance. She was only aware of his turning back, his outstretched arm, his effortless movements exactly mirroring her own.

Only at one point was their equilibrium disturbed. Miranda, red-faced and cross at her inability to pick up the steps, spun out of control and bumped fiercely into Maggie, who found herself thrown into David's arms. He clutched at her elbows, then, in consternation, they both lurched backwards. Maggie found suddenly she was breathless.

The dance ended, finally. Flushed and giggling, Will turned to Alice, pulled her close and spontaneously planted a huge kiss on her forehead.

'That was great!' he said.

Normally Alice would have shrugged backwards and stepped away from such contact with a boy. But in Will's strong arms, the faint, sweet smell of young sweat from his shirt, his smiling face and his eyes locked on to hers . . . she found herself standing, unmoving, in his arms, looking up at him.

*

141

As the music ended, David turned to bow to both of his partners. Miranda was clearly pissed off, her face was puce and her dress was tugged off at one shoulder. He couldn't look at Maggie, although he could still feel her small hand in his, the lightness of her movements. Dancing with her had been like . . . Well, he had felt like he could have danced for ever. He hadn't wanted it to end.

He turned to her, as was customary. Maggie was pink-cheeked and biting her lip, and David bowed to her deeply. She curtseyed too, and, rising up, met his eyes. Their gaze held just a touch longer than necessary, but they still had not spoken.

Suddenly, a scream rang out.

All the teachers charged across to that side of the room. Crumpled on the floor, like a tiny doll, was Felicity Prosser. It was Alice who had screamed.

Maggie knelt down and put a hand to her forehead. The girl had obviously fainted and was already beginning to stir. 'Get Matron!' she heard somebody shout. Maggie gratefully took David's outstretched jacket and covered Fliss's painfully thin limbs, then as Fliss opened her eyes and stared up uncomprehendingly at the crowd surrounding her, allowed him to lift her and carry her to the san.

'One of these years we're going to have a Christmas event without you rendering yourself unconscious,' Maggie heard him joke. The previous year, Fliss had fallen off the stage protesting against school rules.

Once in the calm of the san, deathly quiet after the noisy ballroom, Matron came bustling forwards.

'Have you been drinking, child? Taking anything? Just tell me, you shan't get a row.'

Maggie raised her eyebrows at that. Fliss shook her head in mute misery.

Matron looked her over with a sniff. 'I said it already: this child is not eating enough. Dr Deveral didn't think it would be a problem in this school, but it obviously is.' Matron lifted a lifeless arm. 'Look at her arms, they're like pins!'

'Uh, I'd better get back,' said David, looking uncomfortable. Maggie glanced up at him and they exchanged apologetic smiles.

Maggie crouched down next to Fliss's bed. They'd never been the best of friends, but under the circumstances she'd have to do.

'What's up, Felicity?' she said, in the gentlest voice she could muster. 'Is something making you unhappy?'

Alice, hotly pursued by Will, stuck her head round the door.

'Are you all right? Fliss, Fliss, are you all right?'

'Alice Trebizon-Woods! No boys in here, you know the rules!' barked Matron. But it was too late.

Seeing them together, Fliss felt her eyes glaze over with tears, and let her head sink back on the bed.

Maggie cottoned on immediately. 'Out, you two,' she said. 'Go back to the dance. It's just the heat and the excitement. She'll be fine.'

Alice looked hurt, and guilty.

'Come on,' Will said.

'I'd better go on my own, thanks,' said Alice, grudgingly.

Maggie didn't need to ask any more, and Fliss was disinclined to tell her, but she felt comforted by Miss Adair just sitting there holding her hand and for once not peppering her with questions about how she was doing, where she was in the class and the usual things she heard from her mother and father once a week.

Of course Miss Adair, being totally ancient and, like, nearly married and everything, couldn't possibly imagine what it was like being in love with someone who was in love with someone else. Nobody could. Nobody could understand. Everyone else was having a huge laugh – she could hear the disco starting up downstairs. See? Nobody cared about her.

Drenched in self-pity, Fliss took a great heaving breath and let out a shuddering, choking sob. Maggie squeezed her hand tightly.

'I know,' she said. 'I know.'

'You can't!' said Fliss melodramatically. 'You couldn't possibly.'

'What, you think I've never been fourteen?' said Maggie. 'Not only have I been fourteen, but when you get to my age you won't even think it was that long ago.'

Fliss sniffed sceptically. 'It's all . . .' She wondered whether she could try a swear word out in front of a teacher. 'It's all so shit.'

'I know it feels that way at the moment,' said Maggie. 'But it will get better. I promise.'

'I don't see how,' said Fliss pitifully.

Matron entered the san carrying two plates of sandwiches and some tea. She gave one to Maggie, who was surprised to find herself tearingly hungry. Fliss, however, looked at hers with an expression close to terror.

'I don't want them,' she said. 'I ate before.'

'That's right,' said Matron. 'Skinny people who've just had a good meal often faint on the dance floor. Unless you want me to call the doctor, Miss Prosser, as well as your parents, you'll eat that plate right now.'

'Don't call my parents!' said Fliss, her eyes wide.

Maggie patted her on the hand. 'Fliss, you know . . . you know you've lost too much weight, don't you? That you look frightening?'

'I don't look frightening,' said Fliss. 'I look like girls in magazines. I look like a model.' She sniffed. 'And Will still didn't like me. Maybe he thinks I'm fat.'

Maggie and Matron exchanged glances.

'I'm not happy about this,' said Matron. 'Not happy at all.' She sat down beside Fliss on the chair. 'Now listen, madam,' she said. 'How you look is no concern of mine. You could grow a horn in the middle of your forehead for all I care. But your health is my concern.' She leant over. 'When was your last period?'

Fliss squirmed awkwardly. 'I don't really keep track.'

'Was it recently?'

Fliss shrugged. 'Not really.'

'And have you been having dizzy spells?'

Fliss shrugged again.

Matron wrote something on a piece of paper. 'All right,' she said, 'sit up.'

Matron leant in and smelled her breath. 'Just as I thought,' she said. 'Halitosis.'

'I don't have halitosis!' said Fliss, horrified.

'Oh, of course you do,' said Matron. 'It's really horrible. Your breath really stinks. All people who get funny about their food get gum disorders. Have you got blood on your toothbrush?'

Fliss flushed and went silent.

Matron shook her head. 'What people will do to themselves,' she wondered. 'I suppose you don't really care yet whether you might want babies one day. But, you know, this could make it very hard for you to conceive. Speaking of which' – she turned her attention to Maggie – 'you want to get a move on.'

'Ehm, one, I'm getting married; two, I'm only twenty-six; three, you're treating someone else and four, it's none of your business!' said Maggie. 'Doreen, honestly!'

'I'm just saying,' muttered Matron.

Maggie shot Fliss a quick conspiratorial smile and was gratified to see that her lips almost twitched. Then the seriousness of her situation reasserted herself and her face was drawn back into gloom.

'Have you started to get really hairy yet?' asked Matron.

'What do you mean, hairy?' asked Fliss, looking alarmed.

'Oh yes, when you get too thin your body produces fur to keep you warm. Have you been feeling the cold?'

Terrified now, Fliss nodded. She was freezing, all the time.

'Yes, people with eating problems get covered in fuzz, like monkeys. It's quite funny really. Not that there'll be anyone around to point and laugh, so don't worry. It's not like you'll be here.'

'What do you mean?' said Fliss.

Matron looked sad. 'I'm sorry, Felicity. I don't think you're well. I don't think you're well at all. You may have to leave us for a little while.'

Now Felicity was white with horror. 'You're not going to send me to an asylum?!'

Maggie leant in, worrying that Matron was being very hard on her. 'Doreen, don't be terrifying. Fliss, you'll need to be checked out by a doctor. If they agree you're having trouble eating, we may have to send you home for a little while to get well, that's all.'

'But I'm *fine*!'

Fliss was shaking now. Didn't they understand that she *had* to be thin?

Alice glanced again nervously in the direction of the san.

'Will, it's not really . . . My friend really likes you.'

'Well, I can't help that, can I?' said Will reasonably. 'Anyway, I've known her since she was a kid. It would be, like, paedy or something even if I did fancy her. Which I don't.' He gave her a piercing look. 'I fancy you.'

'It doesn't matter,' said Alice, who was having, so far, the most dramatic night of her life and was enjoying it all immensely, even the bad bits. 'We just can't.'

Will glanced at her with regret. But he could wait.

'OK,' he said. 'But you can come dance with me. Come on. Just a dance.'

Alice glanced towards the san again. 'Just a dance,' she said. 'As friends.'

'As friends.'

As he pulled her into his strong arms she reflected on her noble self-sacrifice.

After ascertaining that Fliss wouldn't be requiring a wheel-chair to get back to her dorm, Maggie took her arm and walked her down the quiet back passageways. The disco was in full swing, but the heavy walls of the old school blocked out most of the noise. They walked in silence, Maggie wanting to wait until Fliss felt ready to talk. She knew under normal circumstances that she would be one of the last people Fliss would choose to confide in, but these were very far from normal circumstances.

'They're not . . . I'm not really going to have to go to hospital, am I?' she said, with a tone of bravado she didn't feel.

Maggie looked at her. 'I don't know,' she replied, 'I'm not a doctor.' *But you should have called one in*, a voice inside was telling her. *You should have noticed*.

Fliss fell silent again.

Maggie reflected on the views of eating disorders at her old school, Holy Cross. Skinnyness was definitely not an epidemic there; quite the opposite in fact. Being too slim was seen as being a 'snobs' disease, something only spoiled rich girls could get. Ridiculous, of course, and very cruel. Still, she wondered if there might not be something in it. No, of course not.

Maggie suddenly remembered the little alcove, a bench set underneath the circular staircase. It was a good place to be private in an environment where privacy was a rare commodity, and she had used it to comfort Simone the previous year. She steered Felicity there now.

'What happened?' she asked.

Fliss swallowed hard. She wondered if maybe it might be better, might feel a bit better if she did tell someone. She couldn't tell her so-called friends – who knew what Alice was doing *right now*. And she wasn't going to tell her evil bloody sister or her parents, that was for sure. Her mother never ate anyway, she'd probably approve.

'It's nothing,' she said.

'Is this to do with Simone?'

Fliss shrugged. 'Well, Zelda put her on this big special makeover programme and it was like everyone was like, Hey, you guys, look at Simone, she's so gorgeous and let's make a big fuss.' Fliss knew she was sounding childish.

'What about Alice?' asked Maggie gently. She knew how delicate and passionate the ties of girls' friendships could be.

Fliss shrugged. 'Oh, I think she's getting like some kind of new boyfriend. Some boy from my village. I don't care though, anyway.'

'Ah, the boy with Alice.'

This time, Fliss's bravado couldn't hold. She tried to speak but her sentence faded away in a blur of a large sob.

Maggie paused. Oh well, here was the nub of it. Alice and that boy. She hadn't liked Matron's harsh approach too much, but maybe it might help. And maybe the Christmas holidays would be enough time away from the other girls to help Fliss get over a little bit of heartbreak.

She wanted to take Fliss in her arms, tell her it didn't matter, that there would be so many other boys, nice ones, ones who would like her. So many fun times she could have with her friends, too. But she couldn't have any of them locked up in her room, starving herself.

'There, there,' she said.

Fliss let out long, loud sobs now. 'I thought . . . I thought if I were really thin he'd like me . . . think *I* was the glamorous one.'

'Well, I'm not surprised, that's what every stupid magazine in the world tells you,' said Maggie, patting her shoulder.

Fliss sobbed on. 'Does everyone think I'm some kind of scrawny nut job?'

'*Noo*,' said Maggie. 'Oh, Felicity. I wish . . . I wish I could tell you that things will get better in a way that you could believe. But they will. There'll be other boys, much nicer. Who'll see you for what you are, not how tiny your waist is. I promise. I promise.'

'What's going to happen?'

Maggie sat her up. She couldn't lie. 'Your parents will have to fetch you. We'll explain the situation, and hopefully they'll find you a doctor. You won't be suspended, Felicity, we'll send your work on, but you won't be able to return until you're fit and well.'

Felicity broke down into huge sobs.

'Come on,' said Maggie, trying to lighten the mood, 'I thought you hated it here anyway.' Felicity just sobbed harder, and Maggie held her tight.

'I'm so sorry,' she whispered. 'I should have noticed earlier. I'm so, so sorry.'

Fliss was still snivelling. Then she paused.

'I just want to fall in love with someone nice one day and get married and get to be happy. Like you, miss.'

'Do you see?' said Ash.

They were lying on their backs in the copse, staring at the clear, starry night sky. It was freezing, but they had heavy coats on top of them and were huddling together to keep warm.

'There she is. It would be about a million times better with a telescope,' he added grumpily.

Simone squinted her eyes upwards. She did see. A tiny, circular sweep of yellow gaseous cloud in the far corner of the night sky.

'Cassiopeia,' she said. 'It's a beautiful name.'

'After the Queen of Ethiopia,' said Ash. 'Well, according to the Greeks.'

'Yeah, all right,' said Simone. 'Do you always have to know everything?'

There was a silence. Simone sensed him feeling tense.

'I don't . . . I don't know what it's like to kiss a girl,' he said finally. His voice went a little high and squeaky.

Simone felt her chest tighten. But . . . Ash? She hadn't even considered it, had really thought that it would be interesting to see the stars, seeing as she wasn't going to be doing any dancing. Her heart began to pound fiercely.

'Uh . . . no?' she said.

'Hmm,' said Ash uncomfortably.

They lay in silence for a few minutes more, both of their faces turned up towards the cold bright sky. Finally, Simone decided.

'You can kiss me if you like,' she said.

'Really? You wouldn't mind?'

'Well, I won't know till you try,' she said, trying to turn her awkwardness into a joke.

'I've read about it,' he said. 'Apparently I should put my hand on your face, like this.'

His hand was cold and a little damp. Simone pressed her own hand on top of it.

'Don't do it like the book says,' she said. 'Just do it how you think you would like to.'

And she closed her eyes as they moved closer, the steam from their breath mingling in the dark air. He smelled of mint tea and shampoo and something else she couldn't identify. And suddenly, the night was not so cold any more.

Chapter Eight

I sent away for the application form for you in case you forgot was written on the bright yellow Post-it enclosed with Anne's letter.

Maggie shook out the paperwork from the envelope. The application form for the school liaison officer in Govan was about ten pages long. She glanced at it. There was room for three essay questions. *Describe one situation in your professional life when you made a positive contribution to equal opportunities*, it said. Maggie groaned and decided to deal with it later. She had to talk to Felicity's dorm this morning, and wasn't looking forward to it. She was going to do it before class, just to get it out of the way. Felicity's parents had arrived, looking harried and confused, early that morning, and driven a wan-looking Fliss away. Joan Rhys had said she'd managed a couple of pieces of toast before she left, which Maggie was taking as a hopeful sign.

Zelda knocked quietly on her door. Miss Adair had asked to see her, when all she'd done was try and gussy up fat old Simone. She was feeling victimised. Maggie was quasi-ambivalent herself, given that the effects on Simone – her shiny hair, new figure and newfound confidence – were so obviously good. But it had to stop.

'Good morning, Zelda,' she said, welcoming her into the cosy office-stroke-study she shared with Claire.

'Morning,' said Zelda. 'Can I have a cup of coffee?'

'No. Only fourth-formers can have coffee.'

'Oh, cool. More rules. Excellent.'

'Don't be cheeky, please.' Maggie stopped herself. This wasn't how she wanted things to go. It wasn't a disciplinary matter.

Zelda plonked herself down in a chair without being asked. 'What have I done now?'

Maggie looked at her grades with some despair. It wasn't that Zelda was stupid, she simply took no effort with her work at all. None.

'Are you happy here, Zelda?' she asked.

Zelda shrugged. 'Been to better, been to worse.'

Maggie leant forward. 'We want to be better, Zelda. There's a terrific education on offer here, if you just make the tiniest bit of effort to grasp it.'

'For what,' said Zelda, 'so I can just get moved on again? Who cares?'

'But you've got so much promise,' said Maggie. 'If you poured half as much energy and creativity into your work as you did to Simone's makeover, you'd be doing really well.'

Zelda looked uncomfortable. 'I thought that was what this was about.'

Instead, Maggie told her about what had happened. 'We're worried about Felicity.'

'She wants you to be,' said Zelda, uncharacteristically sharply, then stopped herself. 'I mean, she's fine. Everything's fine.'

'I know fine, well everything's not fine,' said Maggie. 'And Zelda, I'm asking you. Please take the pressure off the dorm. What you've done for Simone is great. What it's doing to Felicity Prosser is not.'

Zelda sighed.

'And I can trust you not to repeat this conversation?'

In fact, Maggie fully expected her to repeat it word for word. It wouldn't do either Alice or Simone any harm to hear what was approved of and what was not.

'Yeah, whatever,' said Zelda.

Maggie watched her beautifully styled hair leave the room. If she could get just a tiny amount of that attention to detail she put into her appearance into her work, who knew what she could do?

I am going to engage that child, she said to herself. I don't care what it takes.

Another week brought end of term and the school was full of jabber.

Zelda listened to the other girls without joining in. It wouldn't be Christmas for her – four thousand men on a huge army base, sharing catering turkey. She thought wistfully of DC in the snow, the lights glistening on Potterfield drive, their white colonial house festooned with lights, everyone wearing their reindeer jumpers. Here outside it was just grey and horribly cold and miserable.

Simone was just worrying about whether her mother would try and get her to eat too many chocolates. Every so often she would remember back to the night with Ash. It felt like a dream, something that had happened to somebody else. She touched the slight rawness he'd left on her chin wonderingly. Proof that it really happened.

Alice was feeling alternately cross and guilty. It wasn't her fault Will had fallen for her, was it? She hadn't asked for it. On the other hand, she knew in her heart of hearts that she'd considered Fliss's behaviour attention-seeking and hadn't offered to help. She'd ignored it. It gave her an uncomfortable nagging feeling.

Nobody was in the mood for double English.

'Now, I'm not going to make you work today,' said Maggie.

There was a ragged cheer.

'But there is something,' she said. 'I just wanted to send you off on holiday with this. It's a poem I like a lot. It's not a set text, you may just like to think about it. Unfortunately,' she continued, 'if I read it with my accent it will sound totally ridiculous and you will all laugh. Fortunately we have a country woman of the poet here – you have a bit of a southern accent, don't you, Zelda?'

'Ah sure do, ma'am,' drawled Zelda, who'd spent enough time on bases in Georgia and Tennessee to do it well. Maggie was pleased at the response; Zelda couldn't hold a grudge if she tried.

'It's from a great, great countrywoman of yours. Could you come and read it out for us, please?'

Zelda looked as embarrassed as she could, which wasn't very, but the rest of the class cheered happily. This was something different.

Zelda stepped up. 'You could have warned me.'

Maggie shrugged. 'Ah, you'll be great. Do you recognise it?'

Zelda glanced at the book.

'Of course,' she said scornfully, making Maggie more determined than ever to get her marks up.

'Great,' said Maggie. 'Girls, I present . . . Maya Angelou. Also known as Zelda Townell.'

Zelda smiled half-heartedly and began.

'Pretty women wonder where my secret lies.
I'm not cute or built to suit a fashion model's size
But when I start to tell them,
They think I'm telling lies.

I say,
It's in the reach of my arms
The span of my hips,
The stride of my step,
The curl of my lips.
I'm a woman
Phenomenally.
Phenomenal woman,
That's me.'

Zelda's slightly husky tones picked up the verse perfectly. Maggie had been right; it could have sounded risible in her Scottish accent, but with Zelda speaking it made perfect sense. At the end of the verse, a few of the girls even clapped and cheered. Alice sat back, thinking, Yeah, well, chubby women always pretend this is true.

'I walk into a room
Just as cool as you please,
And to a man,
The fellows stand or
Fall down on their knees.
Then they swarm around me,
A hive of honey bees.
I say,
It's the fire in my eyes,
And the flash of my teeth,
The swing in my waist,
And the joy in my feet.
I'm a woman
Phenomenally.
Phenomenal woman,
That's me.'

That's me, thought Simone. Then she flared her eyes wide, amazed she could have even entertained that idea about herself.

'Men themselves have wondered
What they see in me.
They try so much
But they can't touch
My inner mystery.
When I try to show them
They say they still can't see.
I say,
It's in the arch of my back,
The sun of my smile,
The ride of my breasts,
The grace of my style.
I'm a woman

Phenomenally.
Phenomenal woman,
That's me.'

That's not me, thought Fliss sadly, reading it at home two days later, between the nutrition sheets her nice cheerful lady doctor had left her. She was nothing like a woman. She had no hips, no breasts to speak of. None of the lovely bouncing confidence the poet had. She wondered what it must be like to be like that.

'Now you understand
Just why my head's not bowed.
I don't shout or jump about
Or have to talk real loud.

157

When you see me passing
It ought to make you proud.
I say,
It's in the click of my heels,
The bend of my hair,
the palm of my hand,
The need of my care,
'Cause I'm a woman
Phenomenally.
Phenomenal woman,
That's me.'

The class erupted in applause.

'And that's the message I want you to take away with you this year,' said Maggie. 'Happy Christmas, everyone.'

Chapter Nine

Maggie sat round the table with the rest of her family, Stan and Stan's dad, of course. He was drunk and mumbling incoherently about Celtic football team, but that didn't make Christmas any different from usual. They just ignored him.

And they tried to ignore the screams of Cody and Dylan, who'd insisted on having the *Doctor Who* Christmas special on very loudly all through lunch and were waving their new Daleks and screaming along in time. And Anne and her mother, who were loudly discussing floral arrangements and whether purple heather and red roses would go together.

Stan had given her a blue jumper for Christmas. Not a very nice jumper either. It was a lot like something his mother (who was at her new boyfriend's for Christmas) would wear.

'Sorry,' he said, seeing her face. 'I thought you liked those kinds of clothes now.'

Maggie didn't want to take in the whole world of 'those kinds of clothes' he might mean.

'And I thought we should be saving for the wedding,' he added.

'It's lovely,' she said, feeling unexpectedly disappointed. It was only a silly Christmas present after all, who cared? She'd bought him the best of *Top Gear*, the brand new Celtic Away strip, which cost a fortune, a fifteen-year-old bottle of Talisker, a bottle of Hugo Boss and a new watch. She knew it was guilt that was making her spend so much money. He'd looked more and more worried as the wrapping paper had built up.

'These . . . these must have cost a fortune,' he said unhappily as he opened every new gift.

'Don't you like them?'

'Well, yeah, but we've still got a lot of catering to pay for . . . I mean your mum and dad are really helping, but they don't have that much, and . . .'

'It's OK, Stan,' said Maggie. 'You know, I'm making quite a bit more money now, and . . .'

Well, that hadn't been the right thing to say either. Now they avoided eye contact over the sprouts in the small, overheated room. The dining table normally sat against the wall, they only used it at Christmas.

Stan was taking in the plates to the kitchen with bad grace. Maggie was filling in the form with worse.

'You might even get an interview before you have to go back,' said Anne. 'Those ridiculous holidays public school kids get. I suppose they all have to go skiing and things.'

'They have to go skiing and piss on peasants, yes,' said Maggie, sighing. *Describe a situation in which you implemented cultural change management.* What the *hell* kind of questions are these?

'Oh, stick anything,' said Anne. 'As soon as they see your name against that posh school, you'll be a shoe-in.'

'You think?' said Maggie. 'Hmm. Maybe I could write about the time I had to tell Zazie Saurisse that just because she's considered a princess in her home country it doesn't mean she's exempt from wearing plimsolls.'

'I'm doing just fine in here on my own, thanks,' hollered Stan from the kitchen.

'Yeah, that green squeezy stuff?' shouted Anne. 'You put that on dirty dishes to make them clean.'

'Hah ahah,' said Stan.

'What's got into him today?' said Anne.

'Oh, apparently I bought him too nice Christmas presents,' said Maggie grumpily.

She looked out of the window. Kids were on the street, throwing stones at a lamp post. That felt seasonal. Cody and Dylan had already broken their big *Transformers* lorry and were bickering crossly about whose fault it was. All the oldies were asleep on the sofa in front of the blaring telly.

It felt ridiculous, of course, given that she was surrounded by the people she loved most in the world; the people who loved her too. So how could she feel so lonely? She wished there was someone she could ring . . . She thought fleetingly of David. He would be having a wonderful time somewhere, she knew. And schoolgirl fantasies were for schoolgirls.

'Well, it's not jewellery then,' said Miranda, trying to smile but looking a bit tight around the face as she picked up the book-shaped parcel.

'Uh, no.'

David was already regretting agreeing to visit Miranda's parents for Christmas. His mother had died years before, his big brother Murdo was on manouevres in Iraq and his father, who didn't really see the point of Christmas without his wife or his manly elder son, was taking a lecture cruise in the Hellenics.

Miranda's parents, Roy and Pat, were perfectly nice. Their home in Southampton was terrifyingly clean and pastel. Pictures of Miranda, their only child, were everywhere; her

Junior Gymkhana rosettes still covered an entire wall in the sitting room.

Miranda opened the gift. It was a signed first edition of *Follyfoot Farm*. David knew Miranda had loved the books growing up and had tracked it down on a visit to Hay.

'Oh,' she said. 'I think I have this one. But thank you!'

He opened his gifts. There was a trendy Ted Baker shirt, a slim-fitting pink jumper – pink? – and a midnight-blue silk tie.

'Do I wear all these together?' he asked, puzzled.

'No, of *course* not, darling,' she said. 'I'm going to take you sales shopping too! We have to replace those dreadful striped pyjamas. And, you know, nobody wears boxer shorts any more.'

David smiled carefully. He remembered back to when they had first met. Her energy, her enthusiasm, it hadn't seemed like raw ambition then – it had felt fresh and natural, after all the dreamy, bookish girls he'd met at university.

And she'd been impressed then with his love of books, his goal of being an inspiring teacher, had thought it something impressive rather than pitiful. How had they changed so much that they couldn't even choose each other Christmas presents?

Pat and Roy demanded full silence for the Queen's speech, and Roy actually stood up to salute the national anthem.

'She's a wonderful woman,' he imparted to David gravely.

David nodded. Were they actually going to watch television all day? Miranda's parents' house backed on to a golf course and the white frost was crackling invitingly on the ground. Plus Stephen Daedalus wasn't allowed in the house, as Pat didn't like hairs everywhere.

'I have to take my dog for a walk,' he said. 'Anyone coming?'

Roy shot him a sharp look. 'Not during Our Majesty, please, if you don't mind.'

After the speech, Pat passed around shop-bought chocolate biscuits and tea. 'I never cook,' she said proudly. 'I have two personal chefs – Marks and Spencer!' Then she chuckled delightedly like she'd just said something naughty. David had rather a soft spot for Pat, even if he found her heating-up indigestible.

'Now you two,' she said, as the *EastEnders* theme tune lugubriously started up. She turned towards them and clapped her hands. 'It's nearly the New Year! So we must, you know, set the date! When's the date?'

David glanced at Miranda, appalled, but she was sitting there quite comfortably. They'd only been back together a couple of months . . . they'd broken off their engagement, hadn't they? He'd thought this was quite casual, and certainly had no idea her parents thought they were still getting married. But as he looked at Pat's beaming face and Miranda's complacent smile, he realised how naive he'd been.

'Well, you know . . .' he said desperately. 'I really must walk the dog. Miranda, are you coming?'

'Outside, where it's freezing?' she said. 'You must be joking! Anyway, it's the *EastEnders* Christmas special.'

David set out on his own. The contrast between the alarmingly overheated house and the crisp air was extreme, and he stuck his hands in his pockets. In one of them was his seldom-used mobile phone, bought only because housemasters needed to be contactable in emergencies. He pulled it out, ruefully, as he headed for the golf course. There was only one person he could even think that he'd like to call, but she wouldn't want to hear from him. He imagined her surrounded by her loving, laughing family, drinking whisky, singing, dancing, Stan by her side. He snapped the phone closed and, regretfully, put it away.

'Hoy!' shouted a man in a vividly patterned jumper. 'You can't walk your dog here! This is a private members' golf club! Bloody signs everywhere!'

David heaved a sigh and turned back.

Veronica felt her heart pound as she walked up to the house. It was lovely, an old white-washed farmhouse with a bright red door, a holly wreath perched on it jauntily. She took a deep breath and knocked.

Immediately came the tumultuous sound of three young children and their dog, throwing themselves down the stairs to see who it was. Veronica experienced a moment of panic – maybe she shouldn't have come. Maybe this was all a terrible mistake.

Then the door swung open and, standing there, looking just as nervous as she did, were Daniel, Susie, Daniel's parents Ida and John, and three very excited children, all completely oblivious to the atmosphere.

'Look!' shouted Rufus. 'I got a new submarine!'

'Well, that is just fantastic,' said Veronica, kneeling down. 'You must have been a good boy for Santa.'

'VERY good,' said Rufus.

Veronica stood up.

Ida, instinctively kind-hearted, put out her hand. 'It's nice to finally meet you.'

Veronica stared at this woman, who'd had everything she'd always dreamt of. Sometimes she'd hated her, consumed by terrible jealousy for what this woman had got to experience, the things that had been taken away from her.

But at other times, like now, looking at this happy, prosperous, loving family, all she could feel was overwhelming gratitude.

'It's very nice to meet you,' she stuttered. 'I suppose I owe you a vote of thanks . . .'

Ida looked a little wrong-footed. Then she smiled.

'No, you don't,' she said. 'I need to thank you.' She cast a meaningful glance at Daniel. 'It was a pleasure.'

The two women looked at each other, the weight of their lives passing between them.

'Come in, come in!' bustled Susie. 'We'll all catch our deaths!'

Fliss was comfortably wrapped up in a blanket in the sitting room in front of the fire. Hattie humphed past her. She had her mock GCSEs when they went back to school in the New Year and had absolutely loads of studying to do. Fliss, on the other hand, seemed to be watching *Harry Potter* movies back to back and working her way through a selection box.

'Your breath smells,' Hattie said helpfully as she crossed the thick carpet.

Fliss shot her a lazy look. 'Yes, but after I've eaten all this chocolate it won't smell any more. Whereas you'll always have BO.'

'SHUT UP! Mum! Mum!'

Fliss's mother looked at their father. 'I thought they'd grow out of this when they got past five,' she said. 'I feel a migraine coming on.'

Their dad grimaced. 'Is it too early to start on the sherry?'

'And to think,' said their mum, 'that considered not sending them to boarding school.'

They both burst out laughing, then sobered up.

'Do you think she'll be all right?' said Mrs Prosser.

Her husband shrugged uncomfortably.

She controlled her own food intake with an iron fist. Well, you had to these days, didn't you? Keep looking good, keep your man interested. She did wonder if she'd passed her habits on to the girls . . . although Hattie was just such a *lump* at the moment. But yes, she'd need to feed Fliss up, if only to get her back to school. Secretly she thought she looked rather chic.

'She'll be fine,' said Tony. 'A few trips to McDonalds.'

Fortunately Dr Horridge, whom they'd called in at great expense, had slightly better advice than this to give and was to spend a lot of time with Fliss over the coming weeks and months, gently encouraging her to break the link between controlling her food and controlling her life. Fliss's genuine desire to return to school would also be a great motivator, but for now a cosy fire, her dog snuggled up to her, the telly on, her family around and a box of chocolates within easy reach didn't seem like bad medicine.

Veronica had worked very hard on getting it right, and it turned out she had. Her little wooden gifts – a working lighthouse for Rufus to guide his submarines home; a caterpillar and a pull-along dog for the littlies – had been a huge hit without being showy or extravagant, and the carefully chosen books for the adults well-received.

After a wonderful dinner – Susie and Ida had cooked well in harmony, Veronica had noticed – they sat back around the table, the children playing or asleep, and Daniel impressed on Veronica to tell the story once again. Through his eyes, she saw, it wasn't tragic or horrific or shameful, but rather slightly romantic. He was proud of it.

Ida, Susie and John listened with interest. At the end of it Ida clasped her arm and patted it.

'You know,' said John, 'he's probably still out there some-where.'

'*John*,' said Ida crossly. 'Behave yourself.'

'I expect not,' said Veronica. 'Life expectancy for Russian men is very low, and I wouldn't like to disrupt his family, I've already disrupted yours . . .'

There was a chorus of disagreement at this. Veronica felt a little pink in the cheeks and reminded herself not to drink any more wine.

'And anyway, I never heard from him again, although he had my address,' said Veronica. 'So.'

'So,' piped up Daniel's dad again, 'are you going to let the school know then? Stop keeping our boy a secret?'

'JOHN!' shouted Daniel and Ida in unison. Veronica sat back, shocked.

Susie, thoughtful as always, clapped her hands and sug-gested a game of Scrabble. On her way to get the board, she squeezed Veronica on the shoulder. Veronica normally dis-liked over-familiarity. But under the circumstances, she was extremely grateful.

Chapter Ten

A new year!

Lent term began on 9th January. As usual, Veronica had an in-service day for teachers from both schools the day before term started to get them up to date on joint activities for the coming months.

David couldn't help it, he was so looking forward to seeing Maggie. It had been ages. And even though he was sick to death of Christmas and parties and everything to do with it, Miranda wanted him to come to her spring awards bash in February. He had suggested cooling off their relationship a little, but she had looked at him with her huge guileless blue eyes and put on a little girl's voice and it looked like she'd been about to cry, so he'd changed the subject very quickly. It wasn't, he reflected, as if there was much else out there – she was a beautiful girl, and not everyone would be willing to take on a near-penniless English teacher on the wrong side of thirty, whose career prospects would be a lot better if he didn't keep turning down every promotion that would stick him in an office doing paperwork all day instead of doing what he loved: teaching.

Claire was sitting at the back of the ref reading *Paris Match*, dressed in an utterly beautiful new purple coat and looking affronted, as if three weeks in Paris simply hadn't been enough.

'*Salut mon brave,*' said David, slipping in next to her.

'Daveed! Seet with me, we can chat through very boring meeting. Still.' She looked around. 'At least there are none of those *oreeble* pupils.'

'No,' said David. 'Uh, where's Maggie?'

Claire took a quick glance around. 'It ees secret,' she said.

'Excellent,' said David. 'I love secrets.' But something cold clutched at him.

'OK,' said Claire. 'I am very unreliable.'

David raised an eyebrow, then put on his glasses and pretended to be reading the agenda.

'She has an interview,' whispered Claire. 'For a job.'

David bit his lip to make himself look unconcerned. 'Oh really?' he said. 'Whereabouts?'

'But Glasgow of course!' said Claire. 'You know, she gets married, she gets a job at home . . .'

'She always did say she had to go back,' said David. 'I just . . . I didn't expect it to be so soon.'

Claire gave him a shrewd look. 'You will miss her, *non*?'

David found himself caught between a sudden desire to confess everything to Claire, just for a sympathetic ear, but remembered in time that she had said herself she was 'unreliable'. Anything he told her would get back to Maggie. And that would be impossible, wrong. She had chosen her path, and to do anything would be dog-in-the manger . . .

'Oh, well, you know. There's not so many of us under-sixties around that we can afford to lose some.'

'That ees true,' said Claire, mollified.

David picked up the agenda again. But it scarcely mattered; he couldn't read a word of it.

*

Maggie couldn't work out what it was. Was it some kind of dress-down day? Why were the interview panel wearing elasticated trousers and baggy, stained tops?

Then she realised they were just dressed for work. She bit her tongue and smoothed down her smart Marimekko shirt; she was turning into a snob.

'So you've been working in the private sector?' said a woman with a layered haircut so short, precise and unflattering she could only be making some kind of point. 'What made you go there exactly?'

'Well, it seemed a good opportunity to expand my, uh, skill set,' said Maggie, grasping for the right bureaucracy-heavy terminology.

'Don't you feel the private sector is a parasite, sucking away the good marrow from our schools and fostering class war, discontent and inequality?'

Maggie recognised herself from a couple of years ago. Maybe some world views were never challenged.

'I believe every child deserves the best, and none deserves censure for their parent's decisions,' she said.

'But what about a culture that fosters entitlement?' spluttered a very fat woman from the end of the table. She spat a little as she spoke.

'Why shouldn't they feel entitled?' said Maggie, feeling her familiar temper rise – but this time from the opposite side. 'I wish every child could feel as entitled and privileged as the students I've taught at Downey House. I wish every child could feel that the world is there for them, and that they have the potential to succeed in it. That's why I'm here.'

The panel glanced at each other.

'So you think you'd want to bring some of that *boarding school* ethos to your work here as a liaison?' said the woman with the short hair. She was smirking. 'Jolly hockey-sticks? Midnight feasts for everyone?'

The others on the panel laughed.

'I don't see why I can't bring some of the methods used in public schooling to this environment, no,' said Maggie, feeling her voice grow small, even as she tried to keep a lid on her temper. Who were these know-it-alls who were so sure their way was right? If everything they did was so fantastic, they wouldn't need to be hiring someone to encourage kids to attend school in the first place. And she was going to be working with them.

'Things are a bit different up here,' said the fat woman.

'I've worked up here,' said Maggie crossly. 'And I've worked down there. And as far as I'm concerned, kids are just kids.'

Simone was utterly shocked when she learned Fliss wasn't coming back straight away. She'd been under the impression everyone thought Fliss looked as amazing as she did. As far as Simone had always been aware, the thinner the better. But apparently not. So she had a plan for when they were back. Her mother, banned from sending treats to the school under the new regime, and worried that her daughter was looking peaky and thin (never mind the many compliments she'd received, the girl had to *eat*), was only too happy to oblige. Which was why Simone turned up in the old beige Merc with an extra large box for the start of the new term.

'What's that then?' asked Zelda. Their dorm was utterly freezing, and both the girls had jumped into bed in the middle of the afternoon. Simone had noticed that half of the other Plantagenet girls arriving back had their hair styled exactly like Zelda. They looked like they were all about to enter a Miss Young Texas pageant.

And Zelda's mother had actually got out of the car and paraded around the school in a fur coat and cowboy hat! It didn't get much more glamorously exotic than that, as far as Simone was concerned.

'Hon*ey*!' she had said to Zelda. 'How can you *stand* the cold? DuBose, can't you do something?' But DuBose – although an evil soldier, of course, was still so tall and handsome in his uniform that the girls were hanging out of their windows to look at him, until Miss Starling shooed them back inside – had merely grunted and suggested Zelda stopped getting everything her own way all the time.

'And I want to see your grades up,' he'd added.

'But, Pops!' Zelda had imprecated, holding on to his arm in a way he'd always found hard to resist. 'How can I when it's so *cold*?'

And sure enough, a fur coat turned up in the post a week later. Zelda hastily changed it for a fake fur one, after she came across Sylvie Brown crying about all the 'dead polar bears'. There were just so many strange British sensitivities she would never understand.

Back in the dorm, Simone said, 'Aha! The box is for you, actually. Well, all of us. My mum's made us a midnight feast to celebrate when Fliss comes back! I don't *think* that's in bad taste, do you?'

'Truly?' said Zelda, who didn't care about taste one way or the other. 'Fantastic! Will it keep? I hope it's lots of fruit for you.'

'No,' said Simone, proud to be standing up to her. 'You have to eat junk food at midnight feasts. If you eat it at midnight it doesn't count. It'll keep till Fliss gets back.'

Zelda frowned. 'I'll have to get a new toothbrush.' Zelda brushed her teeth for about an hour a night.

'I think you're worrying too much about it,' said Simone.

Suddenly Zelda remembered something.

'I have contraband too!'

'What?'

'I smuggled it in from the base. They've got it all there. Oh God, to show you I'll have to get out of bed. Man, this place is inhuman.'

Steeling herself, Zelda leapt to the cupboard and burrowed around under her suitcase, returning triumphantly with a bottle of Jack Daniels.

Simone looked at it in shock.

'Zelda! No! If we get caught with that, it's just instant expulsion! Straight away, no questions asked!'

That was very much the impression Veronica, Miss Starling and the team attempted to convey to the school. It usually worked quite well on the younger years.

'Simone, we're nearly fifteen. For goodness' sake, live a little! Half the girls our age in this country are pregnant by now!'

Simone still looked at the bottle like it was a poisonous snake. 'I think I'll stick to cake,' she said.

'Suit yourself,' said Zelda, squirreling away the bottle at the bottom of her wardrobe.

Alice, however, thought a midnight feast was a great idea.

'Three weeks and Fliss'll be back – if she can gain three kilos,' she said. In fact, she'd heard it from Hattie. Fliss hadn't wanted to speak to her over Christmas, and Alice hadn't pushed it. Hattie had also said Fliss was loving therapy because she got to talk about herself all day, but Alice had put it down to sour grapes.

What she didn't know was that Fliss had also managed to say hello to Will at the carol service. He had very kindly enquired after her health and said how glad he was she was better and that she looked well and how was her friend? Fliss was more determined than ever to get back to school.

For once, Maggie's heart failed to be lifted as, on her own this time, she saw the four towers of Downey House glistening in the frosty January sunshine as she crested the hill in the cab she'd caught from the station.

She felt guilty and disloyal, going for an interview for another job. She didn't want the job and she didn't want to leave, but what was she going to do? Hide down here for ever as her whole life fell apart? And it wasn't as if she was doing a sterling job. To have one of her pupils suffering near-anorexia on her watch – that was an appalling failure in her duty of care. And she'd not worked the girls nearly as hard as she should have done – too much mooning about her romantic situation. That was another reason to get the hell out of Cornwall. Otherwise, what was next? She'd be at David and Miranda's wedding, smiling and trying to look pleased for them, when all she would feel would be jealousy. Why was it so hard to live in the real world?

But somehow, even with all that, she would still be so sad to leave, she knew she would. She felt so torn.

Well, she could work on doing her best. To pay close attention to the girls, work them hard this term. Be a good teacher. Then a good wife.

So, the following morning, Maggie was pleased to see her class looking relatively bright-eyed and bushy tailed – although there was obvious disquiet at Fliss's empty seat. Maggie had decided the best thing to do was to tell everyone the whole story (apart from the Will parts, of course), then hope they brought any concerns or worries to her afterwards.

'Is she going to die?' asked Sylvie Brown, her big eyes wide.

'No,' said Maggie. 'But recovery can be difficult and we'll all have to support her.'

'Did they force-feed her?' asked Zazie. They were all fascinated.

'Certainly not, she wasn't that ill,' said Maggie. 'It's just important to catch these things early.' She looked round the class slowly. 'So just be aware . . . I'm watching you all, and not just for spelling.'

The class groaned, good-naturedly.

'Now,' said Maggie, 'it's Shakespeare this term. We're going to look at *Romeo and Juliet*. And I think you're really going to enjoy it. It's a love story about people your age.'

Alice's ears pricked up. She was feeling she hadn't quite been getting the credit she deserved for not even mentioning Will since she got back. It was only cruel forces holding them apart.

Simone thought nervously about Ash. She'd only had one email from him since she got home, which hadn't stopped her driving Joel crazy by hogging the computer and keeping him from *World of Warcraft*. She'd memorised every line. It said: *We don't have stupid Christmas. Christmas is culturally stupid, but no Christmas at all is actually worse. Festivals of lights are not the same. And Cambridge and my dad have both said they don't care what my marks are, I can't go till I'm eighteen and have, quote, 'grown up a bit'. . The world is full of idiots and they're all against me. Yours Sincerely, Ashley Mehta (Downey Boys).*

OK, so it hadn't been a love letter as such. But he'd been thinking about her, and that was definitely something.

'Has anyone seen the Leonardo DiCaprio version?' Maggie asked. A couple of the girls nodded. When Maggie was growing up, Leo had been the biggest thing in the world, bar no one. In fact, Leo and Claire Danes were what really turned Maggie on to English literature in the first place. She never told anyone that, of course, pretending it was her love of reading alone that had done it.

'Well, if you all study extremely hard, we'll watch it one day. And if you behave yourself, they're also putting *Romeo and Juliet* on at the Minotaur Theatre in June, so there'll be a joint Downey Boys outing to that – I'll send a consent form to your parents.'

'What are we, six?' whispered Zelda to Alice. But Alice was reading the back of her book with an unusually dreamy expression on her face . . . Two young lovers, held apart by social constraints, even though their love was strong enough to endure . . . It was definitely Will and her!

'We don't know very much about Shakespeare's life,' Maggie continued. 'We don't know where he spent his youth, or much about his love life, apart from the fact that in his will he bequeathed to his wife Anne Hathaway his "second best bed" – which implies at the very least that he had interests elsewhere. But his ability to capture the feeling of young love – and Romeo and Juliet are believed to be very young, your age; Romeo is about fourteen, Juliet too – has resonated down the ages, with almost no one catching it quite so well. So, Simone, can you turn to page eleven and begin reading, please, till we get our heads into the rhythm.'

'*Two households, both alike in dignity,*' read Simone obediently, '*In fair Verona, where we lay our scene.*'

Zelda yawned ostentatiously. Maggie shot her a look. She'd hoped that looking at an American poet might have piqued Zelda's interest last term, but obviously it hadn't. She just wished she could engage the girl in something more than her hair and nails.

*

Veronica sat in her office, grimacing at the form. Evelyn hovered nearby, ready to offer non-intrusive assistance.

'I do *hate* this affair,' said Veronica.

Evelyn nodded sympathetically. The official public school Expo took place in March every year, in Birmingham. Every school had a stall to attract parents looking for the right place to send their children. Veronica understood the anxiety of a parent desperate to do the right thing for their child, but did find it a little wearying answering repeated questions about how they would handle India's wheat allergy and what their programme was for 'gifted' children. She understood this was a selling job, and that her school was also a business. But she found the mercantile aspect a little distasteful, particularly in this tougher economic climate with many families having to tighten their belts. Selling payment-spreading schemes and discussing sibling discounts were not things she liked to get involved in, but her head of finance, Archie Liston, was even more publicity-shy than she was and refused to come to these events. He was an excellent accountant, though, so Veronica didn't feel able to coerce him. Fleur Parsley, the drama teacher, always went down very well at these events – particularly with the fathers – and enjoyed them too, so she would accompany them, as well as Janie James, whose no-nonsense manner was generally a hit. Veronica excused Miss Starling, on the grounds that whilst parents might theoretically approve of strict teaching for their offspring, they occasionally found meeting an austere teacher from their youth a little off-putting.

Dr Fitzroy, of course, would be in his element. Effusive and personable, he also enjoyed the socialising element with other headmasters, swapping war stories and enjoying good brandy. At least he would be nearby, and could often be relied upon to intervene cheerily whenever Veronica's smile looked like it might be about to seize up.

Veronica ticked the boxes on the form for where their stand would be, which conference hotel she would take, how much publicity they would require. She felt tired just thinking about it. Ah well, a necessary evil.

She passed on the paperwork and picked up the form Matron had filled in following Felicity Prosser's unfortunate incident at the Christmas dance. Maggie, however, seemed to have it under control now and there seemed to have been no further cases – eating disorders could often prove infectious. It had been something of a gamble employing her, but she'd proved herself as dedicated to the girls and the school as Veronica could have wished. She was pleased. Although Maggie was showing signs of strain that Veronica didn't think had anything to do with Felicity Prosser. Veronica knew she was getting married – to the quite brash-looking young man who'd visited the previous year – and hoped it wasn't stress from the wedding. She supposed she'd lose her back to Scotland eventually . . . Well, that was another problem she'd deal with as it arose.

'More tea?' said Evelyn.

Veronica glanced up. 'When did they put mind reader on your job description?' she said wonderingly.

Chapter Eleven

In fact the primroses were budded by the time Fliss felt well enough to return to school, four weeks after the start of term. She'd kept up with her work whilst she was away, but still felt a little nervous about heading back into the hurly-burly.

'Just remember, I'm always on the phone,' Dr Horridge had reminded her. 'Just stick to our plan. They'll also arrange for you to see someone local once a week, and Matron will be keeping an eye on you.'

'About four hundred people will be keeping an eye on me,' grumbled Fliss as she went to pack her bag. But staying at home was so boring, and although Simone was keeping her up with the intrigue – she was sad to have missed Zelda's great coat scandal – it wasn't the same as being there.

It felt strange to be dropped off, all alone, but as she rounded the gravel drive and saw Matron, Miss Adair and her dorm-mates all lined up to welcome her, it was all she could do to keep the tears from her eyes.

After a quick pep talk from Maggie, the girls were allowed to take her upstairs. It had been so quiet at home, it was hard to get used to the bustle.

'Tonight!' Zelda was saying. 'At midnight!'

'Well, yes, that would seem to be the point of midnight feasts,' said Alice.

'We're doing what?' asked Fliss.

'I don't want to drink,' said Simone.

'Who's drinking?' said Alice.

'Zelda has booze,' said Simone miserably. 'It'll spoil our feast.'

'Well, that rather depends on the booze,' said sophisticated Alice. 'If it's a sweet white wine, we've no hope.'

'It's Jack Daniels.'

Fliss perked up. 'Ooh! I've heard you can mix that with Coke so it doesn't taste so revolting.'

'We are NOT taking drugs,' said Simone.

'*Cola*. Cola, Simone, don't bust a gut.'

Simone didn't look mollified, but the other girls were excited.

'I'll set my alarm,' said Zelda.

'I don't think I'll sleep anyway,' said Fliss. 'God, it's good to be back.'

'Aren't you worried about getting into trouble?' asked Zelda.

The other girls scoffed.

'Midnight feasts aren't *trouble*,' said Alice. 'At this school they're practically on the syllabus!'

'Stop moaning,' said Miranda sharply.

'I'm not moaning,' said David. 'I was politely wondering what's wrong with my cufflinks.'

'They have dogs on them.'

'Not real dogs.'

'*David*.'

Miranda took out a box from her dressing table. 'Here. I bought you these.'

David opened it. They were plain steel, with *Ralph Lauren* engraved across them.

'My name's not Ralph Lauren,' grumbled David.

'Stop moaning! And zip me up.'

Miranda did look very glamorous for her office night out. She was wearing a very short, tight kingfisher-blue satin dress that would have been unforgiving on anyone in less good shape. David found it a bit obvious for his taste, but on the other hand she did look good, he knew.

'They're having an awards ceremony!' said Miranda. 'I think I'm going to win Senior Sales Rep of the Year.'

'That's great,' said David.

'You need to help me write my speech. I'll have to do it when we get there.'

'You need a speech? Can't you just say thank you?'

'Well, you know. It's a big award.'

'But I don't know anything about sales repping!'

Miranda gave him a look. 'I know how much you care about my job, David.'

David saw his mistake. 'I'm sorry. I will write something for you. Of course. In the car on the way.'

'You know,' said Miranda, 'all the top salesmen in the region will be there. There are definitely openings at entry level ... it wouldn't pay well at first but, with bonuses, within two years you could be en route to making a proper amount of money, and then we could think about getting married. Of course we'd have to move to Southampton, but you know Mummy and Daddy are so excited about doing that and I'm sure they'd help us with a deposit anyway. I'd love to be nice and close to them, that would be wonderful.'

I have to tell her, thought David. I just have to. She's a nice girl, and I was weak, and I gave in, but now I want out. But it's all my fault for leading her on. So how can I?

The hotel, the Princess Royal in Truro, had obviously seen better days. Once a properly grand venue, generations of well-heeled holidaymakers travelling abroad had seen it tip into a slighty dusty, florally decorated neglect, held afloat by weddings and corporate functions, having not yet been targeted for a fawn and beige boutique makeover. As David and Miranda entered, a board with plastic lettering, one 'e' missing, directed them to the Prime Assurance awards.

'The credit crunch really is starting to bite,' sniffed Miranda, but David rather liked the Victorian wrought-iron staircase and the winter garden, with its suggestion of glamour past.

'Oh, come on, it's romantic,' he said.

'It's smelly,' said Miranda. 'And the food is going to be terrible.'

'Let's not go then,' said David. 'Let's have a drink, listen to the pianist then go somewhere else.'

'Could you *be* less supportive?' stormed Miranda crossly. 'This is my *career*. I know you don't care about having a career, but that doesn't mean we're all stuck in the same—'

A row was narrowly averted as a large group of shouting men, already looking pink in the cheeks from bonhomie and beer, entered the foyer. Miranda immediately arranged her features into that of a woman not engaged in a row with her boyfriend.

'Ken! Jim! Declan! Great to see you,' she called, beaming.

'Look at you,' said the beefiest, who had sweat beading on his forehead despite the frosty night outside. 'Corr!'

'Yeah, who crammed you into that dress?' said another. 'Lucky bugger.'

'Uh, that would be me,' said David, trying to make it up to Miranda and gamely sticking out his hand.

'Oh aye,' said the man, as all three of them eyed David up and down. His bought, not rented, tuxedo; his long, thin frame – things that marked him out as not one of them, and both David and Miranda were painfully aware of it.

'What line are you in?' said another of the men, quite aggressively.

'I'm a teacher. Up at the boys' school.'

This was, apparently, hilarious.

'What, little boys and that?'

'What do you teach? Do you like to give them encouraging pats now and then? Just on the bum and that?'

David stared at them. There were bullies in every year, in every walk of life, he'd met them all before and they certainly weren't going to phase him now.

'Do you want a drink?' he said to Miranda, and before she had time to answer he headed for the bar.

'He's a rude bugger, innee?' said the beefy man, Ken, obviously unbothered or unaware that he'd just accused another man of being a paedophile. 'Never mind, sweetheart, you look good enough to eat.'

'You certainly do,' said Declan, who had a reputation amongst the other reps as being a bit of a smoothie with the women. 'Hope you're on my table.'

Miranda was cross with David. Why was he so bloody sensitive all the time? Anyway, he chose the bloody job. He had to know he was a complete embarrassment, surely?

'I do too,' she said, her eyes round.

'Well, come on then,' said Declan. 'Let's go have a look at the table plan.'

David returned from the bar with two gin and tonics in slightly smeary glasses, to find himself alone. He decided the best thing to do was to drink them both.

Stan was nervous. He wished that he'd taken the train so he could at least have had a couple of lagers to calm him, but that would be stupid. He'd finished his early morning shift at nine and jumped straight in the car.

It had been Anne's idea. Be spontaneous, she'd said. She'd even found a hotel on the internet for him to book – a proper posh one, too. Stan didn't feel very comfortable in places like that, but Anne had assured him that Maggie would like it a lot if he turned up, she sniffed, 'looking respectable', which Stan took to mean that his football shirt probably wouldn't do. The hotel had a dinner, bed and breakfast package which seemed expensive, but Anne had really pushed for it.

In truth, Anne was worried. Maggie just seemed a little down about things – not the way a bride should be at all. She liked Stan a lot and wanted to give them a little shove, to remember what they liked about each other, before five hundred miles of countryside got in the way.

Maggie grabbed her mail from her pigeon hole. She liked Friday evenings. No marking to do, she'd sometimes go out with a couple of the other teachers for a quiet drink, or stay in by herself with a magazine, some Maltesers and some television, happy that the responsibilities of the school were, for one night at least, off her hands. Perhaps Claire would fancy splitting a bottle of wine, if she wasn't going out or haring off to try and catch the Eurostar. She was going to put on her cosiest pyjama bottoms, her largest pair of socks, and have a nice, quiet relaxed evening. Let's face it, thought Maggie, she didn't know how many more of these she was going to get.

Humming to herself as she opened her door she was surprised to notice it wasn't locked. But not half as surprised as she was, on opening it, to see Stan, looking embarrassed in a slightly shiny silver grey shirt, in the middle of the room.

'What . . .?' Maggie was careful to keep an accusatory tone out of her voice. 'What are you doing here?'

Then she stepped forward and gave him a hug. 'You gave me the shock of my life. I thought I was being burgled. Not that you look like a burglar,' she added quickly. 'You look great. I like your shirt.'

Stan grinned. 'Thought I'd come and surprise you, aye?'

'Well, you did,' said Maggie.

'Yon headmistress let me up. She's all right that yin. For a teacher, like.'

Maggie reflected that it was just as well Stan had come across Dr Deveral and not Miss Starling.

'So . . . why?' she asked eventually.

Stan grinned. 'Well, maybe – *maybe* – I've booked us into a luxury hotel in town along with a posh slap-up dinner and all that and maybe you have to get your glad rags on because maybe your fiancé is a bit of an old romantic after all.'

He fished in his bag and withdrew a slightly battered, but nonetheless unprecedented bunch of flowers.

Maggie smiled in delight and shook her head. 'You are a dark horse, Stanley Cameron,' she said.

He moved in and kissed her.

'Well, get dressed then, wife to be,' he said, smacking her sharply on the bum. 'Haven't got all night to mess about. And I've got to drive back tomorrow.'

Maggie stopped. 'You drove? You've got to drive all the way back tomorrow?'

'Got the early shift on Sunday, haven't I?'

Maggie blinked. She wouldn't have thought he was capable of such a gesture, or that she would ever receive one. She was incredibly touched and pleased.

'I was going to wear those big fluffy pyjamas you love so much,' she laughed.

'No chance,' said Stan. 'My fiancée looks sexy – or else!'

Giggling, Maggie disappeared into the bedroom.

The Grand Banqueting Hall was filled with tables. Miranda worked mostly with men, and although some of them had brought bored-looking wives and girlfriends along, many had not, seeing the evening more as a chance to get drunk for free, bond with the boys and try their luck with the waitresses. Miranda was certainly the most striking looking woman there, with the fishtail of her blue dress flashing dangerously in the lights. Eyes, already blurry with the free wine, followed her across the room as she found her table, while the other women gossiped. There was to be a dinner (chicken a la King or salmon roulade) followed by the awards presentation, followed by a disco. David checked his heavy watch surreptitiously as the men on the table – including the broad-shouldered Declan – discussed Saturday's match whilst keeping an eye on Miranda's bosoms in the blue dress.

Miranda drank one gin and tonic too quickly to settle her nerves, then another one because it was there. By the time the waitress came round pouring 'Red or white?' she had decided tonight she was going to let her hair down and enjoy herself, particularly if her boyfriend was going to sit there with a face like a bloody wet weekend. You know, he wasn't the best she could do. Not by a long shot. Every man in this room – almost all of whom took home more money than he did and at least had a bloody home to call their own rather than a glorified bloody dormitory – liked the look of her, she could tell. She'd show him what he was taking for granted. She picked up her glass and found it empty again.

'Don't worry about that,' said Declan, magicking up a

bottle from somewhere and filling her glass to the brim. 'You just have fun.'

'I can't wait till midnight,' Fliss said. 'Dr Horridge said I should eat whenever I feel like it.'

'Oh yes?' came Alice's voice in the darkness. 'Can that be now?'

'I could eat,' added Simone. In fact, it was more nerves that made her say that. She was already worried enough that someone would discover the alcohol.

'Yeah, darn it,' said Zelda. 'We can have a nine o'clock feast. Your ma's packed enough that we'll still be eating at midnight anyway.'

There was a general muttering of agreement.

'OK,' said Zelda, directing operations. 'Simone, to the food.'

Mrs Pribetich had indeed done Simone proud. Inside the hamper was every type of chocolate bar imaginable, as well as crisps and nuts. There was even a carefully wrapped and preserved piece of Christmas cake which was just about still edible. The girls, a month into term, were already tired of the general austerity of the Downey House catering service, and squealed delightedly. Alice brought out a two-litre bottle of Coke and four plastic glasses from under her bed.

'Maybe we should have invited the whole form,' said Simone.

'Maybe we *shouldn't* have,' said Fliss, already filling her mouth with chocolate. 'This is amazing, Simone! Your mother is a marvel.'

Simone wouldn't go quite that far, but she did have her moments. She licked honey off her fingers like a bear.

'OK,' said Zelda, passing out cups. 'We don't have any ice, but it will have to do.'

'I'm not having any,' said Simone.

The other girls all groaned.

'No! I'm not! And I don't care if you think I'm square.'

Alice leant off her bed to grab her arm in shock. 'Simone! Are you SQUARE?!'

And the entire room exploded in giggles.

Maggie smiled at Stan while they stood in reception. He looked like he was checking them in as Mr and Mrs Smith. The Princess Royal was the smartest hotel in Truro, she supposed, although it looked a little dated to her and not really like pictures of hotels she saw in magazines. Still, she felt very lucky. She was wearing a pretty green dress she'd found in the January sales and had bought extravagantly without knowing when she would get a chance to wear it. At the back of her mind, she supposed she could justify it as a going-away dress for her wedding, although that was so far away of course. It had a wide boat-neck that framed her face, and a tight waist that drew attention away from her bum. It fell below her knees – and it swished. Maggie had never entirely grown out of the appeal of a dress that swished.

'Do you like it?' she'd asked Stan.

He'd looked at her critically.

'What?'

'No, aye I do, aye. You look good.'

'But . . .'

'But what?'

'Well, it sounded like you were about to say "but".'

Stan shrugged. 'You're a good-looking lassie, Maggie. You should show it off a bit more.'

'What do you mean, "it"?'

'Well, dress a bit more sexy, like. Cause I think you're sexy.'

'Well, good,' said Maggie. 'But I'm not sure I could handle miniskirts and stilettos.'

'Well, maybe you never know until you try.'

Maggie conceded this was indeed the case, but she was still pleased with the green dress.

'We have to hurry if we want dinner,' said Stan, looking worried. 'They're about to close the kitchen and they've got a big function on.'

'Well, nice of them to welcome us,' said Maggie, who'd rather thought they should probably have nookie first – if Stan had too much to drink at dinner, it would be pretty rubbish later on. Best to get it out of the way.

A fifteen-year-old waitress in a nylon shirt and waistcoat led them into a lounge where a fire was crackling.

'Our grand dining room is out of commission,' she said nervously in an Eastern European accent. 'Tonight, we are welcoming guests to our nook.'

Maggie and Stan caught each other's eyes and began to laugh. This could be fun.

'A large vodka and Coke and a large Bacardi and Coke,' he said.

Maggie was about to say that she didn't drink Bacardi any more and would rather have wine, but stopped herself. Tonight, at least, she could drink Bacardi.

Simone could see the difference in them. The laughing was growing more hysterical; the food a little messier.

Alice was talking about the Egyptian waiter who'd fallen in love with her last year and tried to swap six camels for her.

'He just kind of lurked about all day in front of my dad, it was totally embarrassing,' she said.

'How did you get rid of him?' asked Simone.

'Oh, I didn't get rid of him, I snogged him mental up the back of the souk. Have you ever seen Egyptian men? They're *gorgeous*!'

The room collapsed again as Zelda passed around the bottle.

'Simone . . .' she said enquiringly. Simone primly put her hand over her cup.

'*Come* on, Simone,' said Fliss, slurring slightly. 'It's called growing up. Nothing can happen, it's just here, we'll look after you.'

'Si-mone! Si-mone! Si-mone!' Zelda started chanting, and the others joined in. Pink at being singled out like this, Simone finally uncovered her hand from the top of her cup. She was nearly fifteen after all, hardly a child.

'Not too much!' she said warningly, as Zelda sloshed a measure in her glass.

'Of course not!' said Zelda.

Miranda hadn't eaten any of her supper. David kept trying to get her to drink some water, and she called him a boring bastard and batted him away like a fly. He'd sat there like a bloody useless pillock, even when the boys took pity on him and asked him what car he drove. And why shouldn't they take the piss? It was ridiculous to drive an ancient navy-blue Saab at his age. He hadn't even tried to laugh and join in the joshing, just given them a tight smile and not said anything. It was pathetic.

Anyway, it didn't matter now because the awards were starting. A comic that she'd seen on telly was standing up and telling jokes about the Managing Director having sex with a goat; he was hilarious. She shouted out a few 'Yo!'s and tried to give him a standing ovation, but the others pulled her down for some reason.

That didn't matter, it was her category now. And the award for Southwest Sales Rep of the year goes to . . .

Someone was holding her hand in excitement. She glanced down and noticed it was Declan. Oh, that was nice, he wanted her to win too. She took another slug of her wine for courage . . .

'Miranda Carlton!'

The room erupted in applause. Miranda jumped up out of her seat, screaming in excitement. The other men at the table took it in turns to hug her. Then she went for the podium. Her shoes wobbled and she thought she was going to fall, but nobody would notice, would they? There was a great gale of laughter from the crowd, but they were just pleased, weren't they? She turned round and gave them a cheery wave.

The comedian off the telly gave her a kiss and said, 'Well done, darlin'.' He must fancy her too. She took the metal pointy thing off him and waved it in the air, then leant forward to the microphone.

'Thank you . . . Thank you so much, everyone . . . There are some people I would like to thank, of course . . . and you know, I have seen the MD having sex with a goat and you know it didn't look as bad as everyone thinks . . . the goat seemed to be enjoying it.'

The entire room howled with laughter and stamped their feet. David bit his lip.

'So I want to thank Ken, Jim, all the *gorgeous* men who've supported me through this!'

There was a large roar at this too. Miranda couldn't believe she was going down so well.

'There'll be a little treat for you later . . .'

'Get 'em off!'

David got to his feet. This was going way too far, and

Miranda obviously had no idea what she was doing. He headed towards the stage, grim-faced. Miranda saw him.

'And my miserable boyfriend, I'd like to apologise for him . . .'

The audience went quiet. David reached the lectern and jumped up.

'Come on, sweetie,' he said. 'That was a great speech, but I think you can go now.'

'No!' she yelled. The comedian tried to help David get her off the stage.

'Leave 'er alone!' shouted one voice from the audience. David glanced around at a sea of red, howling, drunken faces.

'Miranda,' he said desperately. 'I really think we should go.'

'Spoilsport!' howled Miranda into the microphone. 'Someone get me another drink!'

A great cheer went up as David and the comic finally helped her down from the lectern.

'God, they're noisy next door,' said Stan for the fourth time.

'Mmm,' said Maggie. They'd ordered off the set menu and their food was terrible; a congealed-looking steak and kidney pie, preceded by melon and parma ham, which Maggie thought had gone off menus in the dark ages.

Conversation between them had been stilted, after discussing – yet again – Stan's miraculous journey. The conference next door was certainly very noisy.

Maggie glanced around the room. There were about six other couples dotted about, mostly in their fifties and sixties, the women in pastel suits, the men in brightly coloured golfing sweaters. They had red cheeks, and hair coming out of their ears, and tufted eyebrows, and white hair on the backs of their hands. The women wore glasses and looked anxious; their eyes darting to the waitresses, their mouths a moue of worry. None of the couples were talking to one another except to pass comment on the bread, or the wine, or the whereabouts of the waitress.

Maggie felt a thin line of panic rising in her breast. Would this be them then, one day? Completely lost for conversation, nothing left to say to one another, except to comment on the food and stare with a glazed expression into the fire? She searched in her head for something, anything, to say. Stan was drinking quite heavily, she noticed. It was a sign he was nervous too. She tried to give him a happy smile.

'So, have you heard about that job yet?' he blurted out.

Maggie froze. So that's what this was about. Maybe he thought he was going to cart her off the next morning.

'Have you come to *fetch* me?' she asked.

'No!' said Stan, genuinely wounded. 'I know you'd have to give notice and all that.'

'Well, no, I haven't heard about the job yet, and *if* I got it and *if* I decided to take it' – Stan flinched at that – 'then I wouldn't even *think* about starting until the next academic year. I'd never leave Downey House in the lurch. So don't think you're here to bloody carry me off.'

'I didn't think that!' said Stan, hurt. 'I thought we could just have a nice evening, without you getting so bloody defensive all the time.'

'I'm *not* being defensive,' said Maggie, conscious that they were beginning to attract glances from the older couples at the other tables. 'I'm just sick of this big Scottish conspiracy to kidnap me from this "evil" place, as if I don't know what I'm doing!'

Stan stared at her. 'Well, maybe you know *exactly* what you're doing.'

'And what do you mean by that?'

Stan shrugged. 'Well you've got it all how you want down here, haven't you? Cushy number, nice place on your own, fiancé nicely tidied away up north, everything perfectly arranged so you can be as selfish as you like and do whatever you like.'

'That is totally unfair,' said Maggie, getting angry, even as she realised there was definitely something in what he was saying. She had got used to a compartmentalised life, for sure.

'No messy schools or families or arrangements to deal with. You're living like a bloody schoolgirl yourself. And it's bloody selfish. '

This hit home.

'Shut up!' said Maggie, no longer caring who was looking. 'Just *shut up*!' She stood up. 'I'm going to the bathroom.' The young waitress leapt forward to take her half-full plate.

'That's right,' said Stan. 'Whenever there's a problem, Maggie just leaves. That's your answer to everything. Where next, the Channel Islands?'

'SHUT UP!' said Maggie again, her eyes half-blinded with tears as she ran out of the room.

Simone was feeling woozy and giggly. Oh my goodness, her friends were so funny! They were being totally outrageous, and Zelda was talking about how she'd nearly gone all the way in the summer with a young officer, until he'd found out who her dad was and run for his life. The others were laughing too, except for Alice who was complaining that they didn't have any cigarettes. Fliss said don't be stupid, that would get them thrown out for sure, so Alice had sighed and suggested why don't they play this silly drinking game where if you didn't say the right words you had to play truth or forfeit.

In fact, so excited was Simone that she couldn't even join in the silly game – something about counting in threes – and missed her turn.

'Simone! Simone!' the others screamed.

'No, no, be quiet!' she hissed, as they giggled and tried to make themselves quieter.

'OK, you have to answer a truth question or take a shot,' said Alice under her breath.

'I'll answer the question,' said Simone nervously.

'All right, but if we don't think you're telling the truth you have to take the shot anyway,' commanded Zelda, whose hair had become very dishevelled.

'Those are American rules!' said Fliss, who was lying full-length on the floor. 'No American rules.'

'America rules!' sang Zelda, punching her fist in the air and collapsing in giggles.

'SSSH!' said Simone.

'Come on, we need a question for Simone,' said Alice. She rolled over langorously on the bed, on to her tummy. 'Simone?'

'Yes?' said Simone, feeling a little uncomfortable. The girls at her old school were always asking her stupid questions they knew she couldn't answer, just so they could laugh at her.

'Have you ever . . . kissed a boy!'

Simone flushed instantly. At last! She hadn't wanted to discuss it before, not with the bad atmosphere in the dorm, but now she could reveal it.

'Well . . .' she began.

'She has! She has!'

Fliss sat upright. 'Who?'

Simone flushed even pinker. She felt she was being initiated into a proper grown-up world, where she could talk about boys and drink booze and be a proper member of the gang, without ever having to feel like left-out, bullied, friendless Simone ever again.

'Well, you know at the Christmas party . . .'

Fliss stared in disbelief. 'Not that little midget.'

There was a sudden silence in the room. Alice looked at Fliss crossly. Fliss polished off the last of her drink.

'I didn't mean it like that!' said Fliss, seeing the other's faces. 'I didn't!'

'Yes, you did,' said Simone dully. 'It's all right.'

'What's he like?' said Zelda encouragingly. But it was too late. The moment was gone.

'Well, he's pretty short,' said Simone. She sipped her drink for want of something to do. It didn't taste as repulsive as it had before.

'It always has to be about you, doesn't it?' said Alice to Fliss.

'What?' said Fliss. 'I'm sorry, I just blurted it out. It was a mistake.'

'It's always Fliss's problems, or Fliss's boyfriend, or Fliss's take on Simone.'

'That's not fair,' said Fliss, stung. 'You're the one that's been mooning around like some sad bloody heifer, as if I'm deliberately keeping you apart from some great love affair, instead of some cheap shag – whilst I've been ill, actually—'

'What did you call me?' yelled Alice, mishearing.

'I mean, if you're so desperate to shag him, just shag him. Don't mind me.'

Alice jumped up. 'How *dare* you! At least I didn't try to starve myself to get attention . . . like that's attractive.'

'No, because you just love yourself so much all you have to do is show off all day about how *sophisticated* you are.'

'Well, maybe compared to Guildford, I am.'

196

'Or maybe you're just a bit looser.'

'Looser than what? The dress you were wearing at the Christmas party that you would have been quite happy to take off for him?'

The girls were nearly nose to nose, breathing heavily. Simone hated conflict of any kind, and was staring at them, not knowing what to do about it, feeling terrified. Zelda was watching with curiosity, still eating a Snickers bar.

'Don't you dare talk to me like that!'

'Well, don't you dare talk to me about what Will and I have. Because it's none of your business, and besides, you're too immature to understand.'

Fliss saw red and without thinking, grabbed the closest thing to hand – one of Alice's shoes – and threw it across the room. The lightbulb above the sink immediately shattered, and Alice went for her, pushing her over on to the bed. In a trice they were in a tangle on the eiderdown, pushing and trying to get at each other's hair.

'Stop it!' Simone was shouting in an anguished whisper. '*Stop it!* They'll hear us!'

But Fliss and Alice were too far gone to hear here, and the footsteps were already audible coming down the hall.

Miranda had shaken off David and now he couldn't find her. He assumed – hoped – she was in the Ladies. The awards had gone on but the high point of the evening was obviously over, and the comedian who'd been helpful before was now making lots of unkind jokes about her. David could feel everyone's eyes on him; some of the women's were pitying (and eyeing up his tall dark frame in the shabby tuxedo); the men's scornful that he couldn't control a sexy creature like Miranda. He tried to ignore everyone and ordered a whisky from the waitress, even

197

though he knew it would make him feel maudlin. What a terrible night.

At first, as Maggie staggered into the small ante-room looking for the loos, which seemed to be signposted six miles away, she couldn't quite tell what she was seeing. Her eyes were blurry with tears and she felt an overwhelming sense of frustration and anger. She so wanted to shout at Stan, tell him it was all his fault. But it wasn't, was it? It was her who'd moved away, who'd torn up her roots. He'd never changed. She had. But she couldn't set her life on fire, surely?

Looking for somewhere to have a quiet cry, she didn't notice the couple at first. They seemed to be in a frenzy, tearing at each other's clothes, trying to devour one another. It looked less like kissing and more like almost-violence. As soon as she noticed them, she tried to back away, but it was too late. The woman raised her head. It was Miranda.

David set his glass down with a bang. They were clearing the tables for the dancing. She'd been away for twenty minutes, this was getting ridiculous. He was going to find her and tell her he was leaving, with or without her. He stood up.

Miranda gasped and pushed Declan away. Her head was spinning.

'M . . . Maggie,' she stuttered.

Maggie stared at her in disbelief. 'Uh, hello,' she said, not knowing what else to say.

'Uh, uhm.'

Suddenly Miranda thought she was going to be sick. Declan was still holding on to her elbow.

198

'Come on, love,' he said. 'Let's go somewhere a bit more private.'

Miranda reached a beseeching hand out towards Maggie. 'Please,' she said. 'Don't tell David.'

'Don't tell David what?' came the voice, a tall figure silhouetted in the doorway.

Miranda's face changed suddenly. It grew harder and she jutted out her jaw defiantly. 'I don't need you to tell me what to do,' she hissed.

'Evidently not,' said David, stepping forwards. He took in the whole scene and, although he couldn't possibly have said anything so cruel, he couldn't deny that amid his obvious shock was a distinct feeling of relief. And sadness. Miranda had so much beauty, brains and charm. He wished she could find a man to make her happy. It hadn't been him, and he didn't hold out much hope for the pudding-headed man clasping her by the elbow.

'Come on, love,' whispered Declan again. 'Let's get out of here. I've got the bridal suite.'

Miranda, wobbling in her shoes, walked up to David. 'So, I guess this time I'm dumping you,' she said.

David put up his hands. 'I guess so,' he said. He rubbed the back of his neck with his hand. He hated scenes. Miranda didn't seem to mind them.

'Goodbye, David,' she said. This would have come off as more dignified if she hadn't fallen off one of her shoes. Declan caught her just in time.

Maggie and David stared at the couple disappearing up the stairs.

'Oh God,' said Maggie. 'Oh my God! Are you OK?'

David sat down heavily. 'Yes,' he said. 'Yes, I am. Sorry, what are you doing here?'

Maggie shrugged. 'Uh, just for dinner.' She was conscious of not saying Stan's name out loud. David wasn't listening anyway.

'I just wish it hadn't been so *messy*,' he was saying. 'I should never have got back together with her.'

'She's made a huge mistake,' said Maggie loyally. 'She'll realise in the morning.'

'Well, I think that's immaterial now she has Lumphead Loggins up there,' said David.

'Are you really not that fussed?'

David could feel the whisky in his veins and suddenly felt immensely tired. 'Would you come and sit on the arm of this chair and tell me comforting things?'

Maggie did so.

'It had to end,' said David, staring out of the window into the darkness beyond. 'I just wish . . . I just wish she could be happier.'

'What about you?' asked Maggie softly.

'I, of course, get to drown in whisky and self-pity. It's all rather fun really,' said David. They sat there in silence.

'Oh, Maggie,' he said. 'Oh, Maggie, Maggie, Maggie.'

'What?' she whispered.

Agonisingly slowly, his fingers crept towards hers. She watched, hypnotised, as, like it had a mind of its own, her own hand – her left hand, the one with the small-stoned ring – opened and clasped his.

But Maggie didn't get to hear the end of the thought, and David didn't get to formulate it, for, rampaging in, his red hair sticking up in a fury, his cheeks pink with firelight and beer and self-righteous anger, was Stan.

Stan shook his head in disbelief at the sight of the two of them.

'I can't . . . I can't . . . that poofy English professor from over the hill? All this time? And I thought . . . Christ, Maggie. Every time I see you he's there. Every time I hear about the school it's David this, and David that. And I thought, Oh, that's nice, Maggie's taken pity on the weirdo, she's found a friend to talk to . . . not *once*, not *once* did I ever think you'd be interested in a lanky weirdo like—'

'It's not like that!' said Maggie. 'David's just split up from his girlfriend. We're not doing anything!'

David put a hand over his eyes.

'So you stormed out on me to come and comfort him,' said Stan. There were tears in his eyes, Maggie saw, with a sudden lurch of tenderness. She stood up. She hadn't denied it.

'How could you, Maggie? I trusted you.'

'And I trusted you!' said Maggie.

Stan looked guilty. 'But nothing . . .'

'You know it did,' said Maggie miserably. Stan's silence confirmed her worst fears.

'It was *one time*,' he said eventually. 'So what – you're getting your revenge with spiderlegs here?'

'It's not like that,' repeated Maggie.

'No, it's not,' said David, getting up between them. 'Maggie loves you, Stan.'

Maggie swallowed hard.

David, standing up, revealed the difference between his height and Stan's, but it didn't stop the shorter man. Stan pulled back his fist and punched David hard in the face.

David staggered back. He couldn't believe how much it had hurt. He clutched his hand to his jaw. Maggie's mouth opened in shock. What was Stan *doing*? She suddenly felt herself rooted to the spot, unable to move towards either man.

'I probably deserved that,' David said.

'Yeah, you bloody did,' said Stan, rubbing his knuckles. 'Now what are you going to do, Maggie?' His voice was shaking.

Maggie looked from one man to the other, feeling completely and utterly torn. Stan was holding out his hand.

David was not.

David couldn't do this to another man, especially not one he had always thought of as a decent sort. Look, even Miranda couldn't be with him for five minutes without wanting to pull someone else, and Maggie had been positively avoiding him all year. Stan and Maggie had real love, a history; one day they would have a family. Maggie and he had a stolen kiss on a hillside, and a lot of fantasies built from reading far too much poetry. It was absurd to promise Maggie a dream he couldn't deliver. Tonight had shown him the kind of man he was. Completely inadequate in every way.

His hand wasn't there. Maggie raised her eyes slowly. All the worrying, all the silliness – it had all been for nothing – completely imaginary on her part, just as she'd always thought. She was such an idiot. She felt her face burning.

Suddenly, her phone rang.

'For Christ's sake,' said Stan. 'Who's that, George Clooney?'

The phone stopped, then started again, sounding even more insistent than before.

Maggie picked it up.

'Miss Adair?' It was Miss Starling's voice. She sounded coolly, controlledly, furious. 'We appear to have a situation with your form.'

*

Maggie drove – she'd hardly touched her wine at dinner, and the adrenalin punching through her veins would have cleared the alcohol in any case. Stan stayed behind; David went to catch a cab home before Stan hit him again.

Felicity Prosser, Simone Pribetich, Alice Trebizon-Woods and Zelda Towrnell had been apprehended, completely drunk and having a screaming fight with one another. The room was smeared in chocolate and food products, a light-bulb had smashed and one of the curtains was torn.

Miss Starling was standing in Dr Deveral's office in a long grey flannel nightdress and dressing gown, white with rage. Dr Deveral had managed to get dressed.

The four girls were standing in a line in front of the desk. Simone was sobbing violently, Felicity Prosser more quietly. Zelda looked defiant, Alice uninterested.

'I'm sorry,' said Maggie, rushing in. 'Prior engagement.'

Miss Starling sniffed.

'We understand,' said Dr Deveral, glancing at Miss Starling. 'It is Friday night, after all.'

Maggie looked at the four girls. Why did it always have to be her form causing a commotion, as everyone else cheerfully settled down to prep? She quickly calculated their respective emotional states. No point in asking Simone anything, and Fliss seemed to have tightly drawn into herself.

'Alice. What happened?' she barked sharply.

Alice glanced around tentatively. 'Well, we, uh, found some Jack Daniels.'

'You *found* it?'

'Yes. In the woods. One of the older pupils must have hidden it.'

'You *drank* something you found in the *woods*? Sorry, Alice, please don't treat other people like idiots – and don't think I'm going to believe that.'

Alice didn't look even mildly contrite. Zelda heaved a sigh. This was going to get sticky, she could tell.

'I brought it in, ma'am,' she said quietly.

Maggie turned to her. 'Well. A bit of honesty. At least that I can respect.'

Alice resented that. Protecting your friends wasn't lying, it was the right thing to do. Everyone knew that.

'Simone didn't want to have any,' she said, to show Miss Adair that she could be just as honest as anyone else. 'We made her.'

'Is that true?' Miss Starling shot at Simone, who nodded miserably, her face sodden. 'You girls *forced* alcohol on another?'

'It wasn't like that,' snivelled Simone, but it was too late. Miss Starling was looking at her watch.

'I think we'll have to phone the parents.'

All the girls set up a howling but Miss Starling stilled them with a glance.

Maggie turned to Dr Deveral. 'Can we speak just as teachers for a moment?'

Dr Deveral nodded, and the girls were sent outside.

'And not a *word* from any of you in the hallway,' warned Maggie as they left the room, Fliss and Alice in particular exchanging filthy looks.

'OK, what happened exactly?' said Maggie when the girls were safely outside. She felt unbearably, overwhelmingly tired.

'Well, you'd have known if you were here to supervise,' shot Miss Starling.

'But I arranged to have tonight off,' said Maggie patiently. Miss Starling was being blatantly unfair; she'd had permission for her night off the premises. It wasn't worth getting upset over though. 'But you're right, if I'd been here that would have been better.'

Dr Deveral was impressed with Maggie's cool head under the circumstances. A year ago she'd have blown up at June Starling for the unfair accusation. The fact remained, though, that Maggie's girls did seem to attract way more than their fair share of trouble.

'So is there real damage to the room?' asked Maggie, who'd seen a lot of alcohol abuse in her old school. She glanced at Dr Deveral, who shook her head. 'It's not an automatic expulsion, is it?'

Veronica shrugged. 'It's difficult. Two of the girls are nearly fifteen, which is a slight mitigation, I suppose. And you have to weigh the severity of the punishment against the crime . . . an expulsion from Downey House could hover over their whole next six or seven years; affect their university applications.'

'I'm very keen that doesn't happen to Simone,' said Maggie.

'So am I,' agreed Dr Deveral.

'It's clearly in the rules of the school,' said Miss Starling. 'We can't condone underage girls drinking in the dorms! It's against the law!'

'No one is doing that, June,' said Veronica, taking off her glasses and rubbing her eyes tiredly.

'I suppose this is all all right where you come from, isn't it?' said Miss Starling to Maggie.

Maggie turned round, shocked. 'Ex*cuse* me?'

'Well, it's obvious you have lower standards of discipline where you come from. Obviously the girls are picking up on these habits.'

Maggie felt like she'd been slapped. 'I can assure you, that could not be further from the truth—'

'I mean, you've been out at a bar yourself, it's obvious.'

'June, that is *enough*,' cut in Dr Deveral. The tone of her voice was several degrees below frosty. 'I think Maggie and I can handle this now.'

Miss Starling bristled. 'With respect, headmistress.'

'You are not showing my staff respect, Miss Starling,' said Veronica. 'Perhaps we can have a word in the morning.'

Miss Starling left, but not without shooting Maggie a venomous look.

'Dr Deveral, I promise, I have absolutely *never* encouraged this kind of behaviour in the girls.'

'No,' said Dr Deveral, looking suddenly weary. There was a pause. 'But you must admit, Maggie, yours does seem to be a particularly troublesome group.'

Maggie swallowed hard and bit her tongue. She felt a flare of anger at the injustice – as well as a little voice inside asking, Well, had she perhaps been neglecting her form? With her head full of her love life and her own future?

'Now, what do you suggest we do?'

Maggie did her best to pull herself together and act professionally.

'We need to separate Felicity Prosser and Alice Trebizon-Woods,' she said first. 'Together, those two are nothing but mischief.'

'I agree . . . Goodness, if we even tried to rusticate them, I doubt I could get a Trebizon-Woods to come and pick Alice up. I think they're in Bhutan.'

'I suppose Zelda brought the booze from the base,' said Maggie. 'She just . . . she just doesn't want to fit in here.'

Dr Deveral looked sad. 'I'd hope every girl would be enriched by being at Downey House.'

Maggie didn't say anything. The last thing in the world she wanted to do was let Dr Deveral down.

'I'll try harder,' said Maggie.

Veronica gave her a look. 'Thank you,' she said. Nothing more needed to pass between them.

'All right. What about I speak to all the parents in the morning,' said Maggie. 'Plus detention till Easter, and suspension of privileges till the end of the year.'

Dr Deveral looked up, a sudden glint in her eye. 'Harold Carruthers needs help with his spring planting. He was asking me if he could get a man in. We could put the girls on early morning hard labour.'

Maggie raised her eyebrows. 'That could be just the thing. Make them too tired to get into any trouble. And I'm changing that dorm,' she added. 'I'll take Alice out, she'll cope well elsewhere. Whereas I still need to keep an eye on Felicity.'

Dr Deveral nodded.

'And we'll make it very very clear to them how lucky they are to be avoiding anything worse.'

Maggie wondered if she could say the same for herself.

It was four very sorry schoolgirls who trailed back to bed at midnight. Fliss and Alice had been forced to apologise to one another in front of the teachers, but it hadn't done the trick – they were still refusing to talk. Alice's mouth was set in a stern line. She had a half-day's grace in the morning to move her things, and the prospect of endless hard labour and extra prep stretched well out into the distance, with looming headaches for all of them. Fliss would have some very tough explaining to do to her therapist. Simone wanted to be sick every time she thought of what her dad was going to think when he heard, and how disappointed he would be. Zelda couldn't believe the school was so tight-assed. But there was one thing they all agreed on.

'I'm never drinking again,' said Simone. The others nodded their heads.

Maggie stood in the quiet hallway. The moon shone through the long-leaded window. She knew what she had to do.

She let herself in. Her heart was in her mouth. The figure was dark and prone under the bed covers. Gently, she called his name.

'Hmm?' The figure shifted.

Maggie moved towards the bed. 'Can I come in?' she asked, tentatively.

Stan sat up.

'I just . . .' he said. 'One thing I have to know.'

This was it. Maggie swallowed hard. The thing that had been gnawing at her, tearing her apart.

'Did you . . . did you sleep with him?'

'No,' she said.

'Did you kiss him?'

Her pause told him everything.

'Yes,' she said finally. 'Just once.'

There was a silence. Stan lay down once more on his side of the bed. In horror, Maggie gradually realised that he was crying.

She lay down next to him. 'Are we still . . . can we . . .?'

'Do you want to?'

'Oh yes, Stan. Oh yes. I can't tell you how sorry I am.' She was crying too now.

'But if you ever—'

'I won't . . . never! I promise.'

Slowly their bodies moved closer together, and they held on to one another in a damp salty embrace until, exhausted, they finally fell asleep.

*

At breakfast, which they took late, and quietly, but this time Maggie was thankful for it rather than concerned, she felt in the pocket of her jacket and pulled out the white envelope she'd plucked from her pigeon hole.

'What's that?' asked Stan.

'I don't know, just mail. Oh,' said Maggie, opening it.

'What?'

'*I am sorry to say that your application has been unsuccessful on this occasion* . . . Bugger! Those horrible old witches at GDE haven't given me the liaison job!'

Stan glanced up from his full English. 'Why not?'

'It doesn't say.' Maggie scanned the rest of the letter, which was standard stuff. 'Ugh, it says that if I want, I can call them up to discuss it.'

'Well, do that then.'

'No thanks,' said Maggie. She put the letter down, feeling depressed. 'I know why anyway. They thought I was a toffee-nosed snob for working down here.'

'They're not the only ones,' muttered Stan.

'Yes, I know that, thank you, Mr Working Class Hero. Oh God, how annoying. I didn't even *want* the stupid job.'

'Well, maybe that came across,' said Stan perceptively. 'They could probably tell.'

'I didn't do it on purpose,' said Maggie. 'I'll apply for another job.'

'Course,' said Stan, 'I know. But maybe they could tell you were, you know, a bit reluctant.'

'Well, I'm not reluctant now,' said Maggie. She thought of the horrible looks Miss Starling had given her the night before; her unruly Middle School seconds that she didn't seem to have a hope of controlling. 'I'll finish my year out here and find something new in the summer. I'm sure Dr Deveral expects me to leave anyway.'

'That's the spirit,' agreed Stan. 'Aye, that'll do.'

'Oh God, I have four sets of angry parents to wake up this morning, some of whom aren't even in the same hemisphere,' said Maggie.

'And I have five hundred miles to drive and a nightshift,' said Stan. 'Best get on it, eh?'

Maggie gave a tentative smile. 'Thanks so much for coming down, Stan. I'm . . . I know it was awful, but I feel I got much more sorted in my head.'

Stan nodded. 'You daft lassie. All that bloody mooning around.'

Then he leant over. 'Maggie, if you do it again . . . if you ever do it again, it'll kill me, I swear to God. It'll kill me.'

Maggie swallowed. 'I know. I won't.'

'I don't want you to see him, do you understand?'

Maggie nodded.

'I mean, I've given him a warning he won't forget, but Maggie . . . if it wasn't for me being such an idiot last year, I'd have just called it off, you know?'

'Uh-huh.'

He asked her the same question he'd asked her last night before they'd fallen asleep. 'Just tell me . . . swear on Dylan's life. You never slept with him.'

'I swear, Stan. It was one kiss. You have to believe me.'

'I do,' said Stan. 'I have to believe you.'

And he kissed her and was gone.

Chapter Twelve

Saturday was a blowy and bright February morning, and Maggie wanted it to sweep the cobwebs, and the past, away. She hung up the phone after her calls with some bemusement. With the exception of Simone's parents, who had peppered her with questions, none had seemed that troubled by the girls' misdemeanours. The Prossers just wanted to know if Felicity was eating and said it was fine, Fliss had been drinking wine and water with dinner since she was twelve years old. Zelda's mother had drawled that this was a definite step up from the drugs, but please could they not expel her as she didn't have time to track down yet another school. She'd left a message at the Trebizon-Woods' with a maid that didn't seem to speak much English. And she'd have been even more surprised if she'd seen Simone's mum and dad hang up the phone then hug one another.

'She didn't get sick! She was fine! And she didn't want to drink! But all her friends persuaded her! She was invited to the party!' They were practically bouncing with glee.

Out at 6 a.m. the following Saturday morning, though, following the tracks of Harold the caretaker with small crocus bulbs, the girls weren't in the least bit pleased. Alice and

Fliss were still ignoring each other completely, with Fliss now conversing through Simone, and Alice through Zelda.

'This is *ruining* my nails,' said Zelda. 'I can't believe they didn't let me off – these cost a packet.'

Simone shivered in her thin jacket. 'Does this burn calories, Zelda?' she shouted.

'Sure does, Slim-one!' yelled Zelda back cheerily. 'So, Fliss, don't work too hard.'

Fliss had no intention of working too hard, not like Alice, who was setting out bulbs with a will, if in a slightly strange shape.

'What are you doing, Alice?' asked Simone.

'Why, getting my revenge, of course,' said Alice. 'On that Miss Adair. I always do. You know this was probably her idea.'

'Well, yes, but what?'

'You'll see,' said Alice. 'You know that little secret I mentioned?'

Simone nodded eagerly but, infuriatingly, once again Alice refused to breathe another word.

Veronica fought her way through the Birmingham traffic. Industrial towns reminded her too much of her upbringing; she had a great inclination to dislike them. And after thirty years by the sea, she found it hard to understand why anyone would want to live in a city, even if she had managed to track down tickets to the symphony orchestra for tomorrow evening. It was Tchaikovsky, her favourite. She wondered if Daniel would like to come. She'd offered him a lift to the Expo, but he was popping over to see his mother in Guildford then taking the train from London. She could run him back home, though.

The huge exhibition hall was taken up with hundreds of

stands and tables, all promoting the solid educational advantages of their own schools: those specialising in art, or sport, or helping 'those with varied requirements' (a euphemism for 'who've been expelled from everywhere else'). She saw many faces she'd met over the years at headteachers' conferences, and whilst on good terms with many, she tended to avoid forming close friendships with rivals. She was viewed with respect, but not intimacy, which was exactly what she liked. Spring term, after the Middle School seconds' midnight-feast debacle, seemed to be progressing well, and things were definitely calmer. The mock exams had come off well, too, and they looked set to make a good showing in the league tables, which was a huge relief.

Dr Fitzroy was thankfully at the stand next door, exuding loud bonhomie. He could take the strain. He'd brought along Daniel, and David McDonald, that slightly eccentric English teacher. It was good to include the younger teachers, let parents see that their little ones would be in a modern environment. But of course you needed a touch of gravitas too; Mr Graystock, the Classics teacher, exuded this in spades.

Veronica said good morning politely to all of them, as well as Fleur Parsley and Janie James, who she'd brought from her own school. Always good to emphasise the artistic and sporting benefits of Downey House – the things state schools simply didn't have the resources for.

David seemed a little gloomy, she noticed. Normally he was jumping off the stand and talking nineteen to a dozen, alarming just about as many parents as he enthralled. She wondered why. Dr Fitzroy was bullish, talking about how they were really going to have to fight now, as the credit crunch took its toll; and how school fees, although usually the last thing parents wanted to cut back on, eventually fell victim too.

'Tradition! Honour! Excellence!' he boomed. 'That's what people want!'

As the hall started to fill with anxious-looking parents and their bored offspring, everyone sprung into action. Evelyn handed out beautifully printed leaflets with pictures of the school glinting in sunshine reflected off the sea. It looked like something out of a fairytale, and few of the mothers could pass by without exclaiming at it.

Veronica spent the morning discussing whether an asthmatic child would be able to take the summer saltwater swims (she privately thought the child in question, who had purple shadows under his eyes and a rather large bottom, would benefit at Downey House the second she put her Nintendo DS down); as well as a mother who was very loudly enquiring about stabling her daughter's horse. Veronica wasn't sure if this was for her benefit or that of the other parents passing by, but she did the best she could. Far more questions came about spreading payments and costs; discounts for siblings and potential scholarships. Veronica felt bad telling nicely-dressed, but obviously feeling-the-pinch parents that Jessica, good as she was at writing stories, was very unlikely to win a scholarship if up against the sixteen-hours-a-day-in-the-library, pulling-themselves-up motivation of a Simone Pribetich – these nice girls from nice schools just didn't have quite the same desire to escape, and scholarships had to be kept for those in genuine need.

By the end of the morning she was quite exhausted, and had been delighted when Daniel had suggested lunch somewhere nearby that he'd read about online. She hated to push the advantage, squeeze herself into his life. Their obvious proximity meant she was constantly terrified of becoming a nuisance to him and his family.

On Daniel's part, he was finding it, though extraordinary,

a very rewarding experience getting to know his clever, prickly birth mother, so different from warm, uncomplicated Ida. Somewhere in the back of his mind he even had a plan forming, a stray thought, about perhaps even just looking into the possibility of just finding out – just to see – if his father was still alive. One day. But he didn't want to scare her with that yet. He enjoyed her company and, if he were honest with himself, was flattered by her obviously over-whelming interest in his life and family, however much she tried to hide it. Just like their two other sets of doting grand-parents, no detail of Rufus, Josh or Holly's dealings were too small for Veronica's ears. A generous man, Daniel saw a sur-feit of love and affection for his children as nothing but a good thing. And he felt, with some awe, pleased that he so enjoyed the company, as an adult, of his mother.

'Sneaking off again, you two, are you?' boomed Dr Fitzroy as they left at the same time. 'People are starting to talk.'

Veronica winced with exquisite distaste. Daniel didn't look too happy about it either. But the subject of telling the world hadn't come up again, and that suited Veronica fine.

'Look at them go, eh, David?' said Dr Fitzroy, nudging his colleague. But David could do nothing more than shrug weakly. The sparkle had gone right out of him. Was he sick?

Choosing a high-profile restaurant near the Expo centre in the middle of a headteachers' conference was obviously a terrible idea in retrospect, and both Daniel and Veronica felt it. It seemed every headteacher from the west of England managed to be passing, and of course wanted to drop by Veronica's table for a quick word. Veronica could almost hear them as they left – headteachers, alas, being no less susceptible to gossip than any other sector of society. 'Isn't he dishy?' 'Who'd have thought it?' 'Well, *I* always thought she was a . . .'

'Sorry about this,' she grimaced to Daniel, waylaid for the sixth time. Daniel shrugged; it was impossible to have a conversation anyway, with the sense of being constantly eavesdropped. They finished hurriedly, both refusing pudding or coffee, and Veronica understood immediately when Daniel said he had some errands to run and did she mind terribly if he didn't accompany her back to the exhibition hall?

After a long afternoon standing and smiling, Veronica had made up her mind. That night was the headteachers' dinner. She was scheduled to sit next to Daniel already, they'd arranged it. Something would have to be done.

Later, after a long bath which had done nothing to quell her nerves, Veronica put the final touches on her make up. A grey fine cashmere twinset and a soft red skirt and boots looked elegant and discreet; her hair was the same refined pale blonde she'd kept it since she started to go grey. Fastening a Links necklace round her neck, she checked her reflection one last time. She didn't *look* nervous. Which, given what she was about to do, was half the battle.

The headmasters' dinner was a hearty annual affair, full of gossip about who was moving where, which famous offspring were misbehaving, why so and so had had nine expulsions in one year, who had poached the King's Choir Chorus Master . . . Normally, Veronica quite enjoyed them. The keynote speeches, usually by retired teachers of esteemed colleges, were amusing and erudite, and the tone light. It was a good break from the harsh financial realities that the trade fair showed up.

216

Tonight, however, she was shaking. She'd had a few words with the toastmaster and, although he looked a trifle confused, had a healthy respect for Dr Deveral and her school, so acquiesced accordingly.

As soon as she took her place next to Daniel, she could feel the room buzzing and muttering – who *was* this young teacher Veronica insisted on touting about everywhere? The idea of being the topic of vulgar speculation was completely abhorrent to Veronica – she'd undergone enough of it in her life – and she felt progressively more uncomfortable. Daniel sensed it and tried to make things easier on her by spending a lot of time talking to the woman on his right, a lady vicar from a high church school in rural Wales, which didn't exactly make his evening go with a bang either.

Finally, as the pudding plates were being cleared away and coffee circulating, the toastmaster rose and tinked his glass. The hubbub gradually died away.

'Now,' he said, 'before I welcome you most respected ladies and gentlemen with a few of the choicer selections of Britain's youngest and brightest this year, we have in our midst a lady who wants to say a few words: Dr Veronica Deveral.'

There was a rustle of whispering. Veronica, no stranger to public speaking, suddenly felt a hole in the pit of her stomach. Was this a truly ridiculous idea? Was it going to end her career? Turn her into a laughing stock? Ruin everything?

But what alternative did she have?

Rising, she gripped her napkin slightly for support. Only Daniel noticed; he didn't know what she was doing, thought she'd perhaps been scheduled to speak anyway.

'Hello,' said Veronica, her voice a little quiet. 'It's good to see you all here again – I think I know most of you.'

There were some mutters of agreement at this.

'For those I don't know, you must excuse me.'

Veronica took a long pause and a sip of water.

'You know,' she continued, 'I always say to my girls, "Tell the truth, spit it out, it's all for the best."'

Now she had the entire room's attention.

'But of course, when it comes to oneself, it's quite different, I'm afraid . . . It has come to my attention that there has been some speculation as to the nature of the relationship between myself and Daniel Stapleton here, History master at Downey Boys.' She swallowed. 'To stop idle gossip and exaggeration, I will tell you myself. Nearly forty years ago, as a teenager, I, along with many others, had to give a child up for adoption. Now, all this time later, I have been extraordinarily blessed to have the opportunity to meet him again.'

Daniel's mouth was hanging open.

'Good Lord!' Dr Fitzroy was heard to say.

'By coincidence also a teacher, I'm lucky enough that he works nearby, and I'm so proud of the exceptional man he has become, thanks to his wonderful adoptive parents. I'm so lucky to get the chance to get to know him. And that's all. I'm sorry for interrupting your evening. Thank you.'

Veronica sat down, to a stunned and silent room.

Daniel took her hand just once and squeezed it.

'Thank you,' he said, with tears in his eyes.

'I should have done it before,' said Veronica. 'It was ridiculous that I would treat your kindness with secrecy.'

'What's going to happen now?' said Daniel.

'I have absolutely no idea,' said Veronica. 'You know, I can't bear drinking, but do you think you could ask the waiter to get me a brandy?'

To her surprise, the waiter was back in two seconds with a large balloon of Cognac. 'On the house, ma'am.'

'What?' said Veronica.

The waiter looked at her, his large dark eyes glistening, then spoke in rich Brummie tones. 'I'm adopted, ma'am. I tried to find my birth mother, loike, but she just didn't want anything to do with me. So, you know. He's lucky, right. And my mum and dad are great too.'

'Oh,' said Veronica. She glanced up. Ernie Fisher, a very smart grammar school boss from East Anglia, was standing in front of her, twisting his fingers.

'Veronica,' he said.

'Ernie.'

'I know we don't know each other well, but I wanted to tell you that both our children, Mae and Angus . . . you know, we couldn't have our own. If someone like you . . . Well, we'd never have known . . .'

He, too, seemed about to break down. Veronica found herself clasping his hand too.

The toastmaster tried to continue with the speeches, but there was a steady stream, it seemed, of people in the room who'd had their lives positively touched by adoption, or who merely wanted to sympathise with how things were back then, or to tell her she was brave, or to say how happy they were for her. Veronica felt completely taken aback by the amount of human interest and warmth; the number of similar families out there that, because of her own desire for secrecy, she'd never met, because she'd carried herself around like a locked box for so many years.

Daniel was quite pink, and pleased, too, as people came to look at him standing next to his mother.

'You know,' he said to Veronica quietly, 'I really think this is going to work out all right.'

Chapter Thirteen

Why was it, Simone wondered, that the first term of the year seemed to take so long, then the rest just whizzed by? Spring term – made dreary by Fliss's absence and punctuated by hard labour – had gone in a blur, and now the Easter holidays were coming. She'd only realised how the seasons were changing when Miss Adair sidled into class one morning, looking slightly embarrassed.

'It's such a lovely day,' Maggie had announced, 'that we'll put *Romeo and Juliet* to one side just for a moment.'

This didn't please Alice, who was revelling in the doomed romance of it all.

'And celebrate this glorious morning.' She handed out photocopied sheets. 'This is one of the oldest songs or poems that we have in English. Does anyone recognise it?'

Astrid Ulverton, the class's most talented musician, raised her hand at once.

'It's a round, miss.'

'It is indeed a round, yes,' said Maggie.

It was such a beautiful morning, and Maggie was desperate for the Easter holidays. Knowing they weren't far off, she'd felt entirely jolly waking up.

Painstakingly she took them through the Middle English words – they particularly liked 'bucke uerteþ', 'the stag farts' – and, once she was sure they understood it, started up the song.

'So, I'm not much of a singer, but, Astrid, if you can help me, I'm going to split the class into three groups and we're going to go for it.'

The class perked up as they always did when they were doing something different.

'OK, you lot, follow me.'

And Maggie's wobbly but sweet alto started on the ancient words:

'Sumer is icumen in,
Lhude sing cuccu!
Groweþ sed and bloweþ med
And springþ þe wde nu
Sing cuccu!'

After a few times around, the class managed to get the three different parts and joined the voices together. Across the school, windows were opened at the sweet sound, and all the classes enjoyed a little more of the beautiful morning. In her office, Veronica threw open the French windows and sighed. She would miss that Scottish teacher, if she really did go.

'And oh,' Maggie added, as her smiling class was leaving, 'I've had some good news. We've had our outing to the theatre approved. If you lot work extra hard over the Easter holidays, you can actually go and *see Romeo and Juliet.*'

There was a good-natured cheer.

Easter in Scotland was chilly, both outside and in. Maggie and Stan dutifully visited the hotel where they would be getting married, and approved wedding invites. They were polite to one another; affectionate, even, in company. Only sometimes at night would Maggie lie, looking at his so-familiar outline in the sheets, and wonder if it was possible to be getting married and to feel lonely. Then he would turn to her and embrace her, and she would banish those thoughts to the back of her mind. There were the girls to think about: exam term was coming up. If she was going to leave Downey House, she wanted to do it with her head held high; show Miss Starling and everyone that she was perfectly capable of taking on a smart school and doing well with it. She wasn't going to scuttle back to Scotland with her tail between her legs. So why did it feel like that?

'I have now answered every essay question on *Romeo and Juliet* – ON EARTH,' said Fliss with horror, banging her text-book closed. Still at least detention was over now they were back for summer term; no more back-breaking gardening and the detentions had gone on for so long now that practically everyone had forgotten what they were for. Although Zelda hadn't smuggled in any more contraband, so presumably it had worked, to a point.

And, the only exception being Simone, whose marks were always excellent, all of the girls had seen an improvement in academic performance – Fliss in particular, who had some ground to make up from the term before. So the rhythm of the school indicated that their work-load was about to ease up a little, just as some breathtakingly good weather arrived – soft, spring breezes pushing puffy white clouds above the sky; the sea looking warm enough to swim in (although, as Janie James had sternly warned everyone, it was most certainly *not*). The older girls moaned as they poured over revision texts for their exams, but for most of the Middle School seconds, it was a time for lounging in the grounds, attempting to cultivate early tans and not complaining too much about Janie James' term of hockey.

There were two flies in the ointment, as far as Simone could see. One was that Alice and Fliss were still not speaking. Astrid Ulverton had moved into their dorm in place of Alice, and they all missed her spiky asides. Astrid was nice, but all she cared about really was playing the clarinet and practising. And, though Alice could be bitchy, she was so funny too.

Fliss tried to pretend she didn't care, but it was obvious she did. Alice looked like she really didn't care, and probably didn't, but as far as Simone knew, she wasn't seeing Will.

Simone had been co-opted into taking Fliss's side, against her will – she thought if Alice and Will fancied each other, it wasn't fair to keep them apart just because Fliss used to like him. Whenever she'd tried to explain this to Alice, however, Alice had brushed her off as if she couldn't be bothered to discuss it with a kid like Simone, and that hurt. Why couldn't they just all be friends again?

The second thing was that, after sending a friendly email to Ash, she'd never heard from him again. It was keeping her awake at night. Was it because of her weight (which seemed to have stabilised and made her a pleasantly curvy, if not stick-insect, size for her height – Matron and Miss Adair kept going out of their way to tell her how good she looked now, and instructing her to eat white bread)? Something she'd said? Was she not smart enough for him?

She'd avoided going to the lecture society or the inter-school debating league in case she ran into him. It was horrible to think that he'd just wanted to take advantage of her with a casual snog, but had absolutely no interest in ever seeing her again. That hurt so much to think about that she had to quickly pick up a book or a cake if the thought ever crossed her mind. She wished she had someone to confide in, but Fliss had just been mean and no one else took her seriously. So she'd used the detention time to catch up on some pretty serious prep, and was already quite well-advanced into her GCSE work for the following year. *Romeo and Juliet*, however, made her cry. Imagine, a boy who loved you so much he would do anything for you; risk death, climb balconies, cross countries and deserts. Simone felt absolutely convinced in her fourteen-year-old head that there would never ever be a boy who would feel that way about her.

Maggie read the words again. The euphoria she'd felt as term ended seemed to have dribbled away up north. The weather, glorious in Cornwall, had been dank and miserable up in Scotland, although she and Stan were carrying on as best they could.

She was scandalising both families, but Stan had only snorted when she'd suggested adding part of the old English prayer book to their wedding ceremony. The priest had been resigned, indicating that most people wanted it these days; they just liked it. The Catholic service was ecclesiastical and restrained, but Maggie felt she wouldn't really be married until she said the more famous words: *With all my wordly goods I thee endow/With my body I thee worship*. A binding promise. That was what they would have. *To have and to hold, for richer, for poorer, for better, for worse*. Her and Stan. Just as it had always been.

She picked up her corrections. Felicity Prosser was much improved. Simone was of a high standard, as always. Zelda's work was still dashed off with only the barest care for spelling or punctuation.

She felt it scarcely mattered any more. Miss Starling had

still treated her like dirt, ever since that awful night the dorm had been caught with booze. She couldn't make it any clearer that she didn't feel Maggie belonged at Downey House. However many corrections Maggie did, however much she had thrown herself this term into teaching and imparting knowledge – there had been no more DVD fests – she couldn't help feeling the same way sometimes. That it would be best for everyone – absolutely everyone – if she was no longer there. That she belonged somewhere else.

What God has joined together, let no man put asunder.

She closed her eyes, remembering when Stan had kissed her off on the train.

'For the last time,' he'd said.

'Yes,' said Maggie, feeling a weight in her heart. 'For the last time.'

'See you soon, wife.'

Chapter Fourteen

The morning of the play outing dawned perfectly; a beautiful June day. Maggie wondered if her wedding, now only two months away, would be so lovely. Everyone was relieved – going to an outdoor theatre was one thing, having to sit there through a howling gale was quite another.

The Minotaur was an entirely outdoor theatre, hewn from Cornish rock, that sat at the very tip of England. On a beautiful day like today it made a wonderful setting for a play, and the Roman columns that made up the amphitheatre suited the Italian tone of the traditionally staged version.

Maggie had woken absolutely determined not to be phased by seeing David. That part of her life was over, and it had done nothing but cause everyone misery. So when the Downey boys dismounted from the bus for their pre-show tour of the theatre, she was able to nod to him politely.

'Hello,' he said, equally politely. She gave Stephen Daedalus a scratch. 'I thought he'd be wearing a ruff,' she said.

'Ha, very good,' said David. 'Uhm, how are you?'

'Good!' said Maggie. 'I meant to say . . . sorry about everything last term . . .'

David waved his hands. 'Not at all, don't even mention it. I did deserve it, after all, and it's in the past . . . Can we be friends though?'

'Of course,' said Maggie, more heartily than she felt.

Alice Trebizon-Woods watched their exchange with interest. Alice hated her new dorm. Her new roommates were a bunch of ninnies. She missed her friends and felt she'd been unfairly singled out. OK, so she went for Fliss, but it had been Zelda's Jack Daniels. She'd still show that snotty Miss Adair.

'Great. Great,' said David. 'Right, I'd better round up my shower.'

'Course,' said Maggie, watching as David turned round.

'All right, everyone,' he said loudly. 'By the way, I've heard it said that those who think *Romeo and Juliet* is too soppy are always the ones who end up crying the most.'

There were snorts at this.

'And I hate to conform to gender stereotypes, but the stage director has offered to give you a masterclass in stage fighting if any of you would be the least bit interested in that . . .'

He was drowned out by the hearty cheer that went up and raised an eyebrow at Maggie as he carted the boys inside.

'Yes, us too,' said Maggie, before the girls could ask the inevitable. 'Line up, please.'

The girls paired off, Fliss and Simone at one end of the line; Alice and Zelda at the other. Although Maggie thought it was a good thing that they were no longer influencing each other, she was also sad. Girls' friendships were such fragile things, after all. She would have thought that with every successive post-feminist generation things would get easier, and their self-esteem would improve, but it didn't seem to be going that way at all. It reminded her, too, to call her sister. Anne had thought the same as Stan; that she'd messed up the interview on purpose, but in fact she was going to ask if she would clip some more jobs out of the paper for her. It was time to go.

'What's this?' Zelda was asking. It wasn't like her to be curious about something academically related.

'It's hair and make up,' said the friendly tour guide who was showing them round. 'Do you want to take a look?'

'*Do* I?!' said Zelda, and dived in.

The tiny make up room, with three stools crammed in next to each other, looked like a treasure trove to Zelda. It was stuffed full of every conceivable type of cosmetics, boxes upon boxes of different shades, false noses, wigs and hair pieces of every colour and type. There was putty to build different face shapes, hair to make moustaches and beards, even warts that could be stuck on.

'Oh. My. *Gawd*,' said Zelda. '*Look* at this stuff. Do they use it all?'

'Lots of it, yeah. If you like, you can have a word with our make-up supervisor later.'

'I sure would like that, ma'am,' said Zelda, still looking around as if she'd been let into Santa's workshop. Alice looked at it and yawned. She wanted to meet some actors and see the boys.

On the round stage, the stage fighting demonstration was going extremely well, as Will Hampton volunteered, to the catcalls of the other boys, to take on a plywood broadsword.

'Now, you want to lunge straight at me – but miss, please,' said the instructor. 'See my arm under here? That's what you're after.'

Will slowly, but deftly, parried and made a good show of attacking the instructor, who immediately faked his own death to a mixture of cheers and groans from the watching pupils. Fliss caught Alice's eye watching with rapt interest and flicked her eyes away.

Alice didn't care, as Will turned towards her and, in one smooth movement, plucked a handkerchief out of his top blazer pocket.

'Will you hold my colours, milady?' he said, bowing towards her. All the girls thought this was the most romantic thing they'd ever seen. All the boys wanted to be sick, though many of them envied Will his confidence.

'Is this clean?' said Alice.

'Come *on*!' hollered the instructor, hauling his pike above Will's head. 'You'd be dead by now!'

Fliss turned away, but not before she'd noticed Alice carefully tucking the handkerchief into the top pocket of her blouse.

'Are you the form teacher?' asked a friendly looking woman of around forty with bleached blonde hair. 'Only, you all look so young these days it's hard to be sure.'

'That,' said Maggie, 'is about the nicest thing anyone's said to me in months.'

'Oh dear,' said the woman. Maggie liked her immediately. 'I'm Ailie, the make-up artist. Trish told me you had one of your girls interested.'

Suddenly Maggie had an idea.

'Ailie,' she said. 'Can I ask you an absolutely huge favour?'

'Really?' said Zelda. 'You're kidding me, right?'

'No,' said Maggie, Ailie standing beside her, both their faces absolutely guileless. 'Ailie usually has an assistant.'

'There are a lot of assistants in state-funded theatre,' said Ailie, coughing.

'And she's sick. And we were chatting and she asked if I knew of anyone who was good at putting on make up . . .'

The longing in Zelda's face was so strong, Maggie wished she could take a picture. Ailie had loved the idea, saying if it went well, she might make it a permanent feature for student tours; she could certainly help with the dull bits like mascara, and washing the sponges. When Maggie had explained that Zelda had trouble getting interested academically, kind-hearted Ailie was only more keen to help.

'That's exactly what I was like,' she'd said. 'I wished someone had taken the trouble to give me a leg up. Would have saved me a lot of time. I suppose that's what you schools can do, isn't it? When you've got tiny classes and time to think about your students, and lots of good teachers, and trips like this . . .' She sounded a bit wistful. 'OK, send her up.'

The performance was played out against the backdrop of the setting sun over Crean bay, the setting of the sun matching perfectly the darkening mood of the piece. Maggie watched with some satisfaction her brood get increasingly engrossed; it helped that the main parts were played by very young-looking actors. This wasn't always the case, but it definitely helped. The very thorough work she'd thrown herself into in the term leading up to Easter had obviously paid off; every single face was engrossed, even Zelda's, who was eyeing up the well-mascara-ed dancers with an eye she fancied was now becoming professional.

But there was something more. The sunset, the words, the music and the astonishing setting somehow conspired to place a magic on the stage and wreathe an enchantment around the audience; in the warm, sweet-scented night air, everyone could feel and sense it, as insubstantial as fairy dust, but somehow rendering the drama being played out on the stage as all-important, as the niggles of everyday life retreated into dreams.

Fliss's mouth was wide open. This was all her romantic sensibilities thrown to life. As Romeo declaimed, *My lips, two blushing pilgrims, ready stand/to smooth your rough touch with a tender kiss*, she shivered. This was what she had dreamt of. This is what she had wanted with Will, two people so mad, so crazy for each other, even though the rest of the world wanted to tear them apart.

She looked at Alice, who was looking at Will, who was looking back at her, and felt a sudden stab of shame. Did they feel like that? It wasn't right to keep someone from someone else just because you liked them first. Will was never going to like her. And now she was being just as bad as the Montagues and the Capulets. Under a pink sky, where the stars were just beginning to pop out, Fliss hung her head. How could she have been so mean? No wonder she was so unhappy. She wanted Alice back as her friend, she thought. Very much. She would fix it. She would.

Maggie had started off watching the girls but, as it went on, found herself increasingly drawn into the familiar tragedy. She didn't see David watching her either, or see his lips move, almost unconsciously, to the crushing line, *Oh, I am fortune's fool.*

Simone and Ash were seated almost directly across from one another. Every time she noticed him, he seemed to be glaring at her. She tried to stop looking, but she couldn't help it.

At the interval, people were reluctant to move, still caught in the spell, but Simone wasted no time.

'What *is* it?'

Ash pouted and looked at the ground.

'You didn't email me.'

'Of course I did!'

'You never emailed me back again,' she said.

'Well, that's because your email was so silly.'

In fact, Simone's missive had been very carefully thought through, and she had tried extremely hard to find the right balance between joviality and letting him know she was thinking about him.

'Fine,' said Simone. 'That's what I thought. Fine. Goodbye.'

She stormed off and plonked herself next to Fliss, who of course, as usual, was far too wrapped up in herself to pay her the least bit of attention. In fact, after two minutes, Fliss stood up and wandered off. Fine. Simone pretended to look through the programme.

Ash came after her with two cups of hot chocolate.

'D'you want a hot chocolate?'

Simone shrugged. 'Not p'ticularly.'

'I bought you one.'

'I didn't ask you to.'

'Fine.'

They sat in silence for a while.

'I didn't mean your email was silly,' said Ash finally.

'Then why did you say those exact words?' said Simone.

'Because . . . I meant, well, I thought you would have said something. About the Christmas party. I thought you were just ignoring it, like.'

'Well, I wasn't going to . . . go into lots of detail or anything, was I?'

'I dunno,' said Ash. 'I thought girls did.'

There was another pause.

'I don't know much about girls,' said Ash.

It was the first humble statement Simone had ever heard

him make. She looked at him. Then she smiled, a little. And he smiled back. And then they both burst out laughing.

'Well, I don't know much about boys,' said Simone, choking back the giggles.

'Boys are easy,' said Ash. 'We eat a lot and then we kill ourselves over a bird. Oh, sorry, did you not want to know the end?'

'I know the end,' said Simone, rolling her eyes.

'Can I come back on your bus?' asked Ash.

'Dunno,' said Simone, slightly shocked. She wondered if Janie James would allow it.

'OK,' said Ash. 'Do you want that hot chocolate?'

Simone started laughing again. 'Why, are you going to give it to some other girl if I don't take it?'

Ash grinned. 'Maybe.'

'Well, all right then,' said Simone, glancing quickly around for Zelda just in case. 'But next time, I want apple juice.'

Fliss ran over to where Will and Alice were standing apart, separated by large groups of boys and girls but still with eyes only for each other. Fliss didn't quite know what to do.

'Alice,' she said.

Alice gave her a snotty look. 'Yes?' she said, as if Fliss were some distant relative she barely remembered, rather than her once best friend.

'Err . . . can I have a word?'

Alice shrugged, and they walked over to the stone wall overlooking the ocean.

'Alice, look. I'm really sorry. About Will.'

Alice nodded as if she didn't really care either way, but inside she was glad this had happened. She missed Fliss, but couldn't let herself step down in an argument; she'd have forfeited Will for ever if necessary.

'What do you mean?'

'I mean, I really . . . I mean I had a big crush on him. But that was nothing to do with you and I shouldn't have asked you not to see him. I'm sorry.'

This was very gracious on Fliss's part, and Alice acknowledged it.

'I'm so glad we can be friends again,' she said, taking Fliss's hand. 'I hated you not talking to me.'

'You weren't talking to me either!' said Fliss.

'Never mind that now,' said Alice, her pleasure only slightly marred by the sense that her delightful martyrdom was going to have to come to an end. 'You really don't mind?'

Fliss shook her head. 'I'll get over it,' she said.

Maggie managed to keep up light and easy banter with the other teachers during the interval, so that was good. And Zelda came up to her with stars dancing in her eyes.

'They need me back down there, miss! And she said there might be some room for me if I wanted to help out in the summer, that I'm really good.'

'Zelda, I could not be more delighted,' said Maggie, honestly.

'There's one thing though,' said Zelda, looking unusually modest.

'What's that?'

'You know the suspension of privileges?'

'Mmm?'

'Well . . . I was *rilly rilly* hoping that I might be able to go and tell my parents . . . and it is Friday night and, well, the bus goes right past the base on the way home . . .'

Zelda looked so contrite and pleading that Maggie smiled.

'All right, all right.'

'Yeah!' said Zelda. 'Can you sign my slip?'

Maggie did so.

'And this one.'

'What's this one?'

'Felicity Prosser's. They invited her over for the weekend too.'

'They did?' said Maggie. 'Don't push me, Zelda.'

'I can't, Miss Adair, I have *work* to do!'

And Zelda pirouetted off towards the stage door.

'You are *meeracle* worker,' said Claire gloomily. 'I have more chance of being eaten by giant bat that ever getting that American girl to conjugate *être*.'

Maggie didn't know what it was. The heady scent of the wildflowers that grew out of the towering rocks; the fading warmth of the sunlight; even, merely, a chance to sit down after the exhausting events of the last few months.

But somehow, the play moved her as it had never moved her before. The plight of the lovers – that could sometimes feel a little plotted in less deft hands – suddenly, on this starry night, so beautiful and young amid the columns of the stage, pushed her beyond measure. By the time Romeo bought his poison from the reluctant apothecary, she was choking back great, weeping sobs; the final moment of catharsis, when Juliet wakes to find what she thinks is her love sleeping beside her, made her so uncharacteristically tear-sodden she had to hide her face in her handbag in case any of the girls saw her. It was unprofessional.

The only person who seemed to notice was Claire, sitting beside her, who squeezed her arm with some concern, but still Maggie couldn't stop crying; through the final scenes, through the applause and the standing ovation and the repeated curtain calls for the actors; through the bustle of standing up and getting the girls out in time, a steady beat of tears fell from Maggie's eyes. Only when she briefly escaped to the toilets could she make the least attempt at pulling herself together. But then she would think again of this beautiful Cornwall night; how this was the last time she would come here and sit under the stars; how love, lost, could never be found; about all the youth and promise around her, and her own, nearly over, and she would start all over again.

After ten minutes, Claire came to find her.

'Everyone ees on the bus,' she said. 'What ees the matter with you? Janie James, that horse of a woman, she has let a few of the boys on. I theenk she is a boy herself.'

'It doesn't matter,' said Maggie.

'What *ees* it?'

Well, it doesn't matter now, thought Maggie.

'Oh,' she said. 'Well. It's just, after I'm married, I'm going to have to leave the school to go home. And . . . well, I kind of had a bit of a thing for David McDonald. And I was just a bit sad, that's all.'

'Beeg long Daveed with the dog?' exclaimed Claire. 'Ah, but he ees *perfect* for you!' She caught herself quickly. 'I mean, well, he likes some things you like . . . No, of course not. I am so sorry, I had no idea. You know, it was the same for me last year.'

The previous year, Claire had had an unhappy love affair with Mr Graystock, the Classics teacher at Downey Boys.

'I know,' said Maggie. 'Please, please, *please* don't tell anyone.'

'Of course not. I know how sad thees ees. But you are pleased to be leaving, yes? To be married and to be in Scotland? I theenk David will be sad.'

'Of course I'm happy to go,' said Maggie stoically. 'It doesn't mean I can't be sad to say goodbye.'

'No,' said Claire. 'I understand. And now, I am sorry. You must come, before they turn into a crowd of storming beasts.'

'I know,' said Maggie, glancing in the mirror and turning on the tap to wash her face. 'Teacher face on.'

The bus wound its way slowly along the curves of Cornwall's landscape. Zelda and Fliss were sitting together. Janie James' relaxed attitude to the doings of boys and girls at the end of term (she believed, having grown up on a farm, that these instincts had to come out one way or another) meant that Simone and Ash, and Alice and Will, were entwined in very separate and private worlds of their own towards the back of the bus.

'I'd have waited for you,' whispered Will.

'What, and not drunk the poison?' joked Alice.

Will shook his head. With infinite slowness, he bowed his forehead down towards hers until they were touching. Then, gently, he brought his hand up to her face.

Fliss stared hard out of the window two seats in front, willing herself not to turn around or look back. A tear wandered slowly down her cheek.

'OK,' said Zelda beside her. 'Are you ready?'

'Ready for what?' she said without enthusiasm.

Zelda reached into her suspiciously large school bag and held up the release form.

'You're coming to spend the weekend with me!'

'What do you mean?'

'I got two passes off Miss Adair. Picked her at a weak moment. It's the base dance tomorrow night.'

'Are you kidding?' said Fliss, excitement mounting.

'Nope! Can you lindy hop?'

'Is it dancing? Then, yes!'

'They are going to *love* you, little miss English peaches and cream.'

'But I don't have anything to wear.'

'*Darling*,' said Zelda, shaking her huge bag. 'Have you learned nothing from your Zelda?'

DuBose and Mary Jo were waiting by the side of the road, next to the Hummer. As Zelda jumped off the bus and started hammering away nineteen to the dozen, DuBose shook his head. He came up to Maggie, who was checking their names off on the list.

'I dunno what you done with my daughter,' he said, putting out his enormous hand, 'but ah sure do wanna thank you.'

Chapter Fifteen

After the wonderful play, Maggie felt more confident than ever that her girls were going to do well in their exams, and, as they had now all been converted by Zelda to ardent pacifists, she'd kept her hopes up for the World War One poets too.

Simone had fretted right up until the last minute of course, but her papers were uniformly excellent – her scholarship certainly wasn't in danger. Alice had done just well enough to avoid attention; Maggie wondered what she could do if she ever pulled her finger out, but blinking into the night over textbooks wasn't Alice's style. And Fliss had slipped a little, but there was evidence in the slightly stained jotters that she was trying extremely hard. Maggie was taking this as a good sign.

Overall they'd done, as a year group, very well, which was almost, but not quite, enough to silence Miss Starling on their disciplinary misdemeanours.

Now bags were packed, trunks ready to be conveyed to the railway station. The next morning was end of term, and everything was ready to go. The dorms were a positive havoc of exchanging of emails and promises of eternal friendships; plans to meet up in Tuscany or Rock, and full scale hubbub as to the whereabouts of hairbrushes and riding boots.

Maggie had gone to bed in good time, she had a very early train to catch. She'd been surprised, a couple of days ago, to get a phone call out of the blue from Miranda, who wanted to chat all about her new beau. Apparently he had a flat in a new development in Portsmouth, and she was taking the train up to London to furnish it! He'd given her his Gold Card and everything. She sounded nervous, but excited and excitable. On telling her she, too, was heading for the train station, Miranda had insisted on giving her a lift; she was changing at Exeter, so they could catch the same train.

Maggie looked around one last time at the neat and comfortable two rooms she'd learned to call home. She'd wanted to go and talk to Dr Deveral, but she couldn't exactly leave yet – she didn't have a job to go to, for a start. It felt horribly cowardly, like running away, but she'd have to see what came up over the summer. Get the wedding over with first, then maybe take a look. Spend some time with the family too. It would be good.

Waking over-early, just at dawn the following morning, Maggie crept out of the school, not even saying goodbye to Claire. Rushing out, she checked her pigeon hole one more time. Just one envelope, internal, with her name on it. Shaped like a book. Probably a suggested text from Miss Starling for next year, that woman *never* let up. Rushing, she thrust it in her bag.

Had she turned back, just for a second, she would have seen the full extent of Alice's revenge. But she did not; instead, she moved smartly towards Miranda's waiting car.

The spring flowers had been very late that year, and only finally, clearly unfurled, much to Harold's disgust, on the very last day of term. It was those clodhopping girls he'd had helping him, he was sure, who'd planted the bulbs far too deep.

By breakfast time it was the talk of an already overexcited school, even faster to spread than the amazing news that Dr Deveral was that Downey Boys teacher's mum! And by ten a.m., one of the victims, on the pretence of giving Stephen Daedalus a particularly long walk that day, had ambled over to see what all the fuss was about.

Dr Deveral had seen it and shaken her head. She'd meant to have a word with Maggie anyway before she left, congratulate her. Her English class had taken the highest test scores in the entire school. Their written Shakespeare and war poets work did her extraordinary credit. She even had a creditable essay from the American girl on the use of disguise on the Shakespearean stage. So a silly little bit of schoolgirl pranking meant very little to her.

David, however, stood stock still and looked at it. In a way it was beautiful. Irises and late primroses formed the shape of a heart, in which, clear as anything, was inscribed: DM + MA.

It was a daft – if quite forward-sighted – prank, he knew, some ridiculous attempt to stir up trouble by the girls. He wondered who knew? All of them? Surely not.

With a sudden grip of panic, David thought of the stupid thing he'd left for her in her pigeon hole. It suddenly struck him as the height of cowardice and meanness. But it was after the theatre; he'd seen her crying. Those weren't the tears of a happy bride, looking hopefully towards the future. He'd thought about it and thought about it and decided that he was going to try, just once more. Just once, before she left, probably, he knew from Claire, for ever.

When he thought of her face that night in the hotel, when

she had looked for his hand and it wasn't there, he wanted to cringe. And now he looked at the flowers: simple, glorious, and, it seemed, screaming a very straightforward message right in his face. He was an idiot. A stupid, bookbeaten coward.

'Good morning, sir. You like the message, *oui ou non*?'

David stared at Claire uncomprehendingly.

'Oh. Hello. Uh, yes, silly, isn't it? But still, I'd hate to destroy flowers . . . Stephen Daedalus could probably eat a few though . . .'

Claire let out a big sigh. 'You know, if I was in France just now I would not have to spell everything out to men who have got the emotional feelings of a *dead snake*. Are you *crazy*?'

'OK, steady on,' said David. 'What are you talking about?'

Claire gave him her hardest stare.

'Maggie, you *eedyot*.'

'Yes, yes, I mean, what has she said to you?'

'That she must go and do what is right for her family and not disappoint everyone because you are not 'ers.'

'I am not *what*?'

Claire sighed and threw up her hands in despair.

'*Elle t'adore! Vous êtes sa sole raison d'être. Chaque jour, chaque instant, elle pense à vous, vous êtes dans sa coeur et dans ses rêves.*'

David stared at her as he desperately tried to work it out in his head. Hope and disbelief were fighting a battle on his face.

'Da-*veed*! *C'est* the language of love.'

David took a quick glance at his watch, blinking rapidly. 'Has she gone to get the train?'

Claire rolled her eyes.

'*Vite! Vite!* You need a new car.'

*

Maggie and Miranda found seats easily. Miranda's idle chatter – she had lost weight and seemed a little nervy – was useful as a distraction. After all, after the train reached Exeter, Maggie could put her head down on the table and cry all she wished.

In some years, she told herself, 'in some years, when I have Stan's beautiful babbies on my lap and I'm jiggling them up and down, and am surrounded by cheeky boys at school and loud, lairy girls full of bravado, and I'm going up Sauchiehall Street with my old friends and we're living in a gorgeous house in the West End or Newton Mearns and my life is all sorted, and Cody and Dylan are doing really well, then I'll look back on this and laugh. I'll tell everyone about the funny couple of years I spent in a weird English boarding school that was like something out of an old book, and how odd everyone was and . . .'

She couldn't imagine telling them about David. She couldn't imagine turning that – turning him – into a funny anecdote. But it would fade. It would fade.

Miranda uploaded a pile of glossy homes magazines.

'Right, you help me pick a bathroom!'

They had touched briefly on David in the car. Miranda had emphasised how fantastically successful Declan was and how pleased she was not to be going out with that loser any more. Then she'd asked, slightly contradictorily, how he was doing, and Maggie had answered, heartwrenchingly, that, truthfully, she had absolutely no idea.

Maggie looked at the magazines without interest, then remembered the parcel in her bag. She lifted it out. Her name on the envelope was typed, but inside was a note, written in a hand she knew very well. Miranda would know it too.

'What's that? That looks boring,' said Miranda.

'Uh, just school stuff,' said Maggie, her heart beating madly all of a sudden. She shielded the book from view.

Miranda sniffed. 'You teachers, you're all alike.'

The note was very stark and very simple. It just said, 'Poem.'

Maggie picked up the book – poems by Houseman – and carefully turned to the marked page.

Shake hands, we shall never be friends, all's over . . .

Maggie stared at it and gasped. So this is what he meant to say – leave me alone, I don't want to be friends with you. Why couldn't he say that face to face? She was only trying to be friendly at the bloody theatre. Bloody hell. Staring out of the window, she felt cross, empty and miserable.

I only vex you the more I try, read the next line. Well, bloody right. Couldn't he even have spoken to her about it? It was so cowardly to give her a book; so not like him. Her eyes glazed over and she couldn't read any more. She wanted to throw the book out the window.

The train hadn't started moving yet. Suddenly, there seemed to be some kind of a commotion outside. Her eyes half blinded with tears, Maggie glanced upwards through the window. Then she blinked again. It couldn't be. It *couldn't* be. But there, vaulting the barrier with his ridiculously long legs and charging up the train . . . It couldn't be. It was. It was David. Hotly pursued by Stephen Daedalus. And about six guards.

'OH MY GOD!' screamed Miranda. 'Look! It's David!'

She stood up dramatically. 'Oh my God. He's looking for me!'

'What?' said Maggie.

'I knew it! He wants me back! I *knew* it!'

David was jumping up and peering in every window as he passed by, but was still a good four carriages away.

'Sod these bloody magazines. Declan's a complete bloody arsehole. I made the biggest mistake of my life!'

Suddenly, they both felt the train lurch.

'Oh my God,' said Miranda. 'What do I do?'

The old lady opposite looked up from her knitting.

'On the wrong train, dears?' she asked worriedly.

Maggie stared at her. 'Yes . . . no . . . maybe. I don't know.'

Maggie swallowed hard. The train had started to move, slowly. David was still way back.

Miranda ran towards the connecting carriage. It was an old stock train, and still had windows you could open. She pulled it down and stuck her head out, ignoring the warning signs not to.

'DAVID!' she shrieked, just as the whistle shrieked. 'DAVID!'

But Maggie thought. How did David know Miranda was on the train today? But he certainly knew it was the last day of term, and that there was only one service to Glasgow. Oh, sod it. She stuck her head out of the window too.

'David!'

David's double take would have been comical, had he not been pursuing a moving train.

'MAGGIE!' he shouted.

'DAVID!' shouted Maggie.

'WHAT?!' shouted Miranda, turning to stare at Maggie.

David looked at them both. He didn't even know what he wanted to say. He hadn't planned anything more than finding out where the Glasgow train was and driving like a maniac to the station. But now he could see her, words, for the first time in a life filled with words, failed him.

'You *are* joking,' said Miranda, finally taking in the situation. 'We're meant to be friends!'

Maggie didn't hear her. The train was moving away, but

she was staring at David desperately, as if that alone would bring him closer. As she was nearly out of reach, he realised what it was he wanted to say. The only thing.

'I love you.'

But his voice was carried away.

'WHAT?' she shouted.

But she was getting too far away, and he couldn't yell any more. Everyone was staring at him. The noise of the train had built up too much, the momentum pulling them apart.

David suddenly felt overcome with foolishness. Stephen Daedalus had panted to a halt at his side; the guards were keeping a respectful distance for the moment, in case he turned out to be a violent nutter.

Maybe it is Miranda, thought Maggie to herself, not daring to believe, then seeing him stop. He sent me that bloody horrible poem. Oh God. Oh *God* how embarrassing.

Closing her eyes, she withdrew her head, then just at the last minute, she waved, feeling foolish and sad.

He waved back.

'I loved you,' she suddenly, stupidly, found she wanted to say. But she couldn't, of course. Instead she swallowed hard, closed up the window as the train entered a tunnel, and slowly, miserably, turned to go back to her seat and work out what on earth she was going to say to Miranda.

Which is when she saw the emergency cord.

I couldn't, she thought.

It's not me.

I'd selfishly ruin the day of every single other person on this train, and the next, probably.

I'd get arrested.

I'm getting married.

I'm a *teacher*!

*

Veronica walked through the classrooms as she always did; she liked to be the last one here, carefully closing up and double-checking everything before she left for the summer. She liked the traces of girls just gone; the faint whisper of their footsteps on the stone steps. And she liked to take time to remember her sixth-form girls, leaving to spread their time here out in the wide world; many to university, some abroad. Araminta Kelly was off to spend her gap year teaching amongst the tribes on the Amazon. Veronica privately thought that what Araminta Kelly could teach Amazonian tribes that wasn't about nail polish and *The X Factor* wasn't going to be that impressive. On the plus side, Shanisa Wallace was off to pre-med at Columbia; Carmen Figue to the University at Heidelberg and Heidi Forrest had finally bowed to the inevitable and was following her father and three brothers to Sandhurst.

Veronica hoped, as always, that she'd done enough. That they'd learned enough, not just from examinations and textbooks, but from the team-playing ethos of the school to stand up for themselves without being overbearing; to be confident without being insufferable. Well, perhaps a *little* insufferable – they were still teenagers, after all.

Veronica picked up a discarded sparkly eraser, and considered keeping it for little Holly. She smiled. Her offer of babysitting services had been readily accepted by Susie. It looked like Daniel's littlies might get to see quite a bit of their Granny V.

But somehow, this brought her a fresh sadness. It was ridiculous, of course. But when she was all alone in the world, defiantly making her own way, she didn't mind so much. There was no one who would dare comment on her private life – or lack of one; no one to wonder what she was doing. Now, being drawn into the orbit of a normal, happy family life, she was coming to realise just how lonely she had been. She hadn't even known before. And she was a little uncomfortable with this side of herself showing. It was a vulnerability. Veronica disliked showing vulnerability; it had not saved her.

Then she thought of Rufus's face two Saturdays ago when she'd taken him to the local library and let him pick out his own book about submarines. It was worth it.

She gently turned the key in the lock of the final classroom, watching the spring sunshine highlight the motes of dust drifting gently in the empty air; a faint dusty echoing of all the girls gone by; girls linked to the school, and to their families, often through generations; their pasts and their futures tumbling past just as she, now, too was linked – broken from her past, perhaps, but with a clear way into a future.

Maggie's poems

My Boy Jack

'Have you news of my boy Jack?'
Not this tide.
'When d'you think that he'll come back?'
Not with this wind blowing, and this tide.

'Has any one else had word of him?'
Not this tide.
For what is sunk will hardly swim,
Not with this wind blowing, and this tide.

'Oh, dear, what comfort can I find?'
None this tide,
Nor any tide,
Except he did not shame his kind—
Not even with that wind blowing, and that tide.

Then hold your head up all the more,
This tide,
And every tide;
Because he was the son you bore,
And gave to that wind blowing and that tide!

Rudyard Kipling, 1915

Dulce et Decorum Est

Bent double, like old beggars under sacks,
Knock-kneed, coughing like hags, we cursed through sludge,
Till on the haunting flares we turned our backs
And towards our distant rest began to trudge.
Men marched asleep. Many had lost their boots
But limped on, blood-shod. All went lame; all blind;
Drunk with fatigue; deaf even to the hoots
Of tired, outstripped Five-Nines that dropped behind.

Gas! Gas! Quick, boys!— An ecstasy of fumbling,
Fitting the clumsy helmets just in time;
But someone still was yelling out and stumbling,
And flound'ring like a man in fire or lime . . .
Dim, through the misty panes and thick green light,
As under a green sea, I saw him drowning.
In all my dreams, before my helpless sight,
He plunges at me, guttering, choking, drowning.

If in some smothering dreams you too could pace
Behind the wagon that we flung him in,
And watch the white eyes writhing in his face,
His hanging face, like a devil's sick of sin;
If you could hear, at every jolt, the blood
Come gargling from the froth-corrupted lungs,
Obscene as cancer, bitter as the cud
Of vile, incurable sores on innocent tongues,
My friend, you would not tell with such high zest
To children ardent for some desperate glory,
The old Lie; *Dulce et Decorum est*
Pro patria mori.

Wilfred Owen, 1918

Longing

Come to me in my dreams, and then
By day I shall be well again!
For so the night will more than pay
The hopeless longing of the day.

Come, as thou cam'st a thousand times,
A messenger from radiant climes,
And smile on thy new world, and be
As kind to others as to me!

Or, as thou never cam'st in sooth,
Come now, and let me dream it truth,
And part my hair, and kiss my brow,
And say, My love why sufferest thou?

Come to me in my dreams, and then
By day I shall be well again!
For so the night will more than pay
The hopeless longing of the day.

Matthew Arnold, 1864

Vitae Lampada

There's a breathless hush in the Close to-night
Ten to make and the match to win
A bumping pitch and a blinding light,
An hour to play, and the last man in.
And it's not for the sake of a ribboned coat,
Or the selfish hope of a season's fame,
But his Captain's hand on his shoulder smote
'Play up! play up! and play the game!'

The sand of the desert is sodden red,
Red with the wreck of a square that broke;
The Gatling's jammed and the Colonel dead,
And the regiment blind with dust and smoke.
The river of death has brimmed his banks,
And England's far, and Honour a name,
But the voice of a schoolboy rallies the ranks –
'Play up! play up! and play the game!'

This is the word that year by year,
While in her place the School is set,
Every one of her sons must hear,
And none that hears it dare forget.
This they all with a joyful mind
Bear through life like a torch in flame,
And falling fling to the host behind—
'Play up! play up! and play the game!'

Henry Newbolt, 1897

Summer is Icumen In

Sumer is icumen in,
Lhude sing cuccu!
Groweþ sed and bloweþ med
And springþ þe wde nu,
Sing cuccu!
Awe bleteþ after lomb,
Lhouþ after calue cu.
Bulluc sterteþ, bucke uerteþ,
Murie sing cuccu!
Cuccu, cuccu, wel singes þu cuccu;
Ne swik þu nauer nu.
Pes:
Sing cuccu nu. Sing cuccu.
Sing cuccu. Sing cuccu nu!

Anonymous, c1260

Phenomenal Woman

Pretty women wonder where my secret lies.
I'm not cute or built to suit a fashion model's size
But when I start to tell them,
They think I'm telling lies.
I say,
It's in the reach of my arms
The span of my hips,
The stride of my step,
The curl of my lips.
I'm a woman
Phenomenally.
Phenomenal woman,
That's me.

I walk into a room
Just as cool as you please,
And to a man,
The fellows stand or
Fall down on their knees.
Then they swarm around me,
A hive of honey bees.
I say,
It's the fire in my eyes,
And the flash of my teeth,
The swing in my waist,
And the joy in my feet.
I'm a woman
Phenomenally.
Phenomenal woman,
That's me.

Men themselves have wondered
What they see in me.
They try so much
But they can't touch
My inner mystery.
When I try to show them
They say they still can't see.
I say,
It's in the arch of my back,
The sun of my smile,
The ride of my breasts,
The grace of my style.
I'm a woman

Phenomenally.
Phenomenal woman,
That's me.

Now you understand
Just why my head's not bowed.
I don't shout or jump about
Or have to talk real loud.
When you see me passing
It ought to make you proud.
I say,
It's in the click of my heels,
The bend of my hair,
the palm of my hand,
The need of my care,
'Cause I'm a woman
Phenomenally.
Phenomenal woman,
That's me.

Maya Angelou, 1978

The Night Mail

This is the Night Mail crossing the border,
Bringing the cheque and the postal order,
Letters for the rich, letters for the poor,
The shop at the corner and the girl next door.
Pulling up Beattock, a steady climb:
The gradient's against her, but she's on time.
Past cotton-grass and moorland boulder
Shovelling white steam over her shoulder,
Snorting noisily as she passes
Silent miles of wind-bent grasses.

Birds turn their heads as she approaches,
Stare from the bushes at her blank-faced coaches.
Sheep-dogs cannot turn her course;
They slumber on with paws across.
In the farm she passes no one wakes,
But a jug in the bedroom gently shakes.

Dawn freshens, the climb is done.
Down towards Glasgow she descends
Towards the steam tugs yelping down the glade of cranes,
Towards the fields of apparatus, the furnaces
Set on the dark plain like gigantic chessmen.
All Scotland waits for her:
In the dark glens, beside the pale-green sea lochs
Men long for news.

Letters of thanks, letters from banks,
Letters of joy from the girl and the boy,
Receipted bills and invitations
To inspect new stock or visit relations,

And applications for situations
And timid lovers' declarations
And gossip, gossip from all the nations,
News circumstantial, news financial,
Letters with holiday snaps to enlarge in,
Letters with faces scrawled in the margin,
Letters from uncles, cousins, and aunts,
Letters to Scotland from the South of France,
Letters of condolence to Highlands and Lowlands
Notes from overseas to Hebrides
Written on paper of every hue,
The pink, the violet, the white and the blue,
The chatty, the catty, the boring, adoring,
The cold and official and the heart's outpouring,
Clever, stupid, short and long,
The typed and the printed and the spelt all wrong.

Thousands are still asleep
Dreaming of terrifying monsters,
Or of friendly tea beside the band at Cranston's or
    Crawford's:
Asleep in working Glasgow, asleep in well-set Edinburgh,
Asleep in granite Aberdeen,
They continue their dreams,
And shall wake soon and long for letters,
And none will hear the postman's knock
Without a quickening of the heart,
For who can bear to feel himself forgotten?

W. H. Auden, 1935

David's poem for Maggie

Shake Hands

Shake hands, we shall never be friends, all's over;
* I only vex you the more I try.*
All's wrong that ever I've done or said,
And nought to help it in this dull head:
* Shake hands, here's luck, good-bye.*

But if you come to a road where danger
* Or guilt or anguish or shame's to share,*
Be good to the lad that loves you true
And the soul that was born to die for you,
* And whistle and I'll be there.*

A. E. Housman, 1910

Dance Instructions

The Dashing White Sergeant

Tune: Original.

Time: 4/4

This is a circle reel-time dance. Dancers stand in a circle round the room in threes. A man between two ladies faces a lady between two men. The man between two ladies moves clockwise, and the other three counter-clockwise.

Bars description

  1–8: All six dancers make a circle and dance eight slip-steps round to the left and eight back again.

9–16: The centre dancer turns to right-hand partner. They set to each other and turn with two hands, four *pas de basque*. Centre dancer turns and does the same with left-hand partner, and finishes facing right-hand partner again.

17–24: They dance the reel of three, centre dancer beginning the reel by giving left shoulder to right-hand partner. Eight skip change of step. They finish facing their opposite three.

25–32: All advance and retire, then pass on to meet the next three coming towards them. They pass right shoulders with the person opposite to them. The dance is repeated as many times as you will.

Strip the Willow

Tune: Any good jig

This is a long-way figure dance in which a new top couple begin on every repetition.

Bars description

1–4: First couple give right hands, turning each other one-and-a-half times with twelve running steps. They finish with first lady facing second man, and first man standing behind her.

5–6: Advance again and dance back-to-back, passing right shoulder. First lady turns second man with left hands joined, with six running steps. First man runs six steps on the spot as he waits for her.

7–8: First couple giving right hands turn each other in the middle, then six running steps. First lady repeats these last four bars until she has turned all the men, and at the last turn of her partner. They finish with first man facing bottom lady, and first lady behind him. First man turns each lady with his left hand, and his partner with his right, until he has turned the last lady. Then he turns his own partner with the right and they finish with first lady facing second man, and first man facing second lady.

First man turns second lady with his left hand, while first lady turns second man, with six running steps. They turn each other in the middle with right hands, with six running steps.

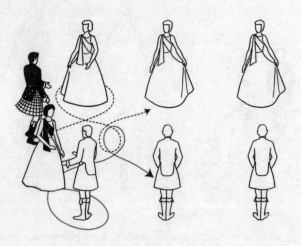

They repeat these two turnings till they have turned everybody in the set, and then turn each other with right hands eleven times, with twelve running steps, to finish on their own sides of the dance at the bottom of the set.

The next couple begins to turn each other at the same time as the first couple are doing their last turning.

Eightsome Reel

Tune: A variety of good reels

This is a round reel for four couples. It is better to treat it when dancing as a square dance, and always stand in the square formation when not dancing. A good plan is to change the tune each time a new dancer goes into the middle.

Bars description

1–8: All four couples make a circle and dance eight slip-steps round to the left and eight back again.

9–12: The four ladies, keeping hands joined with partner, give right hands across to make a wheel and dance four skip change of step round.

13–16: Advance again and dance back-to-back, passing right shoulder. First lady turns second man with left hands joined, with six running steps. Ladies, drop hands, and men, still holding partners' hands, swing them out and give their left hands across in the wheel. They dance round for four skip change of step and finish in own places, facing partners.

17–24: First couple, giving right hands, turn each other in the middle six, running. All set to partner twice, join both hands and turn once round four *pas de basque*. Finish a little way apart, facing partner.

25–40: First lady repeats these last four bars until she has turned all the men, and at the last turn of her partner. They finish with first man facing, each hand-giving.

41–48: First lady goes into the middle and dances eight *pas de basque*, or any reel-setting step, while the seven other dancers make a circle and dance eight slip steps round to the left and eight back.

49–56: First lady sets to and turns her partner with both hands, then sets to and turns the opposite man (third man). Eight *pas de basque*.

57–64: First lady dances reel of three with these two men. She begins the reel by giving left shoulder to her own partner.

Repeat bars 41–64: First lady dancing this time with second and fourth men.

Repeat bars 41–64 until all the ladies and all the men have had their turn in the middle. The dance is finished by a repeat of the first forty bars.